BAD
PATHS

A NOVEL

JUSTIN BEHRENS

iUniverse, Inc.
New York Lincoln Shanghai

BAD PATHS

iUniverse books may be ordered through booksellers or by contacting:

iUniverse
2021 Pine Lake Road, Suite 100
Lincoln, NE 68512
www.iuniverse.com
1-800-Authors (1-800-288-4677)

Because of the dynamic nature of the Internet, any Web addresses or links contained in this book may have changed since publication and may no longer be valid.

This is a work of fiction. All of the characters, names, incidents, organizations, and dialogue in this novel are either the products of the author's imagination or are used fictitiously.

ISBN: 978-0-595-47570-4 (pbk)
ISBN: 978-0-595-71175-8 (cloth)
ISBN: 978-0-595-91836-2 (ebk)

Printed in the United States of America

BAD
PATHS

PART ONE

LOCKED DOORS

CHAPTER ONE

Greg Dameron's mother died on his birthday. A brain aneurysm killed her almost instantly. Greg was thirty-one. Katherine had been forty-seven. Greg's mother was young when he'd been born, and Greg was young when she died. He didn't feel young, though, as he looked out the small window of the commercial airliner that was bringing him back to the place of his birth.

Greg did not want to dwell on the chaotic events of the last three days that had led to his current impromptu trip back to Iowa. As was always the case, thoughts of his mother left him feeling empty and confused. Over the years, Greg had trained himself to think as little as possible about his childhood, but it was difficult to suppress childhood memories when his life had recently become consumed with thoughts about the lead female character in the early chapters of Greg's life story.

In a vain attempt to distract himself from his thoughts, Greg removed his attention from the tendrils of cloud that seemed to cling to the wing of the plane like haunting, ghostly memories outside the square window. He turned his head and glanced at the elderly woman to his right. Even as he did so, he knew it was a mistake. His trepidation was confirmed when the old woman made eye contact and smiled.

Greg was not antisocial, and could even be charming under the right circumstances. But explaining why he was on a plane traveling halfway across the country to attend the funeral of a person he had not seen or spoken to for over ten years, who also happened to be his mother, could be a bit of a challenge. Greg had made up his mind to lie even before the old woman spoke.

"Going home?" she asked.

Greg nodded. "Something like that," he mumbled, averting his gaze and feigning interest in the clouds that had so recently brought back childhood memories.

The elderly woman was not daunted by Greg's lack of conversational enthusiasm. "Me too. I'm going to visit my daughter. She just had her second baby. A girl. Named her Abigail, after me. Ain't that a hoot?"

"That's a nice name," Greg said.

"Well, I wouldn't go quite that far, but it's the thought that counts, right?"

"Sure is," Greg agreed, hoping that Abigail would let the mostly one-sided conversation become *completely* one-sided.

"Where's home, young man?"

"It's a little town in southeast Iowa. You probably wouldn't know it. Lost Haven."

"Wouldn't know it!" Abigail said in apparent delight.

Greg felt the old woman gently place her palm on top of his hand. Her skin had been worn softer than silk with age. The human contact made him feel obligated to look at her. Resigned to the inevitability of conversation, Greg brought his full attention back to the woman and managed a weak smile. She smiled back.

"I'm from Ottumwa. My daughter still lives there. Winters got too cold for me, so I migrated to Florida."

Greg's lack of recognition must have been obvious.

"Ottumwa is just a hop, skip, and a jump away from Lost Haven."

Greg nodded. "Sorry, I didn't grow up in Lost Haven. I moved out of state when I was young. I don't remember much about Iowa."

Abigail patted his hand. "It's okay. Small towns are easy to forget. Did you tell me your name, young man?"

"Greg. Greg Dameron."

"Dameron. That name's familiar. Where have I heard that name?"

There was merciful silence, but only for a few moments.

"Oh!" Abigail exclaimed. "Oh," she repeated softly. She removed her hand from Greg's. She looked up at him with an expression that seemed almost sly. "Do you know Katherine Dameron?" she asked in a conspirator's whisper.

Greg's heart began to pound like a fist in his chest, pumping his blood faster, warming his face in a blush. What were the odds of this woman knowing his mother? Even in her death, he could not escape the connection. He cleared his throat. "She was ... she's my mother."

"Oh, dear," Abigail said, once again patting the top of Greg's hand with her silken-skinned palm. "You poor dear. It's a shame what happened to her. And she was still just a girl, really. Wouldn't wish something like that on my worst enemy."

Greg brought his gaze to the back of the seat in front of him. He had no idea what the old woman was referring to, nor did he want to know. Yet another strange mystery to add to the chaotic scrapbook of oddities that was his mother.

Greg felt sick to his stomach. "Excuse me," he said, rising and taking back his hand from underneath the palm of the old woman. Her skin no longer felt like silk, but like cold, wet tissue paper, or perhaps the liver from a corpse, tacky with half-congealed blood.

Greg made his way to the bathroom. Once inside, he locked the door, sat on the closed lid of the small stool, closed his eyes, and leaned his head back against the wall. He only had about a half hour left of the flight, and he planned to stay in this bathroom for the remainder. Could you land a plane if a passenger was on the toilet? Was there some kind of law that prevented urinating and landing at the same time? Greg didn't know. But he was going to find out.

Greg rubbed his closed eyelids and sighed. *Probably should be some kind of law. So you don't piss all over your leg.*

CHAPTER TWO

Just because people are family doesn't make them good *people. Bad people have families, too. But us, little man, we have each other, and that's it. We don't have a family. You hear me, Gregory? We have no family.*

Greg forced himself to loosen his grip on the steering wheel of the Ford Taurus he had rented at Des Moines International Airport. For some people the act of driving has a tendency to make the mind wander. Greg was one of those people. And as he drove east on Interstate 235, away from Des Moines and toward the family he had been told for so many years that he did not have, his thoughts kept returning to his mother.

He had been six years old when his mother first made him repeat what would become a mantra over the proceeding years: *We have each other.*

They had been standing outside a local ice cream shop in one of the many small towns they passed through in their constant traveling: Greg wanting ice cream, his mother wanting to teach him one of her abnormal life lessons.

Kneeling in front of him on one knee, her chocolate brown eyes filled with a mixture of equal parts stern authority and hopeful compassion. Greg could deny his mother nothing. Even at six he had known she was beautiful.

Say it, Gregory. Tell Mommy what we have.

We have each other, Greg had repeated.

Why do we only have each other? What did Mommy say?

Because we don't have a family.

His mother had hugged him, enveloping his face in the sweet, candylike scent of her long hair. *That's right, little man. You're a good boy. You go tell the nice lady over there what kind of ice cream you want.*

"Mint chocolate chip," Greg said, startling himself with the sound of his own voice, no longer that of a child. Greg took a deep breath and straightened out his back as best he could while driving—the base of his spine had begun to ache.

Sometime while he had been lost in his thoughts, Interstate 235 had changed to Highway 163. He glanced over at the printed Internet directions that lie on the passenger seat. He was still heading in the right direction. So why did he feel lost?

CHAPTER THREE

The first thing Greg noticed about Lost Haven was not the town itself, but the autumn colors of the trees. He had driven for over two hours to get here, but had failed to notice that autumn in Iowa was full of blazing colors of crimson and gold. As a resident of Florida, Greg was accustomed to two seasons: hot and hotter.

As he drove toward the center of town, Lost Haven gave Greg the quaint impression of the all-American small town in a Norman Rockwell kind of way. The center of town featured a town square: old-fashioned brass lampposts sporting green patina, amiably performed sentry duty guarding the wood and iron benches, picnic tables, and a central geyserlike fountain that erupted skyward with the zeal of a miniature Old Faithful.

From across the road, storefronts faced the square on all four sides. Most of the buildings were solid-looking one- and two-story structures, bricked in various shades of red and brown. One of the few exceptions to the brick motif was an ice cream shop that practically screamed for attention. A rainbow splashed across its white-painted front in a wide arch, leaped up from one corner, traveled over the two adjacent ordering windows, and fell to the ground on the opposite corner. A girl of about ten sat on one of the four round, dark green, plastic benches that occupied the concrete in front of the shop, eating an ice cream cone. She sported long blonde hair that glowed with the same deep richness of the leaves and late autumn sun. She looked up, noticed Greg looking at her as he drove by, and waved. Greg waved back. She grinned a clown grin that had been painted on with chocolate ice cream.

After passing a few more nondescript brick storefronts, Greg came upon a bar. The standard collection of neon signs glowed from the windows, promising liquid counseling. What was *not* standard about The Bonfire Bar & Grill was the fact that the building had been painted to look like an actual bonfire. The brick had been coated with a layer of flat black paint. On top of this dark canvas, an artist of some talent had created roaring, licking flames that leaped up toward the second story of the structure in slithering hues of yellow, orange, and red.

Easing past the front of the bar where vehicles occupied the handful of parking places available on the street, Greg saw an alley that ran beside the bar and a red sign bolted to the corner of the building that proclaimed BONFIRE PARKING IN REAR. Greg turned into the alley.

Internet directions had gotten him this far, but lacking a specific street address, Greg had not been able to pinpoint the location of his aunt and uncle's house during his Internet search. In the brief phone conversation with his aunt, whose voice sounded hauntingly similar to her sister's—Greg's mother—she had assured him that anyone could direct him to the "Dameron house," as she had called it. The bar seemed as good a place as any to get directions. Besides, it had been a long last few days. A quick, cold Corona would help take the edge off before Greg met his aunt and uncle for the first time in his memory.

The back parking lot was covered in the same type of gravel as the alley. Greg pulled up next to a Chevy pickup truck, parked, and got out. The soles of his tennis shoes crunched softly on the gravel like the sound of a languid mouth eating potato chips.

The lot was almost exclusively filled with pickup trucks, most various Ford and Chevy models, a few Dodges and GMCs mixed in, many with decals in the back windows of mischievous-looking cartoon boys pissing on rival truck emblems as they looked over their shoulders and smirked.

Greg thought he heard country music drifting out of the screen door at the back of the bar. It grew louder as he drew closer.

As he opened the door, Greg's presumption was proven correct by Garth Brooks's proclamation that he had friends in low places. An acrid haze of cigarette smoke wafted toward Greg, stinging his eyes, nose, and throat, mixing with the smell of beer and fried food to create an odor akin to a pair of unwashed feet thrown on a coal-burning grill for a cannibal barbecue.

"Yee-ha," he mumbled, and walked into the gloom.

CHAPTER FOUR

The interior floor plan of The Bonfire Bar & Grill was a horseshoe that featured the bar at the center of the bend with fifteen barstools of which six were currently occupied. A pair of black machines sat on top of the bar at both ends, each about the size of your average computer monitor. The one farthest from Greg was turned away from him, its screen facing a slightly overweight, brown-haired young woman who alternated between sipping whatever dark mixed beverage she held and tapping the screen with the index finger of her free right hand. The machine closest to Greg cycled through pictures of topless women in various positions of frozen sexual ecstasy. A parade of red-lettered sentences moved across the top of the screen from right to left, promising to pay out tickets that could be spent at the bar and reveal the digital women in their full naked glory if you could determine what was different about the two pictures that alternated on the screen before the timer ran down to zero. It reminded Greg of an adult version of the old *Sesame Street* game with the song:

> *One of these things is not like the others,*
> *One of these things just doesn't belong ...*

Although he was unable to see around to the farthest end of the interior from his current vantage point, the telltale crack of pool balls striking one another told Greg that digital breasts were not the only form of entertainment present.

A few people, including the mixed-drink-sipping, game-playing young woman, gave him a cursory visual once-over before going back to their chosen drinks.

Although all the booths that ran against the wall across from the bar were empty, save one that held a young couple eating an artery-hardening, deep-fried dinner, Greg decided to sit at the bar since he only planned on a quick beer and a little direction.

Greg took a seat and glanced up at the television that was mounted close to the ceiling above two men who sat at the far left corner of the bar. The television silently showed a college football game. Captions scrolled along the bottom of the screen, translating into words the silenced comments of the announcers.

The middle-aged female bartender who approached him had a plain, honest face, neither pretty nor ugly. "What can I get you, hon?" she asked.

"Do you have Corona?"

"Sure do. You want a glass with that?" she asked, reaching under the bar.

"Nah, the bottle's fine."

"Lime?"

Greg nodded. "Please."

The bartender brought up a bottle of Corona, and with a practiced motion as fluid and quick as a magician performing a slight-of-hand illusion, popped off the bottle cap with one hand, put a white square napkin on the bar in front of Greg with the other, and placed the open beer atop the napkin. A thin wisp of chilled air rose over the lime wedge that stuck out the top of the bottle.

"You got skills," Greg said.

The woman laughed. "Hon, when you've owned a bar for going on thirty years, you learn a trick or two."

Greg nodded, tipping the bottle toward the bartender in a salute before tipping it to his mouth and taking a long swallow. "That's what I needed," Greg said, and put the bottle back on the bar.

The bartender studied him for a moment, and then smiled. "Glad I could help. Can't trust a man who doesn't like a good cold beer once in a while."

Greg took another cold swallow of Corona. "What about alcoholics?"

The bartender smirked. "Oh, alcoholics *especially* like a cold beer. They just shouldn't have one, because if they have one, they're gonna have them all, until they get their fill."

Greg nodded. "I guess I can't argue with that."

"My name's Deb. You let me know if you need anything else."

"Actually, I'm looking for—"

"You stupid shithead!"

Both Deb and Greg turned to look at the source of the outburst. The young game-playing woman had given up on her game, and instead repeatedly smacked the shoulder and arm of one of the men who had previously sat under the television. At some point during the last minute or so, he had moved over to the barstool beside the young woman.

The man was stocky, built low and solid. His wide shoulder and thick arm did not seem any worse for wear from the woman's repeated abuse. He reached over with his other arm and grabbed one of her ample breasts in his thick-fingered hand, kneading it.

The woman laughed and smacked him again. "Stop it, you shit," she said.

"Hey!" Deb barked, getting their attention instantly. "None of that stuff in here."

The young woman turned her nose up toward the fondler as if to say, *I told you so.*

The stocky man gave Deb his best *Ah shucks, I was only messin' around* expression. He removed his hand from its upper female anatomical location and raised it above his head like a kid in school. "Sorry, Deb. Gina needs another Captain n' Coke. She ain't ready to put out yet," he said with a slight slur, and grinned.

Gina laughed.

"And I need another beer," he added.

From Gina's body language (leaning a little closer to her fondler), and the sly sideways glance that she gave the man, Greg guessed that she had already decided that she would be "putting out" before the night was over.

"Jimmy, I think you've had about enough," Deb said, her hands squarely planted on her hips.

"But, Deb, I'm thirsty. I'm practically dyin' of thirst. You don't want to see a hard workin' country boy like me die of thirst, do you?"

Deb smirked. "If I get you another beer, will you shut up?"

"Does a whore put out on prom night?"

"I don't know, why don't you ask your mother?"

The retort had come from Jimmy's partner in crime, the man still seated at the corner of the bar, under the television. He took a drink of draft beer, draining the half-full glass in one swallow.

The bar grew silent, an uneasiness hanging in the air. Greg looked from Jimmy, to Jimmy's friend, back to Jimmy. Jimmy's expression was one of half amusement and half rage. A moment later it became all amusement. Jimmy grinned and said, "You're just jealous cuz she charges your ugly ass extra."

"Todd, Jimmy, you two settle," Deb said, like a mother scolding two rowdy boys.

Greg drained the last of his own beer. He stood, shaking his head a little and smiling.

"What's so funny, there, guy?"

It took Greg a moment to realize the question had been directed at him. His hand on his wallet in his back pocket, he looked at Jimmy.

Greg shrugged. "You guys are funny. That was funny. The whole fuck-your-mother thing."

"So what the fuck're you laughin' for?" Jimmy asked. A distinct edge had entered his voice. He rose from the barstool.

"Now you settle, Jimmy. I mean it," Deb warned.

Jimmy shook his head. "I asked the man a question," he said, staring at Greg.

"I didn't mean any offense," Greg said. "I just thought … I thought it was funny. I was laughing with you."

"I know Todd. We work together. He can laugh," Jimmy said. "You don't laugh when someone calls a man's mother a whore when you don't even know him. Who the hell are you, anyway? Where you from?"

By this time, Jimmy stood in front of Greg. Although Greg was easily five inches taller at six foot two, Jimmy more than made up for it in width. The man was built like a bulldog.

"Now you stop it! You leave him be or I'll call Bill. Don't think I won't," Deb said. To validate her threat, she picked up the receiver on the cream-colored phone at the end of the bar beside Todd.

Greg raised his hands, palms open, facing Jimmy. "Listen, I don't want any trouble."

"Yeah? Well, how's it feel to want?" Jimmy said.

The last thing Greg heard before everything went black was Gina screaming, "Jimmy, don't!"

CHAPTER FIVE

"Jimmy's in a world of shit now."

"He didn't know who he was."

"Well, maybe he should've thought about that before decidin' to be an asshole."

Greg heard the two female voices as if from a long distance, like phantom whispers from a dream. He was not positive he even heard anything until after he blinked a few times, opened his eyes completely, and felt a thumping pain blossom on the entire left side of his face. The pain made the moment solidify with stark clarity. Dreams did not hurt this much.

"He didn't know," Gina said again.

Lying on his back, Greg looked up at Gina. Her face loomed over him like a pudgy moon. "I'm real sorry. Jimmy didn't know who you were."

Greg brought his hand up to the left side of his face. His fingers came back wet. "Shit, I'm bleeding."

"No you're not. You relax, hon. It's just water," Deb assured him. She pressed a plastic bag full of ice against the left side of Greg's head. He winced, relaxing a moment later as welcomed icy numbness dulled the pain.

Headlights swept the back window from left to right. A car door slammed shut. Gina turned her head to look out the window. "Bill's here."

Greg took a deep breath and rose to a sitting position. His vision gave a sickly black pulse, like a heartbeat pumping darkness. Then his vision cleared again. Greg took over for Deb by taking the bag of ice from her and pressing it against his head.

Almost everyone had left the bar, excluding himself, and Gina and Deb were the only two who remained. Greg assumed the man who walked in through the back door a moment later was Bill. His assumption was confirmed when Deb sighed and said, "Bill, thank God."

To Greg, Bill looked like the mold used to make Hollywood drill sergeants. He had the close cropped, no-nonsense military haircut that could not really be called a hairstyle. His features were sharp and hard, chiseled. The lines that traveled out from the corners of his eyes and across the tan skin of his forehead put him somewhere in his mid-fifties. Although not a big man, Bill carried himself like Greg imagined a professional boxer would, with an easy confidence that conveyed more than words could say about his ability to physically handle a situation if the need arose. He looked directly at Greg, raised his eyebrows, and said, "Well, fuck me runnin' backwards in a windstorm. Little Gregory Dameron all grown up."

Before Greg could respond, Bill walked with a slight limp over to where he sat and held out his hand. Greg grasped it. Bill hoisted him up from the floor. Bill gave him a firm, economical handshake, one pump, up-down-release. Standing face-to-face, Greg and Bill were the exact same height. "I see you met the town bully," Bill said, and winked.

Greg touched the side of his face before he realized he had done it. The swelling had already begun, and when he applied even light pressure, pain erupted through his face and eye. The thought of going to his mother's funeral with a giant black eye made Greg angry.

"Jimmy didn't know who he was," Gina repeated.

Greg looked at her in annoyance. "What the hell does that mean? What does who I am have to do with some good-old-boy shit-kicker sucker-punching me?"

Gina cringed as if she expected Greg to walk over and take his anger out on her, perhaps punch her in substitution of her boyfriend. Seeing her cower like an abused dog made Greg's anger evaporate. He wondered how many times shit-kicker Jimmy had kicked the shit out of *her*. "How do you know who I am anyway?" Greg asked, his voice calm.

Deb held out his wallet. "We wanted to check and see if you had some ID. We know you're not from around here, so we guessed you were probably visiting someone. Lost Haven's not a big town. Most people know most people. And everyone here knows the name Dameron."

"Why's that?" Greg said, putting his wallet in his back pocket.

Deb gave him a look of disbelief mixed with a touch of suspicion, as if he had asked her a trick question, testing her.

"We don't need to talk about all this stuff now," Bill said. "We need to get this boy home."

"What's going to happen to Jimmy?" Gina asked

Bill shrugged. "Well, after I drop off Gregory—" He glanced at Greg. "You still go by Gregory?"

Greg shook his head. "Greg."

Bill nodded. "Good. Truth be told, I always thought Gregory was a little nansy pansy, if you know what I mean."

"Sure," Greg said, although he was not sure he *did* know what Bill meant. What was wrong with Gregory?

"As I was sayin'," Bill continued, "after I drop off Greg, I'll swing by you and Jimmy's place. You might want to stay with your mom tonight, Gina. In case I have to put a hurting on Jimmy for being a pain in the ass, you don't need to be around for that."

"You want to press charges on Jimmy's dumb ass?" Bill asked Greg.

Greg looked Bill up and down. He was wearing brown leather loafers, sand-colored slacks, and a dark brown, long-sleeved button shirt, the top button casually undone. "Are you a cop?" Greg asked.

Bill smirked. "Not very official looking, huh? I'm the sheriff."

Greg was not an expert on the law, but if half of what he had seen on TV shows was true, if he pressed charges, he would probably have to fill out reports, maybe appear in court. He wanted to be out of Lost Haven the day after tomorrow. Once his mother's visitation and funeral were complete he had no intention of staying any longer.

"No, I'm not going to press charges." Greg expected Gina to be relieved, but she still appeared to be ready to burst into tears at any moment.

"Well, in that case," Bill said, "I'll stop on by and have a little heart-to-heart with Jimmy. I think I might still throw his ass in jail for a few days."

"No," Gina whispered. "That's not what I mean." She looked at Greg with glazed eyes. "What's going to happen to Jimmy?"

The hollow expression on Gina's face was eerie. She looked as if she already knew what was going to happen to Jimmy, and was only asking as a formality. What Greg found most unsettling was the fact that only a few moments ago, Gina had appeared ready to burst into tears. Now she had all the emotion of a corpse. Greg had a mental image of a big metal winder sticking out of Gina's back, slowly turning, making her repeat the same brainless question. A life-size doll housed in human skin.

Once again, Bill took control of the situation. "We don't need to stand here talkin' nonsense. I'm going to get Greg home. Gina, you go to your mom's. Deb, good job callin' me so fast." With that, Bill ushered Greg toward the back door.

Greg let himself be ushered, having no desire to spend any more time with the windup corpse-doll that was Gina.

CHAPTER SIX

Although Bill did not wear an official police uniform, he did drive an official police vehicle: a white Chevy Blazer with a light-bar bolted to the roof. Across the doors, two wide, diagonal blue stripes ascended from left to right. Across the stripes, printed in large black letters, was the word SHERIFF. Under that, in smaller letters, WAPELLO COUNTY. On the rear quarter panels, above the wheel wells, was stamped EMERGENCY 911.

As Greg opened the front passenger's side door to get in, Bill called from the other side of the Blazer, "You got to sit in back. It's regulation."

Greg looked over at Bill, leg bent, foot resting on the side rail, half in and half out of the vehicle.

"It's regulation," Bill repeated solemnly, and nodded.

Greg glanced at the back bench seat. The front and back seats were separated by a dark metal grill that formed a diamond-patterned barrier from floor to roof. A steel plate lay sandwiched between the metal diamond grill, running halfway up from the floor to cover the back of the front seats. The interiors of the back doors lacked handles to open them, or buttons to lower the windows.

Greg did not like the idea of riding in the back of the police vehicle as if he were a criminal. Nevertheless, he stepped back, closed the door, and shrugged. He cleared his throat. "Well, if it's regulation, I guess."

Bill laughed. "Ah, I'm just bullshitting you. That backseat's seen more piss and puke than a drunk whore at a homeless shelter. You can ride up front with the big boys."

Bill drove back around the square, retracing Greg's path into town. Just outside of town, he took a right onto an old blacktop road that wound through the colorful surrounding timber. "You payin' attention to where we're goin'?" Bill asked.

"For the most part," Greg answered. He glanced over and noticed Bill alternating between looking at him and looking at the road. He seemed to have an approving expression. "What?" Greg asked.

Bill shook his head, grinned, and returned his attention to the road. "Oh, nothin'. Just haven't seen you since damn near forever. Now you're all grown up. You and your mother left town before you were three."

"So, you knew my mother," Greg said.

"Small town, everyone knows everyone. Our two families go way back. I'll give you a little history lesson. Lost Haven's an agricultural town, built around farming. Iowa's got good soil. You can grow ears of corn around here bigger than a donkey's dick. At one point, Lost Haven damn near went under, financially speaking. The bank, owned by my family, was forced to start foreclosing on farms. Families lost their homes, their land, everything. That's where the Dameron family comes in.

"Your great grandfather, Cyril, couldn't stand to see what was happening to this town. You probably don't know it, but Cyril Dameron is still well-known today in agricultural circles. He invented and patented a couple of early hybrid corn seeds. He was one of the first people to introduce disease-resistant corn seed by crossbreeding various strains. And in addition to bein' an inventor, Cyril was also the town doctor. That's important to know because it shows his character— Cyril was a healer, a caregiver." Bill glanced at Greg. "You followin' me so far?"

"Yeah," Greg answered.

"So, by this time, Cyril had made a sizeable fortune. He struck a deal with *my* grandfather, and bought up all the land deeds that the bank had foreclosed on. It damn near bankrupted him, but he bought them all. And then you know what he did? He told all those families to come back to their homes. No strings attached. Don't worry about mortgages, don't worry about bank payments. Your grandfather told them, 'You farm the land just like you always have. Assign ten percent of the profits to me, and I'll take care of keeping everything afloat.' Turns out Cyril wasn't just an inventor, he was a financial genius. Not only did none of the farms go under, they flourished and grew."

Bill turned left onto a gravel road.

"The Dameron family owns damn near all the land that makes up Lost Haven. You're a multimillionaire, Greg, and didn't even know it."

Greg shook his head. "That can't be right. I … don't … it's not my money. Is it?"

Bill nodded. "Bet your ass *some* of it is. You probably personally have access to close to a million dollars. You like apples? How you like *them* apples?"

"Shit," Greg said.

Bill laughed. "Yeah, that about sums it up."

"So I guess that explains why people at the bar were making such a big deal about who I am," Greg said after a few moments of silence.

"Makes a little more sense now, doesn't it?" Bill said.

Greg nodded. "I guess so. But what was Gina talking about with all of that 'What's going to happen' stuff?"

"Simple fact of the matter is Gina's kind of slow upstairs. She's a nice girl, has a heart of gold. But the elevator doesn't go all the way to the top, if you know what I mean."

Bill took another left onto another gravel road. Plumes of gravel dust trailed behind the Blazer. "You been payin' attention to where we're goin'?"

"Not really," Greg admitted.

"We're on Parkhill Road. Little more of a history lesson for you. Per capita, Parkhill Road has the highest suicide rate in the Midwest. Once every few years, someone swallows a handful of pills, or more often than not, sucks on the business end of a shotgun. So, Parkhill Road has kind of a reputation. Not a lot of people choose to live out this way." Bill braked and brought the Blazer to a stop.

Ahead stood an old steel bridge rusted to various shades of brown and orange that matched the colors of the autumn foliage. The bridge spanned about twenty feet. A small stream ran underneath between steep banks that ascended to the height of a man, revealing raw, dark earth veined with tree roots and dotted with the occasional exposed rock.

"They say all the suicide shit started because of this bridge. It's supposed to be haunted," Bill said, sounding like a Boy Scout troop leader telling a ghost story around a fire.

Greg looked at him and smirked. "Really?" he said sarcastically.

"I shit you not. It's in the town history books. Not long after Iowa was made a state back in 1846, a girl died here, Mary Riley. She was sixteen, and from what history said, was just about the prettiest creature this side of heaven. So, all the young men in town chased after her. She had more marriage proposals than you could shake a stick at. Now, her family didn't come from money—they were simple farmers—but if you're a beautiful woman, you can open doors with nothin' but a smile.

"As would have it, she fell in love with a farmhand who helped work her family's land—which wouldn't have been so bad, but he was a *black* farmhand. Well, as happens in love, she gave herself to this young man, and became pregnant, but nobody knew that at the time, including her. This was well after the Civil War, around 1886, so this young man came from a free black family. But back then, *free* was a relative term. He was free, but he wasn't free to put his humpstick in the prettiest white girl in town.

"Some of the local boys found out what was goin' on, and for a while didn't do anything. But I think the thought of a black man havin' what they all wanted and couldn't get festered in their heads like some kind of cancer. Eventually, one night when the cancer spread too deep into their heads, a bunch of them got together and they went out after the farmhand. It wasn't anything as dramatic as showin' up on the lawn with torches, pitchforks, and shotguns. They just waited until they caught the young couple together. This was in the summer, and they found them together in the timber."

Despite his earlier disbelief, Greg had been drawn in. Disbelief or not, he focused on the story.

"They beat that young man damn near to death," Bill continued. "He survived, even grew old and died a natural death. But he was never the same. Brain damage left him about as smart as a three-year-old. They beat him so badly one of his eyes ruptured, popped like a balloon right inside the eye socket, leaked out onto his cheek and hung there, a useless sack of bloody mush still connected inside his head."

"Jesus," Greg mumbled.

Bill nodded. "Gets worse. After they finished with him, they took turns raping her. There were eight of them. She got it from all of them at least once in the front door, and took a few in the back door, too. When they were finished, they left the two for dead, which they damn near were. You mind if I smoke?"

Greg shook his head, bewildered. "What?"

Bill wiggled a cigarette between his right thumb and index finger. "You know, another nail in the old coffin."

"No, go ahead," Greg said quickly. He was surprised at his annoyance caused by the story interruption.

Bill lit the cigarette, inhaled deeply, cracked the driver's side window, and exhaled the plume of blue gray smoke out into the evening air.

"So after a while, only half conscious, the girl manages to stumble to her feet. She's not so pretty anymore, the rapists' work tattooed all over her face: broken nose, fractured jaw, missing teeth. Delirious, she stumbles into the timber. Eventually she finds this bridge.

"Now there she is, face smashed, blood and semen seeping from between her legs and backside, standin' on the edge of this bridge, holdin' onto the steel support beams, lookin' over the side, into the water. And she just lets go. Her head smacks a big rock at the bottom of the creek. And that's it for her. Lights out for good. Her head splits like a melon. The water carries her blood downstream."

They sat in silence for a moment. Bill took a drag from his cigarette.

Greg was turned in his seat, looking at Bill. He swiveled to face forward and looked out at the rusty bridge. Now the bridge seemed not to be the color of rust, but instead the color of dried blood.

"Creeped you out, didn't I?" Bill said.

"Little bit," Greg admitted.

"You know what's even creepier?" Bill said. "If you stop on this bridge at midnight, stay real quiet, and listen close, you can hear a baby crying. You can hear her unborn child crying for its dead mother."

Goose bumps rose on Greg's arms.

Bill put the Blazer back in drive and approached the bridge. "But that could just be bullshit. I don't know. I've never had the balls to come out here at midnight and see for myself."

CHAPTER SEVEN

Bill turned into a private drive featuring a black iron gate that ran from two immense square, brick pillars. The vertical bars of the black gate ended in wicked spikes that pointed toward the heavens. A similar fence, on a smaller scale, wound away left and right on either side of the brick pillars to disappear into the surrounding line of soaring evergreen, maple, and elm trees that served to obscure any view of the property from passersby. The blacktop of the driveway and the grandiosity of the gate were in stark contrast to the dull gray gravel road that connected the property to the outside world.

As they approached the gate, it opened automatically. Greg noticed a security camera connected to the top of the right brick pillar. Its dark mirrored electronic eye followed the Blazer past the threshold of the gate. From the sideview mirror, Greg watched the gate close behind them.

The driveway wound through the thick grove of trees like a giant black snake. The trees formed a loose canopy, allowing only occasional beams of dim evening light to find the ground, creating a patchwork of light and dark. In this quilt of light and shadow, the shadows dominated, forming strange angels of darkness and illusions of depth where none actually existed. Combined with the soft quietness, the effect was unnerving.

Greg began to wonder if the Dameron house was in the middle of a forest before the Blazer broke free from the confines of the trees and entered a lawn that needed a bit of attention from a good gardener.

The driveway proved to be circular, and wound around to connect to itself about forty feet ahead. In the middle of the black circle was one of those stone cherub fountains that were supposed to be whimsical but which Greg always found a little strange. The fat, childlike statue held a harp and, with apparent abandonment, produced from its stone penis a steady arc of water that fell into the waiting pool surrounding its central pedestal. The statue's eyes looked skyward. With both hands holding the harp, the cherub's expression seemed to say, *Look, God, no hands!*

Thoughts of proudly peeing statues were washed from Greg's mind as he took in the sight of the house behind the statue.

Employed as a computer programmer, Greg was by no means an expert on architecture, but had taken an introduction to architecture course in college as an elective. The Dameron house was a textbook example of a Victorian Queen Anne. If one word described the house, it was *excess.* The house was three stories, the roof shingled in various shades of gray slate tiles. The front left corner of the house boasted a circular tower, its steeply pitched roof topped with a black iron cross finial that reminded Greg of the front gate.

The bottom story of the house featured a large projecting bay window. Many of the upper story windows held stained glass in various symmetrical patterns of stars, diamonds, and squares. The bright colors of the stained glass were made brighter by the dark background of the house itself. Unlike many houses of its style, which were painted in bright colors of blue, green, yellow, and even pink and purple, the Dameron house was painted a subdued light gray with various dark accents, which included black shutters and forest green decorative trim.

A large brick chimney rose toward the sky in the front of the house, next to the corner tower. The brick was set in a herringbone pattern. Toward the top, a stylized stone D broke up the pattern by jutting forth proudly from the surrounding brick.

Bill drove halfway around the circular driveway and parked in front of the black marble steps with deep veins of crimson that ascended to the porch, which in turn wrapped around the right side of the house to disappear from view. The roof of the porch performed double duty as a balcony for a pair of second-story glass doors.

Standing on the front porch beside Bill, admiring the dark, double mahogany front doors inset with half-length panels of diamond-patterned, clear beveled glass, Greg felt surprisingly calm. He had thought he would be nervous reuniting with the aunt and uncle who had not seen him since he had celebrated his second birthday. Greg had no memory of them at all.

Bill rang the doorbell.

To Greg's right, the chains of a wooden porch swing greeted him with rhythmic squeaks, the light breeze serving to sway the swing lazily.

When Greg heard the sound of someone from inside the house approaching the front doors, he felt a flutter in his stomach—nothing drastic, just a lone butterfly spreading its wings. When he saw a figure appear, obscured by the beveled glass, and watched the doorknob turn, the butterfly in his stomach took flight. When the left door in front of Bill opened, the butterfly seemed to have invited friends to a party. When Greg saw who had opened the door, the butterflies in his stomach almost knocked him over.

There, in the doorway, gazing at him with her big, chocolate brown eyes, stood Greg's mother.

CHAPTER EIGHT

Greg had heard people claim to be rendered speechless by awe, shock, or fright, but had always assumed that being made speechless was, no pun intended, only a figure of speech. Standing on the porch, facing his mother, Greg discovered that it was indeed possible to be literally rendered speechless.

He opened his mouth to say something, but nothing came out. He stood in silence for what seemed like minutes, but what was in reality probably no more than a few seconds, before Bill glanced from his mother to Greg. Recognition seemed to dawn in Bill's eyes.

"Greg, this is your aunt Katelin. Your mother's sister. Your mother's *twin* sister."

Greg let out a long breath, unaware he had been holding it. Before he could stammer out some kind of greeting, his aunt stepped forward and hugged him. She was surprisingly strong for her small size.

Bill laughed. "You looked like you were about ready to shit kittens."

"Bill," Katelin admonished, taking a step back to look Greg over, her hands grasping his arms, "show some manners." She glanced at Bill like a disapproving elementary school teacher. "And what happened to his face?"

As absurd as it seemed, Greg got the impression that Katelin, who stood about five foot four at most and topped the scale at 120 pounds soaking wet, intimidated Bill in a stern motherly kind of way. In reality, Greg felt a bit taken aback as well. Greg felt as if he and Bill were children and had gotten caught roughhousing on the playground. Now they were returning to get punished because Greg had gotten hurt. He felt like a kid about to get in trouble. Glancing at Bill, Greg got the impression that he felt the same.

"Well, you see," Bill began, looking at Greg, his eyes filled with mischief. He seemed to be fighting back a smile.

For the first time in a long time, Greg laughed. It felt good.

Bill smirked. "You see, he …"

"I …" Greg said, trying and failing to help.

Katelin shook her head. "You boys."

CHAPTER NINE

Bill declined to enter the house after asking Katelin if "that dog" was inside. After bidding Bill farewell, Greg followed his aunt into a large living room that mirrored the outside excess of the house. The walls were painted a dark, rich red. A three-inch wide strip of pearl white wooden molding ran around the room about a foot below the top of the twenty-foot ceiling. The crystal chandelier that hung from the middle of the golden yellow ceiling reflected and refracted the light given off from the brass antique gas lamps evenly spaced along the walls. Although the gas lamps had been converted to electric, the filaments had been skillfully hidden inside irregular glass bulbs. Rather than a solid light source, the bulbs created the illusion of dancing flames.

A set of solid-looking, brown leather furniture rested on the hardwood floor. The furniture so perfectly matched the deep brown color of the polished floor that the couch, love seat, and two recliners seemed to have grown out of the floor like oddly shaped, but comfortable-looking, tree trunks.

The furniture surrounded a rectangular, black iron and glass coffee table. Three smaller, square versions of the coffee table served as end tables, one at each end of the couch and the other beside the right arm of one of the recliners. A Tiffany stained-glass lamp sat atop each glass end table. The lampshade by the recliner was a floral pattern of reds, blues, greens, and purples. The two by the couch were golden amber dragonflies. The lamps gave off a brilliant display of colored light like beams of liquid candy.

A massive mahogany bookcase that stretched almost to the ceiling took up the far right corner of the room. Behind the glass doors of the bookcase was a collection of ballerina figurines to rival the dreams of many a ten-year-old girl. The figurines were an eclectic collection of crystal, glass, and painted porcelain. Some twirled and danced solo, frozen in time; others performed in troops or with gentlemanly partners. A dozen or so dancers sprang from music and jewelry boxes.

"Those were your mother's," Katelin said somberly.

This surprised Greg. Although his mother had obviously been a child at one point, Greg found it difficult to imagine her playing with music boxes, giggling in that infectious way that only a little girl can giggle. As an adult, she had been so serious, so intense, so haunted.

A doorway to the left of the bookcase led into what Greg guessed to be the dining room, from what he could glimpse of the table and chairs that lay within. In the middle of the left wall of the dining room was another doorway. From this angle Greg could not see what lay beyond, but assumed it was the kitchen.

Farther along the same wall as the dining room doorway was another doorway. From his vantage point, Greg had a clear view of honey-colored, stained pine cabinets, a white tiled floor, and a granite countertop that housed a stainless steel sink. This confirmed Greg's suspicion that the kitchen and dining room connected.

Katelin motioned toward a closed door in the left corner. "That's the den and a bathroom." Katelin walked farther into the living room, toward a large archway that took up half of the wall. "And in here is the family room."

Greg followed Katelin into the family room. The walls and ceiling were painted a dark forest green. The floor was the same stained wood of the living room. A large, square, white rug in the center of the room hid most of the floor from view. The two love seats in the room were a light brown, suede fabric. They looked soft and comfortable. They sat in the middle of the room, facing a gigantic flat-screen plasma television mounted to the far wall like a painting come to life. The jutting brick fireplace against the far wall, its inside blackened with use, looked out of place in the otherwise modern room.

Although no one sat on the love seats, or at the computer desk in the left corner of the room, the television brought an old episode of *The Muppet Show* to life in large-screen grandeur. Sound filled the room from a stereo system directly under the television. The four towering speakers, two on each side of the stereo, accompanied the smaller speakers placed in the corners of the room near the ceiling. They transformed the noises of the muppet Animal into brilliant stereo sound as he finished pounding on his drum set, panting and slowly blinking his gigantic eyes. The well-placed speakers did such a good job of directing sound that Greg had not even heard the television until he had entered the family room.

"The archway over there in the corner leads upstairs. That's the tower you probably saw from outside. It's a spiral staircase that goes up to the second floor."

Greg nodded. While looking at the spiral staircase within the tower, Greg caught movement from the farthest love seat. The biggest dog that Greg had ever seen rolled off the far left love seat and padded around toward him. It was so large it almost looked unreal, and Greg took an instinctive step backwards.

Katelin lightly took hold of Greg's arm. "Don't worry, he's harmless."

Greg was not sure if his aunt was talking to him or the dog. Either way, he felt little comfort from his aunt's assurance as the dog came closer. Standing in front of him, the dog was massive: over three and a half feet tall at the shoulder and built as solid as a four-legged beer keg. It turned its basketball-sized head sideways and stared at Greg. It was the same color as the love seat: a light brown, like a pair of faded khaki pants. Its eyes, nose, and ears were a darker shade of brown, almost black. It looked kind of like a bulldog on steroids. Greg guessed it had to weigh close to two hundred pounds.

"Spooky, this is Greg. Greg, this is Spooky," Katelin said by way of introduction. "I expect you two to play nice."

Spooky glanced at Katelin and then brought his attention back to Greg.

So, this was "that dog" Bill had asked about. Greg could not blame Bill for not wanting to confront this dogzilla. It seemed that they were at a standoff. It did not appear that Spooky was going to move, and Greg knew there was no way in hell that he was capable of *making* the dog move. Gaze still on the dog that all Chihuahuas dreamed of being when they grew up, Greg asked, "What kind of dog is it?"

"*It* is a *he*. And we believe he's an English Mastiff, although he could be a mix. He's a little big, even by mastiff standards."

"So, uh," Greg said after a moment, "why's he just standing there?"

"English Mastiffs are very protective, but not very violent. They usually won't attack unless provoked. But they will corner you and not let you move away."

As if listening to Katelin, Spooky took a step toward Greg and brought his massive head close to Greg's thigh.

Greg tensed, imagining sharp teeth sinking into the muscle of his leg, viselike jaws clamping down and refusing to let go.

Spooky sniffed once, twice, took a step back, cocked his head to one side, and gazed intently at Greg.

Greg could not help but feel that Spooky was sizing him up, looking for something. The dog was aptly named. As Greg looked into Spooky's eyes, he felt that the dog looked into him, judging him, deciding whether or not he was a good person. The feeling was … well, *spooky.*

Apparently Spooky decided he liked what he saw, or smelled, because no sooner had Greg finished wondering about the apparent canine judging than Spooky wagged his tail, turned, and walked back toward the love seat, climbed on, lay on his side, and resumed watching television.

Greg could not decide which was stranger: the fact that Spooky watched TV, or that he liked reruns of *The Muppet Show*, a program whose target audience was decidedly non-canine.

CHAPTER TEN

In contrast to the downstairs rooms of wood floors and colorful walls, the upstairs hallway walls were a muted gray with matching carpet. Following his aunt down the second-floor hallway, Greg felt as if he were in a motel: the hallway was a long corridor with darkly stained, wooden doors evenly spaced down both sides. Wall sconces similar to those downstairs dimly lit the hallway, throwing onto the walls shadows shaped like strange underwater creatures that were half jellyfish and half angel.

A grandfather clock stood on sentry duty against the center of the wall at the end of the hall, all carved wooden pillars, glass, and shining mechanisms. A brass pendulum ticked off the seconds.

Greg passed four doors, two on each side of the hallway, before stopping beside his aunt, who stood in front of the right side door at the end of the hallway adjacent to the ticking clock. Katelin opened the door and walked in. Greg followed.

Like everything else Greg had seen in the house, the bedroom was on an immense scale, from the armoire in the right corner to the four-poster canopy bed resting against the middle of the left wall that could have provided an elephant with a good night's sleep and room to stretch out. Along the far wall golden velvet drapes covered what Greg guessed to be windows. The walls had been painted to resemble aged parchment: pale yellow splotches randomly played across a background of ivory. In the left-hand corner light shone through an open doorway from the bathroom.

"Sorry you couldn't meet your uncle Ron tonight," Katelin said. "He worked first shift at a pork processing plant for a long time. First shift started at five in the morning. He's accustomed to getting up early and going to bed early. Old habits die hard."

Greg nodded. "That's alright. I'll see him tomorrow."

"Of course you will," his aunt agreed. She patted his shoulder and smoothed out his shirt. "My, you've grown up. Where do the years go?"

"I don't know," Greg said.

Katelin smiled. "None of us know. You make yourself at home. If you need anything, I'm down the hall, right next door. Ron is farther down, first door on the right, but he sleeps like the dead and probably wouldn't wake up if it was judgment day and God himself was knocking on his door."

Greg thought it a little strange that his aunt and uncle slept in separate rooms, but reasoned that maybe they were just old-fashioned. Small town Midwest values or something. "Shit," Greg said suddenly. He glanced at his aunt. "Sorry."

"That's okay. You're a grown man now. You can say shit if you want to."

"I left my luggage in the rental car. And I left the rental car behind the bar," Greg said.

"Oh, don't worry about that tonight," Katelin said, walking over to the armoire. She opened both doors. Inside, on hangers, were enough clothes for at least two weeks: jeans, khaki dress pants, button-down shirts, polo shirts. Below the hanging clothes rested pairs of tan work boots, glossy black dress shoes, and white tennis shoes. Inside the bottom drawers were T-shirts, socks, underwear. Everything was obviously new.

"Wow," Greg said. "You didn't have to go to all the trouble. Don't get me wrong, though, I appreciate it."

"It's no trouble at all. We take care of family around here. You'll find all the toiletries you need in the bathroom."

Standing beside his aunt in front of the armoire, Greg examined the clothes. Everything was the correct size, including the shoes. "How'd you know my sizes?"

Katelin shrugged. "Some things you just know," she said cryptically.

"Well … thanks," Greg finally mumbled.

"You're welcome, honey. Now it's getting past ten and I'm going to head off to bed, unless you need anything else."

Greg shook his head. "No, I'm good."

His aunt hugged him, stood on her tiptoes, and kissed him on the cheek. Greg felt heat enter his face in a blush.

Katelin slowly shook her head. "All grown up. If you get hungry you know where the kitchen is. Help yourself. This is your house, too. You make yourself at home."

Greg waved as his aunt shut the door.

Greg stood staring at the closed door. It felt strange, surreal, to be hugged and kissed by a woman who looked exactly like his mother, who was his aunt, who was his family, of whom he had no memory.

Greg gave up on chasing his own thoughts around and around like a dog chasing its tail, and instead went to the corner of the room by the bathroom and pulled back the end of the golden drapes to reveal two sets of double windows that flanked a set of glass doors. The doors led out onto a balcony. Greg guessed that this was a continuation of the balcony he had seen from the front of the house that ran atop the porch.

Glancing from the balcony to the night beyond, Greg saw a shadowy form, large and low to the ground, slinking in and out of the woods that surrounded the sparse backyard. It would appear for a moment from the tree line, then disappear back into the trees, only to reappear from the tree line a few feet farther to the left. It was approaching a shed that sat under an amber light suspended from a wooden pole that made the shed and surrounding ground appear to be one of those old photos that were not black-and-white, but a grainy yellow brown.

A shadow fell across the ground beside the shed and grew as the creature came from out of the woods. Soon the creature was illuminated by the amber light, and Spooky came into full view, nose to the ground, following the scent-trail of some woodland creature.

Greg laughed, partly in humor, but partly in relief. As a city boy and resident of Miami, Greg was not accustomed to so many trees—woods illuminated solely by moonlight. It was kind of creepy to think about what was skulking through the trees, even if it was apparently only a giant dog who liked to watch *The Muppet Show*.

Greg left Spooky to his moonlight tracking and walked into the bathroom. Two glass globes suspended from chains hung at each side of a large rectangular mirror mounted to the wall above the double sinks. From his reflection, Greg's left eye looked terrible. It had swelled, the flesh from temple, to under eye, to nose a bloody purple. At the slightest pressure from Greg's finger, his face throbbed and spikes of pain pierced his left eye.

"Asshole," Greg said, thinking about Jimmy.

As his aunt had assured him, he found everything he needed in the vanity under the sinks. Everything was what he always used, from his brand of deodorant to his favorite toothbrush and toothpaste. It was weird how his aunt apparently knew exactly what to get him, or that he would even need the stuff in the first place. But Greg had been through enough for one day, and decided to just let it go. Right now, sleep was more important than the mystery of psychic deodorant selection.

After a quick teeth-brushing and a pee, Greg walked back into the bedroom, stripped down to his underwear, and crawled under the weight of the flannel comforter. He left the bathroom lights on, telling himself it would be easier to find the bathroom with the lights on if he had to pee in the middle of the night—which was true, but not the whole truth.

Greg dreams that he sits at the kitchen table with his aunt, who is pretending to be his mother. He is in a high chair for toddlers, but is his present age. The tabletop of the high chair painfully digs into his stomach. His arms are pinned to his sides.

On the table is a banquette of food that is all white: mashed potatoes, turkey and chicken breasts, rice, glasses of milk.

Unable to feed himself, his aunt plucks marshmallows from a huge bowl and shoves them into his mouth. He barely has time to start chewing before she shoves another one in, and another, and another. His mouth full of white goo, he is unable to tell her to stop, his jaw painfully cramping as his aunt continually crams in the marshmallows, telling him, "You can't expect to grow up to be big and strong if you don't eat your marshmallows."

He tries desperately to tell her that he will indeed eat his marshmallows, but he needs time to chew. Involuntary tears begin to fall from his eyes as his jaw creaks and his bottom lip splits, warm blood running down to drip from his chin onto the white plastic tabletop of the high chair. When the red drops of blood hit the high chair tabletop, they turn white.

"You're going to grow up to be so big and strong," his aunt coos as she shoves another marshmallow into his straining mouth.

His bottom jaw dislocates with a wet grinding sound. He opens his throat to scream, but instead chokes on bloody marshmallow mush.

"So big and strong," his aunt says approvingly.

CHAPTER ELEVEN

Greg awoke to the sound of heavy breathing. He figured he had been snoring and had woken himself, which he had previously done on a few occasions when he had gone to bed extremely tired. When he realized that he was awake, could still hear the sound, and that it was coming from the other side of the bed, behind him, he snapped his eyes open and half rolled, half jumped, over. And came face-to-face with a monster.

Greg let out a yelp and lurched backward so fast he fell off the side of the bed, got his legs tangled in the comforter, and landed on the floor face down. Even as he landed he kicked the comforter away. He sprang to his feet, panting, and spun to face his enemy, still blinking away sleep from his bleary eyes.

In the early morning sunlight that managed to creep through the windows and around the edges of the drapes, Spooky opened his eyes, lifted his giant head from the pillow, and yawned, revealing sharply pointed teeth. He looked at Greg for a moment before letting his head fall back to the pillow. He closed his eyes and wagged his tail a few times. Each time Spooky struck the mattress with his tail, it produced a deep *thud* loud enough that anyone outside the room would have guessed that someone was jumping on the bed.

"Jesus Christ, man!" Greg said, trying to catch his breath. He glanced at the bedroom door. It was still closed. He returned his attention to Spooky. "How'd you get in here?"

Spooky replied by thumping his tail against the mattress. A single, powerful *thud.*

"Why am I talking to a dog?" Greg sighed. "Never mind, I'm taking a shower." He headed into the bathroom. "And I wasn't talking to *you* when I said

I was taking a shower," Greg told Spooky from the bathroom. He closed the bathroom door, and after a moment of consideration, locked it for good measure.

Greg walked into the kitchen with Spooky close behind. Katelin stood in front of the stove, stirring something that looked like thick clam chowder but smelled much better. Greg's mouth began to fill with saliva. "What is that?" he asked.

"Sausage gravy. For the biscuits," his aunt said. "You like biscuits and gravy?"

"I don't know. But I think I'm going to like *your* biscuits and gravy," Greg replied.

Katelin smiled. "Of course you will. You're a country boy at heart. It's in your blood."

Katelin's comment about blood reminded Greg of the marshmallow dream. Greg rarely remembered dreams, and when he did they were usually only fragmented pieces, more feelings than actual memories. But the marshmallow dream came flooding into his mind with startling clarity. Greg did not fail to notice that the sausage gravy was white.

Katelin glanced over her shoulder. "I see you made a new friend."

As before when in a room with his aunt and the dog, Greg was not sure if Katelin had spoken to him or the dog. "Yeah, I guess so," Greg said.

Sitting on his haunches beside Greg, Spooky thumped the tile floor with his tail.

"Doesn't that hurt?" Greg found himself asking Spooky.

In reply, Spooky struck the floor again.

"Why don't you go say hi to your uncle?" Katelin suggested. "He's in the dining room. Breakfast will be ready shortly."

"Good idea," Greg said, and headed into the dining room with Spooky.

Greg's uncle had apparently heard Greg speaking with Katelin, because he was rising from the dining room table as Greg entered the room. He put the newspaper on the table and extended his hand toward Greg.

Ron was not a big man, but he had a firm handshake. While Katelin, with her slim, athletic body, could have passed for a woman in her thirties, Ron looked older. Wrinkles ran across the dry skin of his forehead like ancient riverbeds long since forgotten by any source of water. When he smiled at Greg, new wrinkles appeared from the outer corners of his eyes like bolts of lightning. He had a red-tinged nose from burst capillaries, marking him as a drinker. Loose curls of gray hair sprung from around the bottom of a battered black NASCAR cap. Greg guessed him to be about fifty-five.

Handshake over, Ron patted Greg on the shoulder. "Sit down, bud," he said, following his own advice. "Haven't seen you since day before never."

Greg sat and glanced at his uncle. He did not know what to say. Although they were technically family, Greg having no memory of the man made things a bit awkward.

Ron seemed to understand how Greg felt. He reached over and patted Greg on the shoulder again. "I know it's rough, meetin' like this, under the circumstances. We don't need to pretend like we've known each other our whole lives. We'll just take her as she comes."

"Sounds good," Greg said.

"And I'm damn sorry about your mom," Ron said with such simple sincerity that Greg felt a stabbing spike of sadness pierce his chest.

Greg looked down at the tabletop and nodded. "Yeah."

CHAPTER TWELVE

Greg gazed in disbelief at his reflection. He brought his face closer to the mirror, his breath creating rhythmic pools of condensation on the mirror's surface that grew and shrank in time with his exhales.

He ran his finger over his left temple, eyelid, and cheek. What had been a bloody, purple, swollen mess was now normal flesh, the white of his left eye once again white, no trace of the former angry explosion of burst blood vessels that had lit up his eye like miniature red fireworks. Had his face been like this since he had woken? Greg could not remember if he had looked at himself in the mirror this morning. If he had, he was sure he would have noticed that the wound to his face, which should have taken at least the next two weeks to heal, had seemingly healed overnight, as if the wound had been merely drawn on, and then erased in the middle of the night, leaving no trace that it had ever existed.

Greg turned his head toward the bedroom and saw Spooky sitting in the bathroom doorway. Spooky slanted his head and looked at Greg as if to say, *What?*

"That's not normal," Greg said, returning his attention to knotting his tie. With the tie done, Greg put on the black suit jacket. Spooky moved to let him pass as Greg walked out of the bathroom. Greg and Spooky headed back downstairs. Greg did not have time to think about his face. He had to bury his mother.

He met his aunt and uncle in the living room. Both had somber expressions, Ron in a brown suit that looked like it might have been new thirty years ago, Katelin in a simple black dress that reminded Greg of a morbid version of Dorothy in *The Wizard of Oz*.

Greg just wanted to get this over with. He wondered if he should be feeling something: remorse, sadness, loss. But there was only the familiar mixture of anger and confusion that filled him whenever he thought of his mother and their time together: a nomadic childhood of constant chaos and change. Of not knowing where they were going to wake up tomorrow. Of not knowing what new madness he would be forced to listen to and repeat until his mother was convinced that he believed her insanity as much as she did.

His mother had never been physically abusive, but Greg believed that while physical abuse was terrible, it healed; trauma to the fragile, mysterious mind seemed to remain, to linger like a half-forgotten nightmare. A broken arm would mend, but the emotional damage caused by knowing that someone had hurt you, someone who was supposed to love and protect you, hurt far deeper and lasted far longer. They did not make casts for a broken mind, or a broken heart.

"You alright, bud?" his uncle asked.

"Of course he's not alright," his aunt chided.

"Well, that's not what I meant," Ron said. "He looks a little peaked. Like he's gonna pass out or some such thing."

"I'm okay," Greg assured his uncle.

Katelin nodded. "He's a brave boy. He's a Dameron."

Greg followed his aunt and uncle, and Spooky followed Greg, out onto the front porch. "Sorry, buddy, you can't go," Greg said to Spooky.

"Of course he can," Katelin said.

Greg looked at his aunt. "They allow dogs in a funeral home? Isn't that some kind of health-code violation?"

Katelin smirked. "Whose health would a dog be violating in a funeral home? And besides, we're not going to a funeral home. Katherine was buried with the rest of the family."

"*Was* buried?" Greg said.

"Oh, honey," Katelin said, nodding knowingly, "you thought we were going to a funeral. No, your mother never wanted that. Not a bit of it."

"So, my mother is already buried?" Greg asked in astonishment.

Katelin rubbed Greg's arm with her hand. "Honey, that's what she wanted. Now, let's go see her."

Greg allowed himself to be led around the side of the house and into the backyard. A dirt path disappeared into the woods. This was getting stranger by the minute. Greg glanced at his uncle, who shrugged and looked down at his shoes. Greg looked at his aunt. "The cemetery is in *there*?" Greg said, pointing toward the woods. "My mother is buried in the woods? In the fucking woods?"

Katelin frowned for a moment before setting her mouth firmly and looking at Greg. She eerily resembled his mother whenever she had been ready to go off on one of her crazy lectures about how you could trust no one, or that everyone was out to get you, or that you could never go home because you had no home to go to and your family did not exist. Just the thought of it caused Greg to shut his mouth and become silent.

Katelin's expression softened. "Honey, I know this might seem strange to you, but this is how we do things in this family. We're proud and we have a long history." Katelin spread her hands. "This has always been Dameron land. This is our land. This is *family* land. Family means something to us. Your mother is on our land, on *her* land, with family. It's where she should be."

Greg didn't know what to say. He felt embarrassed by his outburst and confused by the surreal quality of the entire experience. He nodded. "Okay."

Greg took his place in the strange three-person, one-dog procession, and entered the woods. Katelin led the way. Greg walked behind Ron. Spooky brought up the rear.

The interior of the woods was darker than Greg would have imagined. It was like the woods formed a barrier that when stepped through, cut off the warm, early afternoon sunlight. Greg did not mind. The woods matched his darkening mood. *Who the hell gets buried without even a funeral?* But Greg knew the answer to his own question: *my mother, that's who.*

In the woods the air was chilly and smelled damp. It was not a clean, crisp odor, like the smell of clear well water or a new chlorine swimming pool, but rather a deeper, more complex smell, like freshly turned, wet earth.

Although the air smelled of dampness, it did not appear to have rained recently, as the path was dry. Greg noticed a light dusting of dirt had covered the front of his previously gleaming, black leather shoes, turning them a dull gray. Oddly, there was nothing on the path *except* dirt: no twigs, no rocks. Not even one fallen autumn leaf marred the perfectly clear path. Leaves covered the forest floor, right up to the edge of the path, where none dared to cross the line.

Greg felt like he was in some childhood story. That if he left the protective boundaries of the path and entered the dim woods, huge hidden monsters would leap out and grab him, hungry mouths filled with sharp teeth and eager clawed fingers grasping at his flesh. The monsters would take him to their home, where if he passed their test, they would make him one of them. But if he failed, they would put him in a pot and make him into dinner: cream-of-Greg soup. Good with crackers.

They passed an oak tree that appeared to have been blasted by lightning. It had been split almost down the middle of its massive trunk; half lay on the forest floor, a fallen monolith, dead and soon rotting, home to insects, while the other half, scorched black by the searing heat of the lightning, fought for survival, branches held high to the life-giving sun. Greg wondered if the tree would live through the winter.

At a fork in the path, they went left. Greg could feel the cemetery before he could see it. He did not know why or how, but he knew that they were close. And then they were there. A black, waist-high, iron fence enclosed the square earth of the surprisingly large cemetery. Greg guessed it to be about sixty feet to the far side of the fence. The path branched off, one branch continuing forward along the outer right side of the fence, while the other branch traveled along the remaining fence perimeter to circle back around and connect to the original path.

Well, at least the path circles the cemetery, so the monsters won't get me in there, Greg reasoned.

CHAPTER THIRTEEN

Greg stood in front of the foot-high mound of dirt that had been covered with green Astroturf, as if the grim fact that a body was buried in the blackness of the ground could be overlooked if only covered over with plastic grass. Spooky sat to his right, and his aunt and uncle stood to his left. The headstone was simple, solid. The stone was as black as ink, and so shiny that Greg could see his sardonic expression reflected back at him. The stone was shaped like the cutting end of a giant chisel, beveled to form a sharp edge that pointed toward the sky. Deeply carved letters on the beveled surface read:

KATHERINE LYNN DAMERON

Daughter and Mother
Missed in Life
Mourned in Death

No dates, no long-winded sentiments. The headstone was simple, so unlike his mother, who had been filled with so many layers of eccentricity that a few mere sentences could never begin to describe her character or personality.

Spooky whimpered softly. Greg reached over and scratched the dog behind the ears. Spooky lay down, put his head on his paws. Maybe death was universal to all creatures, regardless of intellect or emotional capacity. Perhaps on an instinctual level, the loss and finality of death were understood by all those that still lived. Maybe all living things understood on some level that death was final and unforgiving.

It was that finality that hit Greg. The unarguable fact that he would never see his mother again was crushing in its certainty. Yes, they had been estranged for the past decade, but deep down Greg had still known that his mother walked the earth, that she was alive, somewhere, that maybe someday, somehow, their paths would cross again. Now, she was gone. He was *never* going to see her alive again. The certainty of his mother's death did not make him emotional, sad, or filled with grief. In fact, it did the exact opposite: it left a void, a small hollow space inside him that he knew would never be filled—a soft echo of loss that he would carry with him to his own grave.

"I'll never be able to forgive her for taking you away from me," Katelin said, staring at her twin sister's headstone.

"Don't talk shit about the dead," Ron said.

Greg ignored his aunt and uncle, looking past them to the weathered, gray stone mausoleum that stood in the far corner of the cemetery. Stone gargoyles perched around the top of the stout structure, some in stoic observation, others with wings spread, frozen in the second before flight. Greg could not recall ever before seeing actual gargoyles on a structure.

A dozen or so feet away, beside what looked like an apple tree—Greg wondered if anyone would actually eat an apple from a tree that grew in a cemetery—stood a white marble statue of an angel standing on a dais. The statue was at least six feet tall, the dais another two. It was not a benevolent angel, but instead the soldierly fire-and-brimstone type, full of power and vengeance, ready to do battle, square-jawed and muscular. In its left hand the angel held an oval shield with a cross umbo in the center. In its right, a double-edged sword, pointed toward the ground in front of its sandaled feet. The angel's stern gaze seemed to follow the sword's path, long hair and flowing robes billowing in an imaginary wind, wings half spread. Greg was not a religious man, but the statue was an imposing figure nonetheless.

Greg brought his attention back to his aunt and uncle. They were both looking at him expectantly. "Is there anything you'd like to say?" his aunt asked.

Greg thought about it and shook his head, glancing from his aunt to his uncle.

Ron seemed nervous. He pulled at the sleeve of his suit, looked at Greg, and tried to smile. "It's a nice headstone," he finally said. "You know why they call 'em headstones?"

"No," Greg said.

"Well, back in the olden days, people were afraid that dead people didn't always stay dead. That sometimes after you buried 'em, they'd get up and walk away. So they put big stones on top of their graves, above their heads. That way, if the dead tried to sit up, the stones would stop 'em."

"That's not true," Katelin said.

"It sure as shit is," Ron assured her.

Katelin seemed unconvinced. "How do you know?"

"I read it. On the Internet."

"That doesn't make it true."

"Well, it doesn't make it *not* true, either."

"I think I'm ready to go now," Greg said, interrupting the debate.

"Of course you are, honey," Katelin said. She walked over to Greg and took hold of his arm. "Let's get you home."

CHAPTER FOURTEEN

Back at the house, Spooky went off into the family room. A few moments later Greg heard theme music coming from the television. At first he could not remember the show. Then it came back to him from childhood memories: *Fraggle Rock*.

Greg looked at his aunt. "So, he can turn on the TV? And he actually really watches it?"

Katelin nodded. "He only watches kids' shows, though."

"That dog's somethin' else," Ron said, walking over and opening the refrigerator door. "You wanna beer?"

"He's talking to you," Katelin said to Greg. "I can't stand the stuff."

"Yeah, after today I think I need one," Greg said.

"That's what I'm talkin' about. Man after my own heart. Think fast!"

Greg did not have time to think at all, fast or otherwise, before his uncle tossed a silver-colored can at him. It hit Greg in the chest. He fumbled to catch it and managed to get a grip on the cold can of Coors Light before it hit the floor.

"That's why they call it the Silver Bullet," Ron said, laughing at his own joke as he opened his beer. He drank half the can in one long swallow.

Greg did him one better by downing his entire beer. He sat the empty can on the countertop.

"Oh, hell," Ron said approvingly, "we're gonna get along just fine." He brought two more cans of beer out of the refrigerator and motioned for Greg to follow him into the dining room.

Katelin touched Greg's arm. "Now you be careful. Ron can drink like a fish. Don't try to keep pace with him. I imagine after today a few drinks will do you good, though. So, you two go be boys and tomorrow we'll talk about things."

Greg thought about asking his aunt what "things" they needed to talk about, but the first beer had tasted good, and while Greg was not a heavy drinker, he knew from past experience that when the first beer tasted that good, there were going to be a few more to follow.

The second beer tasted as good as the first, and soon Greg found himself drinking his fifth. Or was it sixth? He could not quite remember. Although not drunk, he was well on his way.

Alcohol seems to be the great social equalizer, and the more Greg and Ron drank, the more they talked. Although it can sometimes drive women insane, men have the uncanny ability to communicate by not communicating. What a man does *not* say is often as important as what he does say. And so, neither man brought up Greg's mother, both aware that this evening was about escaping the day, not dwelling on it.

Ron took a drag from his cigarette and peered at Greg through the nimbus of smoke that surrounded his balding head. Out of respect, he was without one of his customary NASCAR caps. "So, you had a big-ass black eye and it just went away?"

"Yeah, it's weird."

"Bullshit!" Ron barked. "You're shitting me."

Greg shook his head. "I shit you not."

"Well, anyway, Jimmy's an asshole."

"That's what I said!" Greg exclaimed. They both laughed.

"His dad used to be a cop around here. Biggest prick you ever met. One time he pulled me over for runnin' the Blackhawk Road stop sign comin' into town." Ron shrugged. "Hell, nobody was around. It's a gravel road. People run that stop sign all the time. So I'm pulled over, with Hard-on Harold—" Ron leaned forward. "We called him Hard-on. He liked it," Ron said, and winked at Greg. He leaned back in his chair. "So, anyway, it's rainin' like a bitch, and I'm pulled over on the side of the road, got my window down, and here comes old Hard-on struttin' up to my truck like King Shit of Turd Mountain. So you know what he says to me, standin' there with that shit-eatin' grin of his on his face? He says, 'So how's it feel to get pulled over for runnin' a stop sign?' Now, I'm not the brightest guy in the world, but I got my moments, and I said, 'So how's it feel to be standin' out in the rain gettin' all wet just so you can ask me how it feels to get pulled over?'"

Greg laughed.

Ron grinned. "Hard-on gave me a ticket. He was such a prick."

"Is he still around here?" Greg asked.

"No, he uh …" Ron cleared his throat. "He killed himself about five years ago. Blew half his head clean off his shoulders with a shotgun. His wife left him, for a *woman*. In small towns like Lost Haven, everybody knows everybody, and everybody knows everybody's business. Guess old Hard-on just couldn't take people laughin' at him behind his back anymore." Ron put the first two fingers of his right hand into his mouth and cocked his thumb back like the hammer on a pistol. Then he dropped his thumb against his hand. "And that was all she wrote."

"So, a guy named *Hard-on* who was a giant *prick* had his wife leave him for a woman, who obviously had no hard-on or prick. That's kind of ironic," Greg said.

Ron seemed to seriously contemplate Greg's statement. He scratched the stubble on his chin. "You know, I never thought about that." Ron grinned. "That's funny. Wrong, but funny."

"I know," Greg said, and grinned as well.

"So, what do you do in Miami?"

"Computer programming. Mainframe stuff. COBOL and CICS mostly."

"Really?" Ron said, and stood. "Well hell, bud, if you like computers I got somethin' to show ya."

Greg stood. He felt pleasantly numb. He raised his beer and nodded at his uncle. "Lead the way."

Ron's bedroom was a lot like Ron: worn and rough around the edges, but still in one piece. It smelled a lot like Ron, too: cigarette smoke and beer. He did not have an actual bed, only a mattress and box spring on a wheeled metal frame. A human-sized depression in the center of the mattress testified to where Ron slept. The jumble of sheets and blankets heaped at the foot of the mattress looked like a miniature plaid mountain range. The battered dresser that leaned into the corner looked like it would have fallen apart long ago if not for the support of the nicotine-stained wall. A hat rack hung on the wall next to the bathroom door, its wooden slats forming a diamond pattern, its wooden pegs holding a collection of NASCAR caps in virtually every color of the rainbow. Greg guessed there had to be at least two dozen caps, some creased and scuffed, others so pristine they appeared never to have been worn.

"Some of 'em are autographed," Ron said, sitting down at a nice glass-topped computer desk, the only piece of furniture in the room that did not look like it had been purchased at a secondhand store that specialized in selling fifth- and sixth-hand furniture. "Got ones from Jimmie Johnson, Bobby Labonte, Kyle Petty, to name a few. My pride and joy's signed by the old Intimidator himself—Dale Earnhardt. God bless him, that man could drive a race car."

Greg studied the impressive computer system that rested on the glass-topped desk. Currently, the two flat-screen monitors were dark.

Ron sat in the black leather office chair. "Dual processors and a shitload of RAM."

Greg nodded. "It's a nice system."

"At first I got interested in computers cuz I found out you can get porn on the Internet." Ron shrugged. "Guess I'm an old pervert, but hell, that's just me. Eventually I started gettin' interested in other things." Ron leaned forward. "Watch this," he whispered. He pushed a combination of keys on the keyboard—Greg guessed it was Ctrl-Alt-Del—and brought up a login screen on both monitors. He typed in a password. The right monitor went through the login process that most PC users are familiar with, while the left monitor displayed another password entry screen. Ron keyed in a second password and the screen changed into four split-screen images, two on top, two on bottom.

Greg leaned forward to get a better view. The monitor displayed four real-time camera images. The upper left corner displayed the beginning of the driveway and gravel road from outside the gate. The upper right image was from the perspective of the right side of the house. It looked out onto the yard. Similarly, the lower left displayed a view of the left side of the yard, while the lower right showed the backyard.

Ron pushed a series of keys and the camera images began to move, panning from left to right and right to left. It made Greg a little dizzy. Ron pushed another series of keys and the camera images split into eight smaller squares. Now Greg could see not only the outside of the house, but the inside as well. He saw small images of the kitchen, dining room, family room, and for the first time, the inside of the den.

Greg looked from the images to his uncle. "Damn," he managed to say.

Ron nodded knowingly. "Katelin thinks I just get drunk and pass out early, which sometimes I do. But not all the time. Sometimes I stay up late and watch things," he whispered.

Greg was not sure if he was uncomfortable because of the cameras or because his uncle was staring at him, his expression suddenly somber.

"Did you really have a black eye that went away overnight?"

"Yeah, I did," Greg admitted, for some reason lowering his own voice to match his uncle's.

"Did Katelin see your face all banged up?"

Greg nodded. "When I first got here I had the black eye."

Ron frowned and shook his head. "That's what I figured. Listen, bud, you need to leave. It's not good for you here."

Greg opened his mouth, but did not know what to say.

"You're leavin' tomorrow, right?" his uncle asked hopefully.

"Yeah, my flight leaves from Des Moines tomorrow afternoon."

"Good. You make sure you're on it. You go home and forget about this place."

Greg shook his head, confused. "What's the problem? You're not making any sense."

Ron stood and faced Greg, his expression grave. "Bud, I don't need to make sense. You just trust me on this. It was nice meetin' ya. It really was. Now you take some advice from an old man, and you get your ass home. And you don't come back here. It's not safe."

"I don't get it," Greg said.

"Just promise me you'll get on that plane and get gone, for good."

"I … I promise," Greg stammered, baffled.

Ron patted him on the shoulder. "Good. Now we should get some sleep."

"Okay," Greg mumbled.

"And, bud?" his uncle said as Greg began to open the bedroom door.

"Yeah?"

"If you hear anything in the middle of the night, like weird noises, or tappin' on your bedroom window, don't go lookin' for trouble. You ignore it and stay in bed."

CHAPTER FIFTEEN

When Greg awoke, it was still dark, and he knew what was going to happen even as he tried to deny the inevitable through sheer will. He noticed that Spooky was once again his bunkmate, then his stomach rolled, cramped, and a moment later Greg found himself in the bathroom, hunched over the toilet. Because he had skipped dinner and had no solid food in his stomach, he vomited a gush of half-digested beer that was like reverse diarrhea: hot, painful, terrible.

The first wave subsided, and Greg gasped for breath, eyes filled with tears. Then the monster inside him squeezed his stomach again. Greg tried to remain quiet, embarrassed that he might be overheard, but the porcelain bowl of the toilet amplified the wet choking sounds of round two, rendering Greg's attempt at sneaky ninja-vomiting impossible. Vomiting was like falling down: you could not control it. There was a grim certainty to both the result of gravity and the result of the inebriated rationale that one more beer cannot hurt.

The third round was a series of dry heaves, a kind of hybrid gag-cough-gasp, a painful signal that the worst was over. After Greg was relatively sure that his stomach had finished its beer eviction, he reached up and flushed the toilet, leaned back against the wall, and wiped the tears from his face with a shaky hand. His throat and nasal passage burned from stomach acid. Greg grasped the sink and pulled himself to his feet. He turned on the faucet and washed out his mouth a few times before taking an experimental swallow of cold water. He felt the chill travel all the way down to his stomach, where it sat, heavy, like a brick of ice. But at least it remained in his stomach, which was a good sign.

Spooky stood in the doorway, his head and shoulders in the bathroom, hind end in the bedroom.

"Maybe I should rename you Shadow, since you keep following me around," Greg said.

Spooky turned his head sideways for a moment and looked at Greg. Then, he glanced back into the bedroom. A moment later, Greg heard the murmur of muffled voices followed by the sound of a door opening in the hall on hinges in need of oil. As the door squeaked closed, Spooky headed toward the bedroom door. By the time Greg followed, Spooky had somehow managed to open the door and poke his massive head out into the hallway, gazing to his left. Greg did the same, imagining they made an odd sight with their heads sticking out from around the doorframe like a doorway totem pole to the creator of giant dogs and the porcelain god.

A young man who had the smooth, fresh look of someone barely out of high school glanced over at Greg, his gaze traveling from Greg to Spooky and back to Greg. His right hand rested on the doorknob of Katelin's bedroom door. He raised and lowered his chin in a hip nod. "Hey."

"Hey," Greg said.

Spooky chose to remain speechless.

With that, the young man walked down the hall and headed downstairs.

Greg decided that he was awake for the day, even though technically the day had not yet begun and the grandfather clock in the hall stoically proclaimed it to be four thirty in the morning.

Back in the bedroom, Spooky followed Greg as far as the bathroom, at which point he sat back on his hind legs and watched Greg. Greg pointed at the bedroom door. "Guard the door and don't let any strange high school kids in," he said, and grinned. He stopped grinning a moment later when Spooky, still sitting, swiveled around to face the bedroom door. Greg shook his head. "You're weird. But I like you anyway."

Spooky thumped his tail on the carpet but did not look away from the bedroom door.

"At ease, soldier," Greg said, and shut the bathroom door behind him.

By the time Greg made it downstairs at a quarter past five, his uncle was already in the dining room, sitting at the kitchen table, reading the newspaper and sipping coffee from a mug with a cartoon cow on it. Below the cow, the mug proclaimed GET IN THE MOO-OO-OOD TO READ! Today Ron had a red NASCAR cap on his head.

"Coffee's fresh. Help yourself," Ron said without looking up from the paper. "Cups're above the sink."

Coffee in hand (his mug was a simple solid blue with no literacy-promoting cows), Greg sat at the table across from his uncle. Greg sipped the strong, dark brew, hoping his stomach would not rebel.

"Sleep alright?" his uncle asked, still reading the paper. He seemed to be tense and uncomfortable.

"Sure," Greg said.

"You know," his uncle said, lowering his voice, "what I showed you last night, upstairs, that's just between us men, okay? I just thought you'd appreciate it, you bein' into computers 'n all."

"No problem," Greg said. He took a sip of coffee and looked over the mug rim at his uncle.

Ron looked up and met Greg's gaze.

"No problem, really," Greg said.

Ron nodded, apparently convinced. He lowered his gaze back to the paper. "Sometimes I get to drinkin' and my mouth gets to flappin'. But you're a good guy. Maybe in another life we could of hung out. But the other thing I talked about, about you hightailin' it out of here, that wasn't me blowin' smoke up your ass. You need to get the fuck outta Dodge."

Greg shook his head in confusion. "Are you going to tell me why?"

Ron cleared his throat. He appeared to continue to read the paper, but Greg could tell he was thinking rather that reading—his eyes were not moving, not scanning words and sentences, but instead staring at the same spot on the page that he held in front of him, obscuring the bottom half of his face. "Let me ask you a question," he finally said.

"Okay."

"You ever been sick?"

"What?"

"It's a simple question. Think about it. Ever had a cold? The flu? You get chicken pox when you were a kid?"

Greg sat in silence. Suddenly he was uncomfortable with his uncle's questions. He felt like a kid who had been seen with his hand in the cookie jar, but did not realize he had been seen. Now, someone was testing his character to see if he would tell the truth, to see if he was a noble cookie thief or a coward.

"Actually, no," Greg said, surprising himself with the realization. He had never given any thought to the fact that he could not recall being sick, ever.

His uncle nodded. "Ain't that a little weird?"

"Maybe I just have a good immune system," Greg said, but the words sounded lame, even to him.

"Well, you see, in order for your immune system to actually *be* immune to somethin', that somethin' has to be introduced into your body so your body can fight it off, build up immunity. You can't really be immune to somethin' you never got in the first place. I mean, hell, the only way *not* to get the flu, is to get the flu shot, which is a strain of the flu virus. So, the only way not to get the flu, is to get the flu."

Greg had assumed his uncle was just your average redneck, all about titties and beer, guns and grenades. And from what little Greg knew about his uncle, he very much was a fan of the female anatomy and six packs of liquid courage, but at times he could also be surprisingly knowledgeable and socially adept.

"And then there's your face. Good immune system or not, ain't no black eye that heals overnight."

"That's true," Greg admitted.

"I'm sure when you were a kid you had your share of accidents. Every little boy scrapes the skin off his elbows and knees so many times it's a wonder it grows back. Now, think back to when you were a kid. Back to when you fell off your bike, tore your new jeans and your knees all to shit. I'll bet dollars to donuts you didn't wake up the next day with fresh new skin coverin' your knees. You woke up with stiff scabs bigger 'n cornflakes."

Greg did not know where this conversion was going, but he didn't like it. He felt a power hanging in the air like the moment before a thunderstorm rips loose and pounds the earth with water. It was like something was coming, something big and powerful, impossible to control.

By this time his uncle was staring at him over the top of the newspaper. "So then you come here and get popped in the face. You go to sleep, and the very next morning, not more 'n twelve hours later, you're good as new. It's like you went to sleep an old junker and woke up with a new paint job and a rebuilt engine."

Ron put down the paper and leaned closer to Greg. For a moment, Greg had the crazy feeling that his uncle was going to reach across the table and either kiss him or punch him. He did neither. Instead, he said, "That ain't normal. That ain't *natural*. This place … this place ain't natural either. This place is *wrong*. And you don't wanna be here."

Greg opened his mouth to say something, *anything*, in protest when he heard his aunt call from the kitchen, "I hope you two are playing nice."

Ron gave him a look that conveyed more than words could say. It was the look of a big brother telling his little brother not to tell. *Don't tell Mom we were looking at the nudie magazine! Don't tell Mom we smoked a cigarette behind the garage! Don't tell Mom we skipped school! Don't tell!*

Ron, still staring at Greg, called out, "We always play nice. Ain't that right, bud?"

"Nice as nice can be," Greg agreed.

CHAPTER SIXTEEN

"Bill may have mentioned your inheritance," Katelin said. It was early afternoon, and she stood over the sink washing the lunch dishes. She had prepared BLT sandwiches and a homemade potato salad that had to be one of the best things Greg had ever eaten. Ron had been silent during lunch, and had quickly retreated to parts unknown after finishing his meal. Greg had volunteered to help his aunt wash the dishes but she had refused, saying that the ritual of cleaning dishes relaxed her. So now he stood behind her and to the right, leaning against the refrigerator, watching her wash a plate with practiced efficiency. The dishwasher sat to her left, below the counter, empty.

"It may not be a fortune by big city standards, but close to eight hundred thousand dollars is nothing to sneeze at."

"That's for sure," Greg said.

"Is there any way you could stay just an extra day or two so we could make all the proper arrangements to take care of the money for you?" Katelin rinsed a plate and put it in the white dish drainer next to the sink. She turned and glanced at Greg. "It'd be so much easier if we could do everything with you here, honey."

"I'd like to," Greg said, hoping that the lie sounded more sincere than it felt, "but I need to get back to work. We can take care of the money over the phone and with faxes."

Katelin shrugged. "And to be honest, I haven't seen you since you were no taller than my knee. It just breaks my heart to see you go so soon. First your mother, now you." Then suddenly she was crying. She grabbed the dish towel she had been using to dry the plates and instead used it to dry her eyes.

Like most men who see a woman cry, for a moment Greg did not know what to do other than stand there, feeling uncomfortable and awkward. In most societies men are taught never to cry, but they are also never taught how to comfort someone who is. Not sure what to do, Greg stepped up behind his aunt and tentatively patted her shoulder. She reached up and put her hand over his.

Katelin dabbed her eyes with the dishcloth. "I'm sorry, honey. I've just been through a lot lately with your mother passing. I know it has to be even worse for you."

Greg felt a twinge of guilt. In reality, Katelin probably felt worse about her sister's death than he did. And it was Katelin who had taken care of everything, made all the arrangements. Hell, he had not even paid for anything. *What kind of son am I?* he wondered. *I didn't even bury my own mother and I can't wait to get the hell out of here. What a selfish little shit.*

And just like that he made the decision. "I have an open plane ticket, so I can leave whenever. I'll stay a few more days."

Katelin sniffled and patted Greg's hand. "You're such a good boy."

"You can't stay here! I told you that!" Ron practically hissed. He took a drag from his cigarette and looked out at the woods behind the house.

Beside him on the second floor balcony, Greg remained quiet.

"What the fuck were you thinkin'? Let me guess, she turned on the water works, got all weepy, and you just caved in." Ron shook his head. "Oldest goddamned trick in the book. A woman knows all she has to do is start cryin' and suddenly a man will do anything to get her to stop. We think it's our fault she's cryin', even when we got nothin' to do with it. And then we gotta try to fix it. We didn't do a damned thing to make her start—"

Ron was really getting wound up. *Off on a tangent,* Greg would have said, had he been able to get a word in. His uncle's ranting brought to mind a horse racetrack announcer: *Here comes Beer-can Ron around turn three. He's gaining ground. Now going into turn four he's only a length behind the leader. He's gaining momentum. He's coming up fast! Wow, is he pissed, folks!*

"—bunch of bullshit! So now we gotta get out the old emotional pipe wrench and tighten up all them loose bolts. Tighten everything down, make sure everything fits good as new—no leaks."

"Sorry," Greg said, but in truth he did not really care about Ron's anger. Greg felt remarkably at peace. Like he had made the right—

(selfish little shit)

—decision. Besides, his uncle's half-cocked, crazy warnings were starting to get on Greg's nerves. The things he said did not make any sense anyway.

Ron's ranting began to remind Greg of his mother and her bizarre practice of trying to control Greg's life by forcing him to listen to her insane lectures in a vain attempt to reach him with what she considered logical reason, but what in reality had been nothing more than paranoid delusions.

Who cared if his black eye had healed remarkably fast? Maybe it had not been all that bad to begin with, the shock of getting punched in the face making it appear worse than it had actually been. And so what if Greg could not remember ever being sick. That was not a bad thing. What the hell was so great about catching a cold that he was missing out on? So much for Greg's peaceful mood.

"Fuck a duck!" Ron sighed in obvious exasperation. "Sorry? You're not sorry, yet. But you stick around here and you will be. Tell you what, bud, since you seem bent on puttin' your own ass in a sling, come by my room tonight, say three in the morning."

Greg looked at his uncle in disbelief. "Three in the morning?"

"Sometimes you can see 'em during the day, but they come out a lot more at night. Besides, what do you have to do tomorrow that's so important you can't lose a little beauty sleep to humor an old drunk?"

Greg ignored Ron's question. "*What* comes out a lot more at night?"

Ron looked at him with tired resolve. "You'll see. I wouldn't have to show you if you would've just listened and left. But you'll see. Tonight."

CHAPTER SEVENTEEN

"What *comes out a lot more at night?*"

With that strange instinctual certainty that comes with some dreams, Greg knows he is dreaming. They are standing on the balcony, but in the dream it is well past sundown. Crickets chirp in the dew-covered grass, and unknown things rustle through the underbrush in the woods.

"What comes out a lot more at night?" he asks his uncle again.

"Piss!" his uncle exclaims and giggles like a girl. He unzips his pants and pulls out an impossibly long penis. It hangs past his knees. He grips the base just above the mass of pubic hair and quickly jerks his hand up and down once, snapping his penis like a flesh-colored whip. When the wave reaches the end, his penis becomes instantly erect. His uncle lets go and puts his hands behind his back, smiling proudly at Greg, his bull-sized manhood throbbing. Then, hands still locked behind his back, Greg's uncle begins to dance in place—a bow-legged little jig.

Abruptly, his uncle stops dancing, reaches down, and cups his balls in his right hand. He yanks. His right testicle comes away with a slick pop! He holds his hand out toward Greg, giving him an eye-level view of the blood and gore. "You can have it," his uncle says solemnly. "I don't need it anymore. Besides, I have to give back this king-sized fuck-stick to the bull I stole it from before midnight. Otherwise it'll turn into a pumpkin. They get mad if you keep 'em that long."

Greg awoke to the sound of his uncle's voice. He opened his eyes, disoriented. He heard a knock from the other side of his bedroom door. The side of the bed next to him was empty. Before going to bed, almost as an afterthought, Greg had locked the bedroom door. As a result, no giant dog greeted him with snoring and doggy breath. "At least he can't walk *through* doors," Greg mumbled as he got out of bed and stumbled toward the bedroom door.

As he had expected, Greg found his uncle when he opened the door. Spooky stood beside him. Greg looked at the dog, shook his head, and sighed.

Spooky wagged his tail.

"You ready?" his uncle asked.

It was obvious from the beer breath that washed over Greg's face that his uncle was drunk. *Piss-drunk,* Greg thought without humor. "You're drunk," Greg said, growing annoyed.

"No shit, Sherlock. What was your first clue?"

Greg sighed again and stretched. "Whatever. Let's get this over with so I can go back to sleep."

Ron gave a nervous laugh. "You won't be sleepin' after what you see."

In Ron's bedroom, Greg stood behind his uncle and looked over Ron's shoulder at the computer monitor that greeted him with its familiar camera images. The current four images were feeds from the outside cameras that watched the yard with unblinking electronic eyes.

Ron took a gulp of beer from his current can. Greg counted at least a dozen empty cans piled on the side of the computer desk. A few had fallen onto the carpet. Ron stared intently at the monitors, his eyes bulging.

Greg alternated between glancing at the computer monitor and glancing at his uncle. He was growing increasingly impatient.

"There's slim pickings tonight. But they'll show. I saw one earlier," Ron mumbled.

After a few minutes, feeling ridiculous and tired, Greg could not take it any longer. "What are you looking at?" he asked.

"You'll see," Ron said, his gaze fixed on the computer monitor.

Greg leaned in closer to the monitor, his head above Ron's shoulder. "I don't see shit."

"There!" Ron said, jerking a finger at the last of the four square images.

"I still don't see—"

"There it is again. On the tree line. Watch it. Wait for it. There!"

Greg did see something. It came out of the tree line. It looked like a fuzzy … well, a fuzzy *nothing.* A vague, oval-shaped, gray fuzz, like a giant amoeba, floated out from the tree line into the backyard, where it hovered for a moment before disappearing back into the trees.

"You see that?" his uncle said. "You saw that, didn't you?" he asked, his voice almost pleading.

Greg nodded. "I saw *something.*"

"That's a monster."

Greg smirked and glanced at his uncle. Ron could not have looked more seri-ous. "That could be anything," Greg finally said. "Hell, it's like that bullshit on TV where someone records little flying balls of light and says it's ghosts. Then they find out it's just specks of dust distorted by the camera lens and illuminated by the camera light."

"Could be ghosts," his uncle said.

"Jesus Christ, this is stupid," Greg said. "You're drunk and sitting in your room looking at what's probably a piece of dirt on your little spy camera lens, and telling me it's a monster." Greg was growing angry. Apparently, it was his turn to be the racetrack announcer. "A monster? What's that mean, anyway? Monster my ass!" Greg looked behind him at Spooky. "Hell, *he's* more of a monster than that thing!"

"It's a monster," was all Ron said. He did not even raise his voice, speaking with a firm conviction that was frightening, as if he were not trying to convince Greg that the fuzzy blob he had glimpsed was a floating nightmare, but rather that the sky was indeed blue, or that grass was green.

Greg thought about his mother, darkening his mood further. *Another crazy in the family. They must breed them in Iowa. Something in the damned water.*

His uncle grabbed his elbow and dug his bony fingers into Greg's flesh. His eyes were wide, quivering. "Not all of them look like that. The strong ones, the older ones, some of them have arms and legs. Sometimes they have tails, and wings, and horns, and teeth. Sometimes—"

Greg jerked his arm back, breaking his uncle's grip and nearly sending the drunken old man toppling off his chair face-first onto the floor. Behind him, Greg heard Spooky whine. "I'm going back to bed. Maybe you should lay off the beer."

"Bud, you've got to believe me," Ron called from behind Greg's back. "I'm tryin' to help you. I'm tryin' to *save* you."

"You should worry about saving yourself," Greg said from the hall, and slammed closed his uncle's door.

His aunt's door opened a few feet and a young man with a mop of chaotic black hair stuck his head out from behind the door. He was not the same one as yesterday. "What's going on out here?" he asked.

"Fuck you!" Greg said.

The young man gave a start and withdrew from the doorway. Greg heard him engage the door lock a moment later.

Greg looked down at Spooky and turned his head sideways.

Spooky looked up at Greg and did the same.

Despite his anger, Greg grinned. "Well, I guess now that I woke everyone up, we should get some sleep."

CHAPTER EIGHTEEN

Although Greg had awakened around 7:00 AM, he did not come downstairs until after nine o'clock. To his relief, his uncle was nowhere to be found. Part of Greg felt apologetic about his outburst last night, but another part of him was leery about dealing with his uncle.

Greg did, however, find his aunt as she came up from the basement by the back stairs adjacent to the kitchen door that led into the backyard. She held in her hand a small oval package wrapped in white paper that you could get at any butcher or the meat section of any grocery store. When she made eye contact, Greg felt instantly embarrassed. He could feel his face flush red. "Morning," she said.

"Morning. I'm uh … sorry about last night," Greg said, hoping the look he gave his aunt was sufficiently sheepish. "I was just, well …"

"You were just pissed off, honey," Katelin said. "That's okay. It happens. A man who never lets out his anger is a man who eventually ends up going on a killing spree. And believe me, I know how much Ron can get on your last nerve sometimes."

Greg realized that his aunt thought he was embarrassed because of his outburst, when in reality he was embarrassed for her. There were very few reasons that a young, shirtless man would be in her room at three o'clock in the morning. There were fewer reasons still that it would be two different young men in two nights. His aunt seemed not to care in the slightest that he had noticed her night-time visitors.

While his aunt was beautiful, athletic and toned, and dark-featured, exactly like Greg's mother had been, Katelin was old enough to be the mother of either of the young men. And *two* different men in two nights? Ron had to know what was going on. Did he just not care? It was becoming clear to Greg why his uncle slept in a separate bedroom: it would be difficult to sleep in the same bed with some young guy on top of your wife, humping her like a rabbit. Just the thought of it made Greg feel dirty and guilty, like being a kid again and looking at the photos of bare-breasted, dark-skinned women in *National Geographic*. Back when he had not been old enough to know exactly *what* he wanted to do with a woman, but old enough to know that he wanted to do *something* with one.

"You have to take what Ron does and says with a grain of salt," his aunt continued. "He means well, but half the time it's the beer talking. And really, Ron's a dirty man with a dirty mind. I do the laundry every week, but sometimes I miss a week. Once, while doing two weeks worth of his clothes, I found one pair of underwear. *One* pair in two weeks worth of dirty laundry. And to think, he used to ask me to put his dirty old thing in my mouth."

Greg rubbed his hand over his face. *Too much information! Didn't want to know that!* Greg, now even more embarrassed than before, glanced out the kitchen windows. Spooky had accompanied Greg downstairs. During his uncomfortable conversation with Katelin, Spooky had wondered off and apparently ended up outside in the backyard, head down, following some unknown scent. Eager to change the subject, Greg asked, "How does Spooky manage to get into rooms with the doors shut?"

Katelin shrugged as if the answer was obvious. "He opens the doors."

Well duh, Greg thought. *Ask a stupid question …*

The kitchen phone rang. Katelin answered it on the second ring. She listened for a few moments, at one point glancing at Greg and nodding. "I'll make sure to do that," she said, and hung up the phone. "Someone stole your car," she said matter-of-factly.

"What?"

"That was Bill on the phone. Seems someone stole your rental car from The Bonfire parking lot. He called to verify that you hadn't went and picked it up."

"No, I didn't pick it up," Greg said.

"I know, honey, I already told Bill that."

Greg sighed.

"Don't worry. Bill said that that's why rental companies have insurance and that he's on top of it. He'll take care of everything."

"What's there to take care of? Someone stole my car. Probably that Jimmy guy."

Greg thought he caught a hint of a smile play across his aunt's lips.

"I don't think Jimmy Elison stole your car. He might be a bully and a dimwit, but he's not a thief," his aunt assured him.

"Maybe he did it to get back at me."

"People like Jimmy don't get back at people by stealing their cars. People like Jimmy aren't that subtle. They just hit you in the face and call it even. You of all people should know that."

"Well, *someone* stole it," Greg sputtered, realizing that his aunt had subtly managed to make him feel both foolish and inferior with a few quick responses.

"Of course they did, honey. That's why Bill's taking care of it."

Greg began to feel angry again. He often felt angry lately, more so than usual, and his aunt talking to him with her condescending tone as if lecturing a child was pissing him off. He had been through enough lectures during his childhood. Lectures that made no sense and taught no lessons. Lectures that had always left him feeling confused and somehow lost.

"I'm going to my room," Greg said, realizing even as he said it how immature, how *foolish*, he sounded. He had meant to add that he was going to his room to get his tennis shoes so he could take a walk, but he did not bother to elaborate.

Although Greg had not found a jacket in his collection of new clothes, he had found a gray sweatshirt, what some would call a hoodie, which he currently wore as he walked along the gravel road, his hands in the sweatshirt's front pockets. The front of the sweatshirt read:

Property of
Indian Hills Community College
Athletic Department
XXL

The sweatshirt did a good job of keeping out the late morning breeze, which still carried a chilly bite from the night before. The crisp morning air seemed to do Greg good, clearing out his head, making him feel more alert, more awake. And it smelled good—not like the city air that Greg was accustomed to. The scent was deep and earthy, complex and yet somehow still pure, still clean. It smelled like the dreams of babies.

Greg did not know where he was going, and with the gravel road surrounded on either side by timber, he could not see much around him. So, head down, hands in pockets, Greg contented himself with watching his feet stir up small clouds of gravel dust as he walked. Once in a while, he would kick a noticeably larger rock out of his way, sending it bouncing off farther down the gravel road, or veering into the tall grass and weed-filled drainage ditch that ran beside the road.

Greg walked along for some time, mind clear, thinking of nothing but the road and his feet before he noticed noises coming from the woods to his right. Greg did not know how long it had been going on before he noticed it, but now that he was aware, it was easy to hear the snapping of twigs, the hissing of something moving past tree branches and underbrush.

An image of his uncle's quivering face came into Greg's mind. *That's a monster.*

Greg dismissed the thought a moment later. To prove to himself his own conviction, Greg stopped walking and turned to face the direction of the noises. The noises did not cease. If anything, they grew louder. Whatever was crashing toward him through the woods was coming fast. And it was big.

Greg could see underbrush being pushed aside, branches being whipped back and forth as something came for him. Despite his earlier conviction, Greg tensed, his muscles as taut as guitar strings, ready to bolt like a deer at the first sight of a mountain lion. At the last moment before the thing broke through the tall grass beside the road, Greg realized he had nowhere to run and nowhere to hide.

Then, Spooky poked his head out from the underbrush on the side of the road. Although Greg could not see Spooky's tail, he knew it was wagging when the grass behind Spooky's head began to sway back and forth.

Greg sighed and laughed. He leaned slightly forward and brought his hands out of the sweatshirt pockets. "Well, come on," he said, patting his knees with his hands. "Come on, big guy, what are you waiting for? Come on, boy."

Spooky needed no further invitation, and bounded out of the grass at a speed that belied his size.

Greg had time to think that perhaps he had been a bit hasty in his invitation before Spooky hit him like a brick wall covered with fur.

Before Greg had time to fully register what had happened, he was lying on his back, looking up at Spooky's panting mouth, the dog's two front canine bigfoot paws planted in the gravel on either side of Greg's heaving chest.

Greg raised his head from the gravel and gazed into Spooky's amber-colored eyes. "I think you did that on purpose."

Spooky wagged his tail.

CHAPTER NINETEEN

Greg sat at the dining room table while Katelin finished preparing dinner. As usual, Ron was not present for dinner. Although Greg usually saw him at breakfast and lunch, by dinner Greg guessed that more often than not Ron was well on his way to drunk, preferring a liquid dinner most evenings, upstairs in his room, surfing the Internet for porn or monitoring his cameras for monsters.

The thought of the cameras made Greg glance around the dining room. Was he being watched right now? Where were the cameras hidden? In the light fixtures on the ceiling? In the wall behind a light switch? Greg tried to remember if the images he had seen were from a high vantage point, looking down, or at something closer to eye level. He could not recall. Were there more cameras that his uncle had not shown him? Was he being watched when he took a leak? Greg had an even more disturbing thought: What if his uncle liked to watch other men with his aunt? What if he spanked it while he watched some young stud give it to his wife?

"Dinner is served," Katelin said, walking into the dining room. Greg was relieved to have something to distract him from his thoughts as Katelin sat a white plate in front of him. A single item sat in the center of the plate: a large steak topped with sautéed mushrooms and onions. Katelin went back into the kitchen and returned a moment later with a wicker basket filled with rolls and a tall glass of milk for Greg. For some unknown reason, it was always milk with dinner.

Greg found it a little odd that Katelin prepared all meals, every day. Breakfast at seven o'clock, lunch at noon, dinner at six o'clock—no exceptions. If you missed a meal, you were on your own. He was not complaining—he had eaten better while in her culinary care than at any other time in his life. But the whole thing was old-fashioned, and in a way, almost controlling, as if his aunt were the alpha female of their small pack and decided when and what they were allowed to eat.

Katelin sat across from him, a similar steak in front of her on the table. Greg watched her cut off a slice of meat and pop it into her mouth. She chewed slowly, and with her steak knife, motioned for Greg to dig in to his own meal. "Nothing beats a hunk of red meat," his aunt said a moment later after swallowing.

Greg cut his steak in half, down the middle. It was cooked medium rare, just like he preferred. Regardless of whatever else was going on in his aunt's seemingly strange life, she was a great cook, and Greg wasted no more time.

The onions were sweet, the mushrooms robust and earthy. The steak had a wild, gamey flavor. It did not taste bad, just foreign. Greg ate half of it before asking between mouthfuls, "What is this, venison?"

Katelin shook her head. "It's your mother's placenta. From your birth."

Katelin had said it with such flippant ease that for a moment Greg was not sure he had heard her correctly. He stopped chewing, the half masticated piece of meat sitting on his tongue, and glanced up at his aunt.

Katelin nodded and smiled.

Greg felt his stomach cramp and lurch. He spit the meat from his mouth back onto the plate. There was a sour taste on his tongue and a protective coating of saliva washed over his mouth in anticipation of the vomiting that threatened to commence.

Greg looked from his aunt's face to the plate in front of her.

Katelin pointed at her steak with her fork. "I'm not eating the same thing as you. Katherine wasn't *my* mother."

When Greg remained silent, Katelin continued. "I was beginning to think we'd never have the opportunity to follow tradition. Do you know how hard it is to keep a placenta edible for over thirty years?" Katelin glanced from Greg to the piece of meat he had spit onto his plate. When she looked back up at Greg, she seemed sincerely concerned. "Does it taste that bad, honey? I mean I'm pretty good in the kitchen, but it's been thirty-one years. Is it too tough? Do you want some ketchup?"

Upstairs, Greg hunched over the toilet for the second time in so many days, but all he seemed to be able to do was gag. Nothing came up. He stuck his finger down his throat, causing himself to gag harder, a thin line of drool running from his bottom lip into the toilet bowl water, tears running down his cheeks.

Spooky stood in the doorframe between the bedroom and bathroom.

Greg heard his aunt call to him as she entered the bedroom. "Honey!" She came into view from the bedroom. "Honey, it's not all that bad," she said, and walked toward the bathroom. Greg tried to protest, but a round of stomach-ripping gagging prevented anything he may have managed to say.

Spooky turned to face Katelin, and when she tried to enter the bathroom, he refused to move. She actually ran into his head. She stumbled back and looked down at the dog in shock. "Get out of my way," she ordered, taking a step forward.

Spooky growled deep in his throat. It sounded like he had swallowed a diesel engine that had suddenly kicked over and chugged to life.

At that moment Greg loved that dog. In his mind he cheered, *Good boy!*

Katelin, apparently shocked into silence, stared at Spooky, her big brown eyes filled with hurt. Realizing her mouth hung open, she shut it, only to open it a moment later. Then she closed it again.

The crazy bitch is speechless, Greg thought, and would have laughed had he not been preoccupied with gagging.

The look of surprised hurt in Katelin's eyes changed to cold understanding. She stared down at Spooky, apparently having completely forgotten about Greg. She folded her arms across her breasts. "So that's the way it is," she said, and sat her mouth into a firm line, making her lips nearly disappear, small lines shooting out from around her mouth. She looked her age suddenly.

Spooky remained motionless like a guard on sentry duty.

"Fine!" Katelin screeched, and stormed out of the bedroom.

Greg watched Spooky turn his head to follow her progress. Only when she had apparently left the bedroom did Spooky once again return his attention to Greg.

Greg gave up on vomiting. He composed himself enough to stand, although every time he thought about what he had eaten he was forced to suppress a gag. He wiped his chin with the back of his hand and looked at Spooky. "This is one fucked-up family."

This time, Spooky did not wag his tail.

Greg remained in his room for the rest of the evening. That night, he locked the bedroom door. There was no longer any debate. Tomorrow he was leaving Lost Haven. As crazy as his uncle was, he had been right about one thing: Greg did not want to be here. Not anymore.

PART TWO

CLOSED WINDOWS

CHAPTER TWENTY

Greg was awoken by the familiar sound of the squeaking hinges of his aunt's bedroom door as it was opened, then closed. Ten minutes later, Greg opened his own bedroom door and stepped out into the hall. Part of him wanted to walk downstairs and leave, hopefully by borrowing a car if his aunt and uncle had one, but he would walk if he had to. But another part of him, a more defiant part, wanted to tell his aunt face-to-face that he was leaving. To show her that she could not just do whatever she wanted without ramifications. In his own somewhat childish way, he hoped he would hurt his aunt by telling her that he was out of here. Like being a kid and telling someone that you were not going to be her friend anymore. With that in mind, Greg knocked on his aunt's bedroom door.

"Yes?" Katelin said, her voice muffled.

Greg cleared his throat. "It's me."

"Come in, honey."

Greg did not know what he had been expecting when he walked into Katelin's room, but what he saw was not it. The room could have belonged to a five-year-old girl. The walls and carpet were a stomach-churning shade of pastel purple. The ceiling was painted to look like a child's coloring book rendition of the sky: all blue with white cartoonlike clouds. The clouds reminded Greg of marshmallows, making him frown.

In the corner sat a wooden rocking horse and a tiny, obviously antique rocking chair that might have been big enough to hold Greg's foot. On a large pink bed heaped with pillows like the standard-issue bed assigned to storybook princesses, sat his aunt, a pink sheet pulled up over her chest, her back resting against a stack of overstuffed pillows, all various organlike shades of pink.

"I wanted to tell you that I'm leaving," Greg said after he recovered from the visual overload of colors that only a child (and apparently his aunt) could find appealing.

Katelin looked at Greg, scowled for a moment, and then sighed. "You don't want to leave. This is where you belong."

"No, not really."

His aunt stared at him. Greg stared back, determined not to give her the satisfaction of having him avert his gaze first.

Katelin grabbed the sheet and threw it off, revealing her complete nakedness. Her dark nipples stood erect, like small, accusing pointing fingers. Still staring at Greg, she brought her knees up and spread her legs, revealing the glistening pink sheath of her sex.

Despite himself, some male testosterone-filled Freudian instinct made Greg glance down between Katelin's legs. When he looked back up at Katelin's face, she was smirking.

"You can fuck me if you want," she said.

"You … you're my aunt," Greg managed to say. "And you look like my mother."

Katelin continued to stare at him for a moment before she scowled again and set her mouth in that hard line that Greg had seen before. She reached over and pulled the sheet back over herself. "What, my pussy not good enough for you? You're probably one of those nasty boys who only want to fuck women in the ass because you're really a fag."

Greg stepped backwards out of the room.

Katelin leaned forward in bed. "That's it, isn't it? You're an ass-fucking fag-boy!"

Greg closed the bedroom door.

"Ass-fucker!" Katelin screamed from the other side of the door.

Greg did not wait around to hear more.

Greg found his uncle in the family room. He was sitting on one of the love seats beside Spooky, Lynyrd Skynyrd coming from the stereo. Spooky appeared to be sleeping and took up almost the entire love seat, exiling Ron to a small spot on the end. Ron glanced at him but said nothing, returning his attention to staring at the stereo. As much as Greg hated asking his uncle for a ride at least into town, it was better than the screaming alternative waiting upstairs in her princess bed.

"Do you have a car I can borrow? Or can you give me a ride, at least into town? Dropping me off in Des Moines would be even better."

Ron shook his head and continued to stare at the stereo. "Don't have a car. Katelin doesn't ever go anywhere and I lost my license quite a few years ago."

"How do you get groceries and stuff?"

"Pay someone to go shoppin' and deliver. High school kids want any excuse to drive *anywhere* after they get their license. Hell, throw in some money to boot, and they're in hog heaven."

"Teenagers can't buy beer."

Ron looked at him with a mixture of sadness and annoyance. "No shit. Thanks for lettin' me know that. For your information, I get my beer delivered right from the distribution truck. And you ask too many questions, so don't ask me how or why. Money talks is all you need to know."

Maybe it was because of not growing up with a father, but whatever the reason, Greg always felt strangely uncomfortable whenever any father figure-aged man expressed anger toward him. Regardless of how crazy his uncle was, Greg still felt a twinge of nervousness. "Listen, I'm sorry about before."

Ron's expression softened. "Shit, bud, why didn't you leave when I told you to?"

"I don't know. But I'm leaving now."

Ron returned his gaze to the stereo. "Might be too late," he mumbled.

Suddenly Greg had an idea. "I'll call the police station. I'm willing to bet Bill will give me a ride."

"Yeah, now *that's* a good idea," Ron said sarcastically.

"Well, you got a better idea?" Greg asked.

"Nah. I'm all out of ideas. Live and let live, and all that happy shit. You do what you think's best. I'm gonna sit here and listen to some Skynyrd and not think about a fuckin' thing. I got a feelin' I'm gettin' drunk early today."

"Yeah, well, good luck with that," Greg said, and walked toward the kitchen.

Greg's bet paid off. He sat in the passenger seat of the Chevy Blazer and from the sideview mirror watched the Dameron house recede from view like a memory of a bad dream. Greg would miss Spooky, but nothing else.

Although it was early afternoon and Greg assumed that Bill was on duty considering that he had driven from the police station to pick him up, Bill was once again dressed in civilian clothes: khaki pants, dark blue shirt, long sleeves rolled up over his forearms, brown leather loafers. Apparently, being the boss had its perks. And maybe, Greg reasoned, in a small town like Lost Haven, the regulations governing police officers were less strict. Besides, everyone seemed to know who Bill was, uniform or not, so it was not as if he needed a uniform to identify himself.

Around Bill's left wrist, strikingly out of place, appeared to be a genuine diamond-encrusted platinum Rolex. The diamonds refracted the sunlight into fiery flashes of multicolored brilliance. It was probably worth more than the combined yearly salary of the entire Lost Haven police force. When he noticed Greg gazing at the watch, Bill grinned and shook his left wrist from side to side by the top of the steering wheel, creating explosions of refracted light. "That's my bling," Bill said.

"It's some watch," Greg said.

"The bitches love it," Bill said, and winked at Greg.

When they arrived in town, Bill drove around the square, past The Bonfire Bar & Grill. He turned down a side street that ran next to a white cinder block garage. CARL'S CAR CARE was painted in big blue letters above the double bay garage doors. ALL MAKES AND MODELS—DOMESTIC AND FOREIGN proclaimed a sign hanging from inside the glass door of the small connected office.

At a four-way intersection, Bill turned right. They drove past a two-story sandstone church. The top of the message board that sat on the well-manicured front lawn of the church, constructed of matching sandstone—albeit on a smaller scale—proclaimed: BELIEVERS WANTED. NO EXPERIENCE NECESSARY. APPLY INSIDE. Behind the glass of the message board, in miniature versions of the black, plastic block letters used to raise gas prices, offer milk for $2.29 and giant-sized candy bars for less than a dollar, was the message: JESUS—THE GIFT THAT KEEPS ON FORGIVING.

This part of town was new to Greg. Although he had never driven these roads, he knew that the road out of town, to the highway, lay in the opposite direction.

"Hey, partner, I thought we'd swing by my place for a few minutes," Bill said, as if reading Greg's mind. "Maybe have a quick farewell drink. We could stop at the bar but I'm technically on duty. And besides, you don't have a good track record when it comes to The Bonfire."

Greg glanced out the window at the nondescript row of houses that lined the residential street. They passed a street sign that read ELM ST. Like many people of Greg's generation, an Elm Street sign would forever conjure up memories of Freddy Krueger with his dirty, striped sweater and razor-fingered glove.

Bill pulled into the driveway of a small, easily forgettable ranch-style home with vinyl siding the color of toast. Bill parked the Blazer in front of the single-car garage, turned off the headlights, and cut the engine. "Be it ever so humble, and all that happy horseshit," Bill said, getting out of the vehicle.

Greg was not in the mood to drink. He was even less in the mood to remain in Lost Haven. But since they were already here, and considering that Bill was being kind enough to drive him two hours north to Des Moines, Greg could spare a few minutes to have a drink with the man. He got out, closed the passenger's side door, walked around the Blazer, and followed Bill up the concrete steps onto the small front porch.

CHAPTER TWENTY-ONE

"Here's to heat. Not the kind that ignites and burns down shanties, but the kind that excites and slides down panties!" Bill said, raising his glass of Jack Daniel's toward Greg.

Greg held his own glass out in front of him. "Here's to the breezes that blow through the trees, that blow the skirts off of young girls' knees, which leads to the sight that sometimes pleases, but more often than not leads to social diseases."

Bill laughed and knocked back his drink in one swallow. He sucked in breath through clenched teeth, poured himself another round, and sat the bottle back on the kitchen table.

Greg, being more conservative, sipped his whiskey and glanced around the room. Like Bill himself, Bill's house reminded Greg of a military lifestyle. The house was utilitarian: orderly, neat, sparsely arranged. Clean almost to the point of obsession. Everything seemed to have been placed with a conscious precision: from the TV remote that rested precisely in the middle of the coffee table in the living room, to the towel that hung from the refrigerator handle in the kitchen, both ends of the towel perfectly aligned. There were no dirty dishes in the sink, no spots of grease on the stove top, not a crumb on the counter. If he walked into Bill's bedroom, Greg wondered if he would be able to bounce a quarter off the tightly made bed.

Bill finished his second drink while Greg continued to work on his first. Bill clapped him on the back. "Partner, I've got somethin' to show you. You game?"

Greg shrugged. "Sure."

Bill walked around Greg and down a step onto the landing by the back door off the kitchen. Bill opened the basement door across from the back door, reached into the darkness, and flicked on a light switch. Light spilled up from the basement. "You're gonna love this. It's gonna knock your socks off. You can bring your drink with you."

Greg followed Bill down the steep wooden steps into the basement. Greg was greeted with bare cinder block walls and a poured concrete floor. In the corner of the basement, adjacent to the steps sat a washer and dryer beside a freezer that looked big enough to hold an entire cow. A sturdy-looking wooden workbench, chipped and scarred from use and age, rested in the middle of the basement underneath one of the bare bulbs that hung from the ceiling between the exposed joists. Next to the workbench a round, metal support column ran from floor to ceiling, covered in chipped white paint. And slumped over in front of the metal support column, hands bound behind his back with handcuffs, was Jimmy Elison.

Jimmy raised his head and looked at Greg wearily. His face was bruised and swollen, both eyes blackened. Dried blood from a badly broken nose covered his lower face and stained his filthy, once white T-shirt. Some kind of black gag-ball thing filled his mouth, leather straps running around the back of his head, forcing him to breath around the ball in gasps and pants that swelled up his cheeks and shot spittle out from around the ball each time he exhaled. Greg smelled urine and feces, making it obvious that Jimmy had not been permitted to use a bathroom. The stench of human waste mixed with the smells of fear, sweat, and pain. The basement smelled like a locker room in hell.

Greg became dimly aware that he had dropped his drink when he heard the glass strike the concrete floor. Oddly, it did not break. It bounced a few times, spun in place for a moment, and then became still. Greg noticed this as if he had stepped outside of himself. It was as if none of this was real and he was simply a spectator, watching a show on television. When Jimmy lowered his head and began to sob, shudders of agony shaking his body, Greg snapped out of his initial shock. "What the fuck?" he said, his voice wavering.

Bill walked over to Jimmy, grasped a fistful of his hair, and yanked his head back, forcing him to look up. He stared at Bill.

"What the fuck?" Greg said again. "What have you done? *What the fuck have you done?*" Greg thought he was going to be sick. He could not stop shaking, and his legs felt dangerously weak and loose, as if the bones had melted into unsupportive mush.

Bill ignored him, instead grinning at Jimmy with clenched teeth, his lips pulled back in a predatory snarl. "Don't look at me!" he spit. "Look at *him*!" he said, and pointed at Greg.

Jimmy did as he was told, looking at Greg with eyes that held nothing but defeat. Jimmy seemed to know what was going to happen and had resigned himself to his fate.

"That's right, you piece of shit," Bill continued. "You look at him. You look at him *good*. You know you don't fuck around with the Damerons. You *know*!"

Bill, still gripping a fistful of Jimmy's greasy hair, looked over at Greg and smiled with what appeared to be genuine pride. He seemed to be practically buzzing with excited glee. "You're the boss. What should we do with this piece of shit? Should he live or should he die?"

Greg looked at Jimmy, and for the first time, saw a glimmer of hope enter his eyes. Greg, unable to take his gaze from Jimmy's, continued to stare. He had no idea what was happening, or why he was being asked to make what was literally a life or death decision, but there was no question as to the answer. "He should live. He should definitely live. You should let him go."

Bill lost some of his maniacal grin, but shrugged in indifference. Before letting go of Jimmy's hair, Bill slammed the back of Jimmy's head into the metal post with enough force to make the metal ring like a tuning fork. Jimmy's eyes became unfocused for a moment before his gaze once again locked onto Greg.

Bill strolled over to the workbench and opened one of the utility drawers. "Well, dicky, looks like it's your lucky fucking day," he said, rummaging through the drawer. "The boss man has granted you a reprieve."

Bill's face lit up when he apparently found what he had been searching for. He fiddled with something in the shadows that lingered in the far side of the basement. Both Greg and Jimmy jumped when an air compressor burst to life with a metallic screech, filling the room with a hollow *chunk-chunk-chunk* sound.

Greg had assumed that Bill had searched the utility drawer for a key to release Jimmy from the handcuffs, or maybe a pair of bolt cutters. Instead, when Bill came back into view, limping a bit, he held a nail gun in his right hand. It was not a new model made of plastic and bright colors, run on rechargeable batteries, but instead an ancient gray, steel hulk of a thing, all hard lines and weight. He walked over and once again stood beside Jimmy.

Jimmy glanced down at the nail gun. His breathing quickened into panicked gasps. His gaze shot up to Greg, pleading.

"We're going to let him go," Greg said.

Bill brought the nail gun up to Jimmy's head and put it against his right temple.

Jimmy groaned, but did not remove his pleading gaze from Greg.

"We're letting him go!" Greg yelled.

Bill shook his head. "Nope. Sometimes you gotta make an executive decision, even if the boss doesn't agree. Sometimes you just have to do what's best for the company." Bill pulled the trigger of the nail gun.

There was a sharp crack of air. Jimmy's head jerked to the left. His eyes bulged open, full of shock. About half an inch of a large nail stuck out from his right temple. Blood welled up from around the nail, slid down the side of his face, traced his jawline, and dripped from his chin onto the floor. He stared at Greg with a look that seemed to say, *What happened? I thought everything was going so good.*

"I'm sorry," Greg whispered.

Greg actually saw the life slip from Jimmy's body. His eyes became unfocused. His face relaxed. He breathed deeply. Sighed. And slumped forward, dead.

"No! You fuck! You fucker!" Greg howled, striding toward Bill.

Bill pointed the nail gun at Greg from his hip, like a cowboy in an old western movie, and pulled the trigger.

Greg barely had time to register the nail that stuck out of his left thigh before a searing pain shot through his leg as if a welder was inside his thigh, fusing bone with a white-hot flame.

Greg screamed, grabbed his left thigh with both hands, and fell backward. His butt hit the concrete floor with enough force to audibly clack his teeth together. He stared at his thigh, blood welling up from between his fingers. "I'm going to die, too."

"Relax, you ain't gonna die," Bill said, walking over to Greg. "Shit, if what Katelin says is true, you're chosen. By tomorrow morning you'll be good as new." Bill reached down, grasped the nail head, and yanked it out of Greg's thigh.

Greg felt the nail dislodge from his thighbone. A gush of blood erupted out of the wound like a blood-filled volcano. Greg had not realized that the human vocal cords were capable of making such an *inhuman* sound until he heard it from his own throat. He only stopped when he began to choke.

Bill threw the bloody nail over his shoulder. When it hit the concrete it made a tinkling noise, as if giggling at the pain it had caused.

Greg, his hands tightly clamped over his thigh, glared up at Bill, who stood over him.

Bill hunched forward, resting his hands on his knees. "Buck up, partner. Stop being such a pussy and listen for a minute."

"Fuck you," Greg said.

Bill laughed. "That's better. Get pissed. Be a man. It's good to know that all that time with your mother hasn't made you a sissy. It's good to know you still got a pair." He stood straight, walked over to the workbench, and leaned against it, crossing his arms and looking down at Greg.

"Don't talk about my mother."

Bill smirked. "Yeah? What're you going to do about it? Bleed on me?"

Bill pulled out a cigarette from his front shirt pocket and stuck it between his lips. He pulled out a chrome Zippo lighter from his front pants pocket. A moment later the area between Bill and Greg filled with the smell of lighter fluid and cigarette smoke. "You want one?" Bill asked Greg.

"I don't smoke," Greg said.

"I don't smoke either," Bill said. "The cigarette smokes. I'm just the sucker on the end."

"That's not funny."

Bill nodded. "Yeah, you're right. It is kinda fuckin' stupid."

Greg's hands were beginning to cramp, but he dared not let go of his thigh for fear that without constant pressure, he would lose enough blood to slip into unconsciousness.

"So, anyway," Bill said, "about your mother."

"What about her?"

"I fucked her."

Greg's eyes narrowed. Despite the searing pain in his leg, he could feel heat rising up his neck, into his face. Anger made his jaw muscles ache. "Shut up. You're a crazy fuck. Everyone in this town is crazy."

"Nope, we're not crazy. Just different. You see, we live under a different set of rules in this town. And I did fuck your mother. I gave both of them a hot beef injection. Katelin was easy. Even though she was a virgin, she wanted it. She knew what it was all about. Your mother though," Bill said, shaking his head, "she put up a fight. Kicking and screaming. For being only sixteen, she swore like a sailor."

Bill took a drag from his cigarette. He shrugged. "But in the end, Katherine got what she got. It's the rules. Dameron girls are supposed to produce offspring. This town *needs* Damerons. My … contribution didn't stick with Katelin, but Katherine did us proud." Bill gazed down at Greg. His expression was serious, stern. "Katherine did good."

Greg had forgotten about the pain in his leg. "That's not true. You're full of shit."

"Anyway," Bill continued, ignoring Greg, "I did your mother first, gave her a good dose. With Katelin I barely got my rocks off before that fuckin' dog got into the room and damn near bit my leg off."

Bill put his cigarette between his lips, unbuckled his belt, unbuttoned and unzipped his pants, and dropped them around his ankles. He shimmied around to give Greg a backside view of his legs. Just below the end of his boxers, a chunk of flesh was literally missing from the back of Bill's left leg. A series of angry-looking scars exploded out from the flesh crevice in all directions, like an octopus made of scar tissue.

Bill bent down and pulled his pants back up to his waist. He turned back around to face Greg, zipping up his pants. He removed the cigarette from between his lips and crushed it out on top of the workbench. "Because of that fuckin' dog my Olympic dreams were crushed," Bill said, and laughed without humor.

"They don't have an event for most sick son of a bitch in the Olympics anyway," Greg said.

"Yeah, they don't have a dick-sucking contest either, but you can bet your ass that if they did, I'd be one of the judges."

"I don't believe you," Greg said simply. "You can't be my ..."

Bill brought his hand up to his ear. "What's that, you say? I can't be *what?*" Bill smirked. "I can't be your father? Oh, I can be, and I am." Bill crossed his arms and looked up at the ceiling. "You know, it's funny. They make you buy a license to own a firearm, drive a car, run a daycare, but any couple of dumbasses with a stiff pecker and a willing cunt can squirt out a little bundle of joy. If they really want to make the world a better place, they should license *that* shit."

"So you're saying you're a dumbass?" Greg asked. The pain in his leg was once again making itself known.

Bill looked down at Greg. "Nope. I'm speaking hypothetically. You were planned. And both your mother and I come from good stock. There ain't no hillbilly fuck-cousins in our bloodlines. No retarded dumbasses. No niggers or spicks."

"So on top of all of it, you're a *racist* murdering crazy fucker," Greg said, disgusted.

Bill scowled at Greg. "Shut the fuck up. Jesus Christ, you'd think a son of mine would have bigger balls. You must get your whiney little attitude from your mother. Stop being such a self-righteous little shit."

"*You* shut the fuck up!" Greg yelled. "My mother was a strong woman. You don't know anything about her." Greg would have never guessed that he would have ever defended his mother to anyone, certainly not to a deranged murderer.

"I know what she feels like from the inside," Bill said.

"Everything about you is just wrong," Greg said.

"Yeah, well, you believe whatever you want there, partner. But you better believe this—you're the first Dameron in three generations to be chosen. You have a responsibility to your family, to this town. Your mother did everything she could to run from who she was and to take you away from here."

Bill walked over to Greg, leaned down, almost touching Greg's nose with his own. His breath smelled like whiskey and stale cigarette smoke. "This is your home. You are who you are. You can't deny that. You can't deny what's in your blood."

CHAPTER TWENTY-TWO

The entire trip back to his aunt and uncle's house was made in silence.

When Bill circled around the cherub statue and braked to a halt in front of the house, Greg opened the door and hobbled out of the Blazer, not bothering to even turn around to acknowledge Bill. He slammed the door behind him.

"You'll learn," Bill called from the Blazer. "Pretty soon you'll see things with different eyes. Mark my words, partner. You'll learn."

Greg ignored Bill and walked up the front steps, opened the front door, and walked inside, closing the door and leaning against it. He heard Bill pull out of the driveway.

His aunt must have been watching from one of the family room windows, waiting for him, because she came into the living room and headed toward him. When she tried to touch Greg's arms, he shrugged her off. "Don't touch me."

Katelin took a step back, wringing her hands together in nervous agitation. She glanced down at his leg. The front left side of his jeans was soaked black with blood. "Jesus, why does Bill have to be so blunt about things? I mean, I know he's a man, but a little finesse wouldn't hurt." She looked up, gazing into Greg's eyes with concern. "Does it hurt bad, honey?"

"What do you think? The crazy fuck shot me with a nail gun! The sick son of a bitch *killed* that Jimmy guy with a nail gun!" Greg yelled, his voice beginning to waiver. "He shot him right in the head." Not wanting his aunt to see any sign of emotion that she might interpret as weakness, Greg fought to choke back tears, finally succeeding. He cleared his throat. "We have to tell somebody."

"Who do you want to tell?" his aunt asked.

"I don't know. The police."

"Bill *is* the police."

Greg threw up his hands in exasperation. "So what. He's one cop in one tiny town. I'll call the state police."

Katelin shook her head. "They won't let you do that."

"Who won't?"

"The entities. You may be chosen, but you don't know how to control them. You'll learn, but you don't have that kind of ability yet. Bill's family made a deal with our family a long time ago. They're immune. In return, they protect our family from physical threats."

"Chosen for what?" Greg asked.

Katelin smiled. "There's so much to teach you. It's going to be so wonderful."

Greg wiped his forehead. He was sweating profusely, yet was paradoxically cold at the same time. There seemed to be some kind of gray pulse in his head that blurred the edges of his vision. With each breath the pulse throbbed in his ears, making everything echo as if he was listening to sounds with his head submerged under water. "I'm going to die."

"You're not going to die," Katelin said, her voice filled with deep echoes. "I *do* think you're going to pass out, though. You've lost a lot of blood."

Greg reached out a hand toward his aunt, but for some reason could not quite seem to touch her. "You sound funny," he said, and fell forward. He was unconscious before he hit the floor.

CHAPTER TWENTY-THREE

At first, Greg thought he heard someone knocking on the door. When he realized that the noise was coming from the other side of the bedroom, he guessed that Spooky was in the room, thumping his tail of destruction against the floor, or the wall, or the bed. After scanning the darkened room and finding no sign of the dog, Greg stopped guessing and instead started listening.

Greg's thoughts centered on the waking nightmare that had been—considering it was currently night—what he guessed to be yesterday. Although Greg tried not to think about it, the image of Jimmy, eyes wide with shock, the end of a nail sticking out of the side of his head, would not leave. Every time Greg closed his eyes, the image filled his head like a snapshot from a camera designed to take pictures of the moment before death flips the switch and turns out the lights.

Had he really seen a man die? Although Greg wished it could have just been a dream, he knew that it had been all too real. And was Bill really his father? He still refused to believe that. Refused to believe that some psychotic country cop had raped his teenage mother (and aunt), and had casually decided to share this information with his long-lost son over a glass of whiskey and a smoke, a dead man in the room with a nail in his head, the aforementioned son sitting on the floor in a growing pool of blood, with a nail wound of his own in his thigh.

Greg reached down and touched his bare left thigh. Someone, probably his aunt, had removed his blood-soaked jeans. The thought of his aunt touching him—

You can fuck me if you want.

—while he lay unconscious, unable to defend himself, made Greg shiver in disgust. Gratefully, he still wore underwear, which he took as a good sign. And, for the second time in a week, he had miraculously healed overnight. There was no sign that he had been used as a human two-by-four.

The noise came again. *Dink-dink-dink.* Now that Greg was awake and at least semi-alert, there was no doubt that the noise came from the other side of the velvet drapes, from outside. It sounded like a bird tapping on one of the windows or the sliding glass doors that led to the balcony overlooking the backyard. Greg thought of a big oily-black raven. Did they have ravens in Iowa? Greg didn't know.

Dink-dink-dink. Dink-dink. Dink-dink-dink.

Greg rolled over, his back to the drapes. It would go away eventually. Besides, he had more important things to worry about. Like how he was going to get out of Lost Haven and report Bill for being a murderer.

Greg had already decided that he could not trust the other Lost Haven police officers. Although it was unlikely that the entire police force were a bunch of crazed lunatics, Bill was nonetheless their boss. And who would they believe: Bill, the boss, who they all knew and worked with, or Greg, an outsider from Florida with a family history of mental illness swimming through his gene pool?

Hell, for all Greg knew, they might try to blame *him* for Jimmy's death. After all, Greg had more of a motive to kill Jimmy than Bill did. How many people had witnessed Jimmy punch Greg in the face? Five, ten, a dozen? No, the local police would be no help, and might actually be a hindrance.

Dink-dink-dink.

Greg pulled a pillow from the bed and flung it in the direction of the tapping. It hit the thick velvet drapes with an unsatisfying hiss.

Dink-dink.

Greg threw off the flannel blanket and began to rise out of bed. The sound of the knob on the bedroom door turning stopped him. He looked at the door, tense, blanket in hand. Even in the gloom, enough light seeped from around the curtains and spilled into the room from the amber bulb above the backyard shed that Greg thought he could see the doorknob twist. Regardless of whether or not he could in fact see the knob moving, he could *hear* it quite clearly: the bolt disengaged from the latch plate with a metallic *click*.

The door swung open and in walked Spooky. He did not stop and greet Greg with his customary sideways head turn. He walked past the bed and right up to the drapes, almost touching the golden fabric with his muzzle at a spot roughly in the middle and about three feet up from the floor. He sniffed, growled, and tensed. Then, for the first time since Greg had met the dog, Spooky barked. It was only a single bark, but it possessed the deep booming quality of a shotgun blast.

The bark was so sudden and unexpected that Greg jumped, startled. Heart pounding, he got out of bed and approached Spooky, coming to stand beside him.

Spooky glanced up at Greg before returning his attention to the drapes and the glass door beyond. He growled again, and before Greg could attempt to hush him, boomed out another shotgun bark that seemed to say, *I'm a big dog. Don't fuck with me.*

Greg held out his hands, palms facing Spooky. "Hush. Calm down, buddy."

Spooky growled. Barked again.

Light from the hallway bathed the bedroom, throwing Greg's and Spooky's shadows onto the drapes, both impossibly thin, tall, and distorted. Greg thought his shadow looked like an alien bogeyman—all gangly arms and legs and a big, bulbous head. Another shadow appeared beside Greg's. He turned toward the bedroom doorway as his uncle entered the room. Like Greg, he was clothed only in a pair of tighty-whitey underwear. Unlike Greg, a considerable beer belly bulged from around his middle, supported on spindly, old-man stick legs. His hair stood up in wispy chaos, like gray storm clouds.

"He won't be quiet," Greg said.

"He's got one out there. Spooky can smell 'em," Ron whispered, standing beside Greg, staring at the drapes. "There's one out there."

"I think it's a bird," Greg whispered back, although not sure why he whispered.

Ron shook his head. "Bird my ass."

"Whatever it was, I'm sure Spooky scared it away. He barks like a damned cannon."

As if to prove Greg wrong: *Dink-dink-dink. Dink-dink.*

Both Greg and Ron jumped. Ron grabbed Greg's arm like a high school girl grabbing her date in the movie theater during a horror film. It would have been funny had Greg not been so unexpectedly freaked out.

When Ron realized he was grasping Greg's arm, he let go and smiled sheepishly. "Sorry."

Greg was about to reassure his uncle that all was forgiven when Spooky barked again.

"He's going to wake up Katelin," Greg said.

Ron frowned. "She don't give a shit. She's too busy with one of her fuck-buddies to bother with us."

Dink-dink-dink. Dink-dink. Dink-dink-dink-dink-dink-dink-dink!

Spooky was so tense he looked like he was ready to launch himself right through the drapes and glass door to get at whatever lay beyond. His substantial shoulder muscles quivered. His back was rigid. He growled and revealed a formidable-looking arsenal of wickedly sharp teeth.

Before he could think about it and stop himself, Greg reached out, grasped the edge of the drape, and pulled it aside.

His uncle had been right about more than one thing. It was not a bird that stood outside on the balcony, tapping on the glass. And monsters did indeed exist after all. Greg knew this for a fact, because he stood looking at one.

CHAPTER TWENTY-FOUR

Even more disturbing, it looked back at him.

The thing on the balcony—and Greg could think of nothing else to describe it other than a *thing*—was about half the height of a grown man, which was appropriate since it was in fact half a man. Its skin was the dark gray color of pencil graphite. It had the upper body of a steroid-using heavyweight bodybuilder, all bulging biceps and chiseled pectoral muscles. What it lacked was any kind of lower body, simply ending at the point where a human navel would have been present. It was not as if a human body had been roughly cut in half, the creature just stopped, smooth and efficient, as if a cartoonist had begun to draw a monster and decided to give it up halfway through. Its set of massive arms seemed to perform double duty as legs. The splayed fingers of its hands, firmly planted on the balcony boards, balanced its body.

Although the thing had the body of a man, any resemblance to a human being stopped when Greg stared at the thing's head. Atop the thickly muscled neck was something that resembled a weird hybrid of bird and insect. Most of its face was taken up by a wickedly long, daggerlike beak. The beak was about two feet in length and had a slight downward curve, ending in a point that would have made a needle proud. Like the beak, the entire head appeared to be made of some kind of hard, bony material, hairless and smooth. Bulging from either side of the head were large, orb-shaped eyes that glistened with an alien blackness, beetlelike.

"Oh fuck, it's a nasty one," Greg heard his uncle say.

As if to confirm that it was indeed a nasty one, the thing vaulted sideways, balancing itself on one arm like a gymnast missing half a body. It planted its other hand against the glass of the door with a hollow *thud*, palm facing the group.

Both Greg and his uncle jumped and took an instinctive step backwards. Spooky, apparently fearless, actually pushed his nose up against the glass exactly opposite the creature's hand and growled.

The thing moved its hand a bit farther up the glass door, producing a rubbery squeaking noise, like a bare foot slipping on the bottom of a wet bathtub. From the center of the creature's palm opened a mouth filled with miniature versions of pointed shark teeth. A long, thin tapeworm tongue, the purple color of a fresh bruise, shot out from between the rows of teeth and licked the glass, leaving a thick and cloying path of saliva, like the slime trail of a snail. To Greg the gesture seemed both obscene and hungry. Then, it removed its hand and once again pecked the glass in its version of Morse code: *Dink-dink-dink. Dink-dink.*

Now that he could actually see the thing's beak strike the glass, Greg was afraid that with each new strike, the glass would spiderweb and shatter, destroying the only barrier between them and it.

As improbable as it seemed, the glass did not break, or even crack. Staring at the glass, Greg felt the sudden urge to touch it. To reach out and lay his palm against it. To feel its solid, smooth surface.

"Don't let it in!" Ron yelled.

For the first time since seeing the creature, Greg glanced over at his uncle. "Why the hell would I do that?" Greg asked.

Ron just stared at him.

Without his knowledge of having done so, Greg's right hand had firmly grasped the wooden handle that would open the sliding glass door. Although he had no memory of doing so, he had actually managed to open the door a fraction of an inch. The chilly night breeze blew against his bare legs.

Spooky had squeezed in between Greg and the door, his nose sniffing at the crack of an opening.

Greg shut the door. "Jesus Christ," he mumbled, disoriented. He turned away from the door, running a trembling hand through his hair, and looked at his uncle.

Ron nodded. "It's a nasty one," he repeated, as if the simple statement explained everything. "Let's go over to my room and watch it on camera."

CHAPTER TWENTY-FIVE

While the creature appeared no less appalling when viewed on camera, the distance and two-dimensional camera image did make the thing a bit less frightening, but only a bit.

Greg sat next to Ron, Spooky sat next to Greg. All three of them continued to stare at the camera image on the computer monitor. Thankfully, there was no sound to accompany the tapping movement of the thing's beak against the glass. Even without sound, Greg could still hear the tapping in his head. He wondered if he would ever be able to get the noise out of his memory. Would he be the first person in history to be scared shitless every time he heard a woodpecker tapping away at a tree?

The creature continued to tap out its Morse code for another ten minutes before it finally stopped. Greg watched on camera as it turned away from the glass and launched itself up and over the balcony railing with the speed of a striking snake. It seemed to hit the ground already moving. Running on arms as thick as legs, the creature raced toward the back woods in a strange looping gate that resembled the sway of a pendulum. The movement of its body was so wrong, so alien, that watching it made Greg nauseated. He swallowed back bitter saliva and took a deep breath.

Ron lit a cigarette with shaking hands. "That one was a badass," he said after the creature disappeared from view.

Greg continued to stare at the now creature-free camera image in silence.

There are moments in our lives when what one thought of as reality proved to be in fact *unreality*. Moments that, for better or for worse, change how we view the world, and how we view ourselves. Some of these moments are funny, such as when we get drunk for the first time with teenage friends. Someone—usually the most straitlaced of the group, the one we would least expect—always goes overboard, passes out, and pukes on themselves. And we never let them forget it, even if that unfortunate individual grows up to be a brilliant brain surgeon or CEO of a Fortune 500 company. Some of these moments are sad, such as when we discover the absolute power of death. If we are lucky, we discover this power through a still hamster or a floating goldfish. If we are unlucky, we discover it through a loved one taken from us too soon, always too soon. Other moments are simply facts, like when we realize that our parents in fact do not know everything, and are fallible, just like everyone else.

Greg felt a crushing kind of certainty that made him sick with its truth but that he fought to deny, even though the evidence was impossible to refute. It felt like he had discovered masturbation for the first time, and then halfway through, found out he was on a television reality show and the whole world was watching as he discovered his newfound hobby. *Wave to the camera and say hi to your parents. No, not with* that *hand!*

Greg wanted to disconnect from himself, emotionally unplug. He imagined that if he took a deep breath through his nose, he would be able to smell burning wires as the logic circuits of his brain overloaded and burned out. Maybe small plumes of smoke would drift out of his ears.

Ron nudged Greg's arm. "Earth to Greg, come in Greg. Snap out of it, bud."

"How can that … be real?" Greg asked. "I mean, damn. How?"

"Yeah, the really nasty ones can do some weird shit. The not-so-nasty ones, they just kind of float around like smoke. That's pretty much what they look like, too—smoke."

"What did it want?" Greg asked, gazing at his uncle.

Ron averted his gaze from Greg's beseeching eyes, to the floor.

"What?" Greg said.

Ron sighed and glanced back up at Greg. "It probably wanted somethin' from *you.* I don't know what, but since you're chosen and all, they know about you."

"Chosen for what?"

"Katelin can explain it better 'n me. She's a Dameron by blood; I just married into the family. It's a family secret kind of thing. I don't even know the half of it. By the time I came into the picture and met Katelin, Cyril was dead, and you and your mom were already long gone."

"Well, what *do* you know?"

"I know your great grandfather could do things."

"The one that saved all the farms?"

Ron shook his head. "Bill tell you that?"

Greg nodded. "He's a psycho."

"Oh yeah, he's bug-shit crazy," Ron agreed.

"He killed somebody."

Ron held up his hands, palms facing Greg. "I don't wanna know. I don't want no part of that shit."

Spooky, sitting beside Greg, put his head on Greg's thigh. Greg scratched behind his ears, earning a contented sigh from Spooky. The simple act calmed Greg.

"I'm bettin' Bill told you your great grandfather was some kind of hero," Ron said. "From what I've gathered, he was more like a greedy son of a bitch. He didn't buy any farmland to help anyone out. He made some deals with Bill's family at the bank and bought the land out from under everyone. He had a way about him for gettin' what he wanted. People'd say that if he came around and looked at a family's farm, within a year or two the land would go to shit, crops would fail, equipment would constantly break down. The fucker had the evil eye or somethin'. So, eventually the family would be forced to sell. Then he'd swoop in like a vulture and buy up the property. He'd let the family stay on if they wanted and farm the land, giving them just enough money to survive, and he'd keep the rest."

Ron shrugged. "Hell, even today for most people around here, farmin's all they know. I'm sure most families stayed on 'n farmed. I'm sure the bank got a kickback, too. So the Damerons and Lost Haven have a history together. And it ain't nothin' pretty. People in Lost Haven ain't exactly sure what's goin' on, but they ain't dumb, and they know wherever there's a Dameron, there's some bad shit followin' close behind. People around here don't respect the Dameron name, they *fear* it. And it don't matter that they don't know exactly what's goin' on. Little kids don't have to see the bogeyman to know it's in the closet waitin' to hurt 'em."

"You said the land turned to shit," Greg said.

"Yeah, until your great grandfather bought it. Then, suddenly it was the best damned land money could buy. It was better 'n it was before it went to shit, better 'n it was before he came sniffin' around and ruined it."

"What's that got to do with that thing outside?" Greg asked.

"Well, like I said, your great grandfather could do things. Weird things. I don't know about all the mumbo-jumbo shit, but if your great grandfather called somethin', somethin' answered. I suppose anyone could *try* to do the shit he did, but it wouldn't do a damned thing."

"Not sure I'm following you," Greg admitted.

Ron scratched his chin in thought. Then he leaned forward toward Greg, resting his forearms on his knees. "It's like one of those plastic toy phones kids have. It looks like a real phone, got buttons and everything. You can pick up the handset and put it to your ear, punch the buttons and dial a number, but no one's gonna answer."

Ron leaned back and crossed his arms. "It's like everyone else is callin' with a toy phone. But your great grandfather, he had a real phone. And when he made a call, those fuckin' things out in the woods picked up on the other end of the line. Normally those things don't even pay much attention to people—most people can't even see 'em. But they paid attention to your great grandfather. I think he could communicate with 'em somehow, talk to 'em."

Ron looked at Greg and sighed. "And I think you got that real phone, too. Just like he did. You might not know what numbers to dial yet. But you got the phone. And those things know it."

"Yeah, well, I'm not calling *anything*," Greg said. "In fact, I want to disconnect the phone and throw it away."

"Problem is, I think you're callin' whether you know it or not. You're like a kid with a real phone—you're just punchin' in random numbers like it's a toy. Most of the time you're just gettin' a dial tone, but once in a while you manage to punch in a real number, and somethin' answers."

Greg shook his head. "How is any of this possible?"

Ron shrugged. "Why do men like titties? Why can't you piss and shit at the same time? Why do women always want to know what you're thinkin'? Some things can't be explained. Some things are just fact. They are what they are."

"Where do they come from?"

"Don't really know for sure. But I think they're here because of the old Cooper farm." Ron gestured behind him. "You know the path we followed to see your mother's plot? You know the path that went farther on past the cemetery, deeper into the woods?"

Greg nodded. "Yeah."

"Well, if you keep followin' that path for about ten minutes, you'll come to a clearing in the woods. That clearing used to be a small farm, way before your great grandfather stuck his nose in other people's business. Way before your family ever stepped foot on Iowa soil. Iowa is Indian country, and that place in the woods was known to them, too."

Despite the situation, Greg smirked. "Let me guess, the farm was built on an ancient Indian burial ground and now the Indian ghosts are pissed."

Ron grinned and shook his head. "No. But I'm glad you still got a sense of humor after what you saw. I'd say that's a good sign. Anyway, nothin's left of the Cooper farm except the old barn. That barn seems to be the center of it. Or actually, the barn just happens to be built on the center of it. The damned thing should have fallen over a long time ago, but it's still standin'. Nothing left of the old Cooper farmhouse but parts of the foundation, but that damned barn won't go away." Ron shook his head. "Fuckin' thing," he mumbled.

Ron lit a cigarette. "I'm not sure exactly how it works, but there are paths that crisscross the earth. Some of these paths are literally paths you can see, like the one that leads to the Cooper barn. Some of the paths you can't see, but you can feel 'em when you're close. It's like when you're walkin' down the street mindin' your own business and suddenly you swear someone called your name. Or you get that feelin' you're being watched. I'm not talkin' that *maybe* kind of feelin'; I'm talkin' that *no doubt, bet your ass, you* know *someone called your name* kind of thing. You *know* someone's watchin' ya."

"Yeah, I hate that," Greg admitted.

"Think of those paths as roads and those things in the woods as drivers. Some of the paths are gravel roads that mostly stay empty—only an occasional car drives by. You'd stumble across one of those lonely roads when you hear someone call your name, or you just get a bad case of the heebie-jeebies. Other paths are like cross-country interstates with an ass-load of drivers all tryin' to get where they're goin' as fast as possible. Where you got paths like that you end up with haunted castles and ghost stories."

"Let me guess," Greg said. "The path in the woods is an interstate."

"Yes and no. It's worse than that. The path in the woods *is* like an interstate. And that interstate runs through the Cooper barn, where it connects with a bunch of other interstates. What we've got," Ron said with a frown, "is a damned interstate-crossroads truck stop for monsters. Hell, they don't only pass through this way, they stop for coffee and pie, and a hot shower."

"How come no one knows about this place?" Greg asked.

Ron shrugged. "I guess because no one ever built some monument on the site. Or maybe because not many people travel around it. But you can bet your ass there's other places like it, other truck stops. Some of 'em even got names, like the Bermuda Triangle, or Stonehenge. And a few of the monsters are famous. Ever heard of Bigfoot or the Loch Ness Monster?"

"I don't think the Loch Ness Monster ever knocked on someone's window and scared the shit out of them," Greg said.

"Yeah," Ron agreed. "The Loch Ness Monster don't really seem like a monster. Not compared to the shit that runs around in those woods. I don't think all the monsters are bad, just the ones around here. It's like there's good paths and there's bad paths. Here, we got bad paths."

"Aren't we lucky," Greg said.

Ron crushed out his cigarette. "Yeah, we're about as lucky as a one-legged man at an ass-kickin' contest." Ron rose from the chair. "Well, I'm guessin' you ain't goin' back to sleep, so let's go downstairs and make some coffee."

At the dining room table, they sat in silence. Greg continually glanced into the kitchen, looking out into the early morning darkness through one of the kitchen windows. He half expected something to come crashing through the window, some beaked monstrosity or hairy, fanged beast. Spooky had wandered away to wherever it was that Spooky wandered to. Greg suddenly wished the dog was still beside him. Hairy, fanged beasts were a little less scary when you had a fur-covered beast of your own. Forcing himself to take his gaze away from the window and what may or may not be lurking in the darkness beyond, Greg glanced at his uncle.

"So, what if I just leave?" Greg blurted out.

Ron nodded as if he had been expecting such a question. "Well, I'm guessin' Katelin did somethin' to you. If it's what I'm thinkin', I bet you won't be eatin' anything she cooks from now on."

"That's a bet you'd win," Greg acknowledged grimly.

"Like I said before, I don't know much about all the mumbo-jumbo bullshit, but what she did is supposed to unlock your natural abilities. The eating of ..." Ron cleared his throat uncomfortably. "Well, you know. Anyway, it's supposed to pass on your mother's power to you by some kind of osmosis or somethin'. Like flesh has a memory. I know it sounds like some crazy shit."

"There was this study done somewhere," Greg said. "They took some kind of worms and they trained them to go through a maze or something to get food. After the worms became good at it, they chopped them up and fed them to other worms that had never been through the maze. The worms that ate the other worms went through the maze correctly on the first try."

"That's some weird shit," Ron said.

Greg sipped his coffee and nodded. "You said it was to pass on my mother's power. So she could do this calling thing, too?"

"I think it's in the Dameron blood—some kind of gene or somethin' that's passed down. From what I've been able to gather, not all Damerons—hell, not even most—can do anything unusual. But a few can. I think your mother could a little. And I think you can, too."

Greg had barely registered what his uncle had said. For perhaps the first time in his life, if only in a small way, Greg felt a flutter of understanding and empathy for his mother. Just maybe she had been running not from delusional mental ghosts, but from *real* creatures. Was it possible that his mother was not so crazy? Or had she been crazy *because* of what she had seen. After all, he had only seen what he guessed to be one brief example of what his aunt referred to as an "entity." What if those things had chased his mother? What if they had constantly tormented her? What if they had managed to catch her? Greg could not begin to guess what the things would want, what sick desires fueled them. How would someone cope with those things her entire life? Worse yet, what if someone had a child, a little boy, to take care of and protect?

"You alright?' Ron said, snapping Greg out of his thoughts. "You got that peaked look again."

"Yeah," Greg mumbled. "I was just thinking about … things."

"I don't doubt it," Ron said.

"So, what if I just leave?" Greg asked again, although he had an ominous suspicion that he already knew the answer.

"There's not a whole hell of a lot of paths—good or bad—but there's a fair number of 'em. Enough so that you'd probably run into 'em from time to time. And the things that travel those paths, they'd know you when they saw you, or smelled you, or whatever the hell it is they do to sense you. And they'd come." Ron sighed. "And I don't think those things really exist in this world, at least not completely. It's like they're half here and half someplace else. They can't, for example, walk through a solid object, but some of 'em don't exactly travel within the laws of nature."

"So they teleport or something?" Greg asked.

"I wouldn't go that far. But they can get places a whole hell of a lot faster than's natural. You'll see one of those things way out yonder in a field, a couple hundred yards away. And by the time you turn around to get the fuck outta there, the thing's covered half the distance. By the time you start runnin', it's right on your ass."

The thought of meeting one of those things outside, in the darkness, sent a chill through Greg. "You sound like you're talking from experience."

"Yeah, wish I wasn't," Ron said. "You know what the worst part was?"

"What?" Greg was not sure he wanted to know, but he couldn't help himself.

Ron leaned forward and stared at Greg. "When that thing was on my ass, I knew I wasn't in charge anymore. As human beings, we take it for granted that we're the top predators, that we're the shit. I mean, yeah, a bear can eat us. But compared to us, a bear's stupid. And if you got a high-powered rifle, well, a bear ain't so tough anymore. But those things out there, they're *smart*. And they don't give half a shit about any kind of weapon you got. You realize you just dropped down a link in the food chain. When one of those things touches you, you know without a doubt that you ain't in charge anymore."

Greg glanced into the kitchen, through the kitchen window, and out into the darkness beyond.

CHAPTER TWENTY-SIX

Greg sat on the brown leather couch in the living room. Katelin sat across from him in one of the matching recliners. The glass and iron coffee table separated them. Greg continued to stare at Katelin. She stared back.

His aunt's refusal to answer his question was testing his patience. After being greeted with nothing but more silence, Greg asked again, "Well, did he?"

Just when Greg thought he was going to scream in frustration, Katelin finally answered. "It wasn't really rape," she said.

Greg waited for Katelin to continue but she remained silent. Greg sighed. "Just tell me."

"This has nothing to do with your training. It's just a distraction. You need to learn what you need to learn."

Katelin was not the only one who could test someone's tolerance for frustration. Greg had been doing a pretty good job of evading her attempts to begin or even explain his "training."

"If you answer my questions, I'll concentrate on my training," Greg said.

Katelin stopped looking at Greg and instead looked down at the floor. She crossed her arms over her chest and seemed to consider his offer. "You promise?" she asked after a few moments.

"Promise," Greg lied.

Katelin nodded. "It wasn't rape. It's part of the family tradition. Part of the pact that was made with Bill's family. He didn't rape us. He was doing his duty. Virgin women in our family must have sex for the first time with a male from Bill's family. It increases the chance of producing a chosen child. The emotion of that first sexual experience—the newness of it, the pain—increases the odds that the entities will notice. A chosen child can only be conceived with the first act of intercourse with a man. If it doesn't happen the first time, a new man is needed. Being a virgin and the man being from Bill's family increases the odds in our favor even more."

Greg began to feel sick to his stomach.

"Katherine got to go first," Katelin continued. The contempt in her voice was unmistakable. "She always thought she was too good for family tradition. She was always so ungrateful. We had to hold her down. Even holding her legs apart, Bill had to hurt her to get inside her." Katelin shrugged. "That's what she gets."

Greg sat in stunned silence.

"*I* should have been allowed to go first!" Katelin burst out, startling Greg. "He used up his seed in my ungrateful sister. He should have fucked me first. *I* wanted it. When it was my turn, I ground my hips up under Bill and wrapped my legs around him, making him fuck me deep. I made sure he came deep inside me. But it didn't work. It …" Katelin's voice wavered. She sighed.

For a moment Greg thought she was going to cry. Then she took up where she had left off. "I've never asked for anything. All I've ever wanted was a chosen child. All I've ever tried to do is carry on this family's legacy." Katelin looked at Greg. "You should have been *my* son. Oh, the things I would have shown you. I would have *never* taken you away from here. I would have never taken you away from your rights as a chosen child."

When Katelin noticed Greg's expression, her own facial features softened. She rose from the recliner, walked over, and sat beside Greg. She put his right hand in between both of hers and proceeded to further confirm her unique mixture of denial, mistaking Greg's shocked expression of disgust for hurt at being denied his birthright.

"It's okay, honey," Katelin cooed. "No one's going to take you away ever again. You're home now. Did you know that Katherine and Katelin are versions of the same name? So, in a way, I'm like your second mother." Katelin patted his hand. "I know it's hard to forgive your mother for what she did, but you have to try. We *both* have to try."

Greg pulled his hand away from Katelin. "Don't touch me."

Katelin's expression took on the hard edge of annoyance that Greg had become familiar with. "You don't have to be so mean all the time. Just because your mother was a bitch doesn't mean you have to be one," she said indignantly.

Greg shook his head. "You're unbelievable."

Katelin shrugged. "I'm sorry if the truth hurts, but it doesn't make it any less the truth. You're mother was a self-absorbed, ungrateful little brat. She was given everything and pissed it away like it was nothing."

"Oh yeah, she was given everything all right," Greg said sarcastically. "A family full of psychos chasing a forest full of nightmares. Oh yeah, and let's not forget about the rape—every teenage girl's dream."

Katelin looked away from Greg. "You're really being a shit today."

"Yeah, I don't know what's wrong with me," Greg said. "I should be happy to find out I'm a rape baby."

Katelin returned her attention to Greg. "You'll learn to see the big picture. You've been given a gift. Don't piss it away like your mother did."

"Hey, not only am I a rape baby," Greg said, ignoring his aunt's comments, "but my father is a racist, murdering piece of shit! I'm doubly blessed. Oh wait," Greg added, holding his hands together in front of his chest in a mock gesture of anticipation, "and now that I finally begin to understand why my mother was the way she was, it's too late to try to have any kind of reconciliation, to come to any kind of understanding, because she's dead!"

Now that Greg had gotten on a roll, he found it easy to continue. In fact, it seemed impossible for him to stop. "And my aunt's a whore who's jealous of a dead woman."

Katelin looked away from him again.

"Oh! Oh, and I almost forgot, I can call things that shouldn't even exist. I don't know how I do it, and I don't *want* to do it, but I *can* do it. Yeah, I'm blessed."

"You have no intention of learning anything, do you?" Katelin said after a few moments of silence.

Greg suddenly felt exhausted and empty, like an old, bald tire that had finally given up and gone flat. He rubbed his palm over his face and sighed. "Yeah, it's all about the training. It's all about the family." Greg looked at his aunt. "Glad to know that in your concern for my well-being you have the piece of mind to remember why we're here."

Katelin stood. "I want to show you something."

Greg glanced at his aunt and then looked away. "Yeah, well I don't want to see it."

"It's something your mother left for you."

Despite himself, Greg returned his gaze to Katelin. "And what would that be?"

"I'll show you. It's upstairs on the third floor. It's just for you," Katelin said. She took a few steps toward the kitchen, stopped, and looked over her shoulder at Greg.

Although he did not want to take the bait, Greg rose from the couch and proceeded to follow his aunt into the kitchen. They climbed the wide set of back stairs off the kitchen in silence.

At the top of the final landing was a solid-looking oak door. Katelin produced a large old-fashioned brass key and inserted it into the matching brass mechanism of the door lock. When she turned the key, the lock responded with a series of dry, metallic clicks. Katelin turned the doorknob and pulled. The door came loose from the doorjamb with the protesting cracking noise of a door that had become accustomed to not being used. Musty air, eager to once again be inside human lungs, rushed out to greet Greg.

Katelin stepped to the side, leaving Greg to stand in front of the open door and look into the dim hallway beyond. She made a sweeping motion with her hand. "After you."

Greg took a few hesitant steps forward through the door and into the hallway. He had a moment to wonder if perhaps he should not turn his back on his aunt before the door slammed shut behind him. He heard the metallic *clank* of the lock engage as he turned to face the now closed and locked door. The noise bounced off the hard walls and wooden floor of the hallway, echoing with the finality of a locked prison cell.

CHAPTER TWENTY-SEVEN

For a moment, Greg stood in silence, staring at the door, before his aunt called from the other side, "Are you okay, honey?"

"Am I okay? You just locked me in here!"

"But that doesn't make you not okay. It just makes you locked in."

Greg crossed his arms and scowled, refusing to say anything else.

"The third floor is where your great grandfather conducted his research and experimentation. It contains all his notes, papers, and research material. It's the perfect place for you to learn to use your gifts."

After a few moments of silence, Katelin asked, "Honey, are you there? Are you listening?"

Greg decided it was pointless to remain silent; it was not accomplishing anything. "Just let me out of here. I'll pay better attention from now on."

"No you won't," Katelin admonished. "You're stubborn like your mother. But that's okay, honey, I forgive you. Maybe it's better this way. You can learn on your own at your own pace."

"So, if I don't learn anything, are you just going to leave me up here to starve to death and die?"

Katelin actually laughed. "You're family, I would never do that. There's a dumbwaiter in the right side room. I'll make sure you get plenty to eat. There's plenty of writing material, so you can even make a list of what you'd like and send it down to me on the dumbwaiter if you want. Don't worry, honey, you concentrate on learning. I just want to take care of you and help you realize your potential. Someday you'll thank me for all this. I know you will."

Greg had reached the limit of his patience. His simmering anger boiled over. "I don't want to learn anything! You can't keep me here, you bitch!" Greg struck the door with the palms of his hands. "Let me out, you bitch! *You crazy bitch!*"

Greg struck the door a few more times before giving up. Panting, he stared at the closed door and wished that he could somehow change the molecular structure of the wood, reach his hands through the door, and strangle Katelin. Maybe bang her head against the door a few times for good measure. "Fuck!" Greg yelled, spinning around to face the hallway, putting his back to the door.

"You'll thank me for this someday," Katelin said.

"You can kiss my ass, twice, once for each cheek," Greg said. "I'm not learning shit."

"Of course you will. You're a Dameron, it's in your blood. You'll learn because it's in your nature. And as much as you'd like not to believe it, honey, you can't mess around with nature. We are who we are, and the sooner you accept that, the happier you'll be. The happier we'll both be. I know you're angry right now, so I won't bother you anymore for a while, but I'll leave you with something to think about. I may be a lot of things, but at least I *know* who I am. At least I *accept* who I am. I didn't run away like your mother did. I stayed and faced my responsibilities. All your mother did with her life was run from it and leave a confused, angry young man behind. An angry young man with lots of questions and no answers. That's why I can't really blame you for the way you act—you don't know any better. But you're home now, and I'm going to show you what family is, and how family sticks by each other. How family takes care of family. I love you, honey. And one day, you'll love me back."

CHAPTER TWENTY-EIGHT

Now that Greg had been left alone, he decided to explore the makeshift prison. It seemed that either the third floor had never been completed or a remodeling project had begun at some point and been abandoned halfway through. The third floor was small compared to the lower levels of the house, and it was not difficult for Greg to see into the other rooms from his vantage point because the walls and doorframes of the hallway had not been finished.

The room to Greg's left was separated from the hallway by nothing but two-by-four wood framing. Beyond the skeletal framing members, a simple bed rested on the unfinished pine-board flooring, still rough and in need of sanding, that covered the entire area. Because the bedroom wall had not yet been framed for windows, the room was dark and gloomy, like an overcast day threatening rain.

A white toilet, looking oddly out of place without walls to separate it from the bedroom, was to Greg's immediate left. A matching white sink hung from the only finished wall present, the same wall that contained the oak door that had been slammed shut and locked to bar Greg's escape.

The right side hallway wall was partially plastered in rough, sweeping arches that resembled white waves. The plaster traveled away from the door about half-way down the twenty-foot hallway before revealing a naked wooden lathed wall that had probably waited patiently for decades for someone to finish clothing it in plaster. Through the unfinished doorframe, Greg glimpsed a room filled with bookcases and a large wooden table, a thick and sturdy workbenchlike structure.

Because his aunt had said that the third floor was where his great grandfather had conducted "experiments," Greg half expected to see beakers of bubbling, multicolored liquids belching plumes of smoke and formaldehyde-filled jars of human body parts and deformed fetuses. When he entered the room, Greg was greatly relieved to see nothing on the big table other than piles of paper, opened books, and various writing instruments. A simple brass lamp sat atop the table. Taking a closer look, Greg realized that the table was actually a large desk. From his current vantage point, he could see the backs of drawers and the top of a wooden chair that looked more like an uncomfortable kitchen chair than an office chair.

Overflowing bookcases lined the back wall, the hazy afternoon sunlight falling on numerous leather book spines from the two windows that looked out onto the backyard along the adjacent wall. A first coat of rough plaster covered this wall, making it almost finished. The dumbwaiter his aunt had mentioned hung between the set of windows, its two recessed panel doors partially open, revealing a thick rope that could be used to raise and lower the dumbwaiter on a series of pulleys. Currently, the wooden box was empty. It reminded Greg of a tiny elevator.

Greg walked over to a window and tried to open it, but it wouldn't budge. He checked the locks, flipped them back and forth, and tried again. There was still no movement. He tried the other window, same results. "Yeah, couldn't be that easy," Greg said, and walked over to the desk. Failing to locate what he sought on top of the desk, Greg rummaged through the desk drawers until he found a sturdy yet flexible plastic ballpoint pen.

Back at the window, Greg gripped the pen in his fist, thumb pressed against the end of the pen, point held up toward the glass, his elbow bent as if the pen was a kitchen knife, the glass a not-so-innocent young college girl, scantily glad and about to discover that when you hear a noise in the woods, for God's sake, do not go outside to investigate. Despite the situation, Greg grinned. "Stay in the cabin. Drink another beer. Finish having sex with your jock boyfriend. Do not go outside. And if you *do* go outside, when you hear the spooky music, turn your cute little panty-wearing ass around and run back to the cabin," Greg said.

Although Greg guessed that the windowpanes must be coated glass, and would crumble into nice nonlethal little nuggets rather than great gleaming wicked shards of pointy nastiness, he nonetheless turned his face away from the window, took a deep breath, and drove the pen forward.

When the pen hit the glass, it made a dull *thunk* sound and bounced off. Frowning, Greg stabbed the window again, this time with more force. The pen hit the glass and bent sideways, in the middle. Greg held up the pen in front of his face—it now looked like a boomerang pen. Greg doubted it would return to him if he threw it. Tossing the pen over his shoulder, he confirmed his doubt when the pen failed to sail in a wide arc and strike him in the back of the head.

Greg bent forward and peered at the glass. The only indication that the pen had made any contact was a small blurred white dot where the pen tip had collided with the glass pane. In the right corner of the bottom windowpane was a triangular red sticker that read: BULLDOG IMPACT RESISTANT SAFETY GLASS—STRONGER THAN A BULLET—GUARANTEED. A gray bulldog face, superimposed over the red lettering, stared at Greg.

Greg brought his head forward, rested his forehead against the window, closed his eyes, and sighed. Greg tried to remain calm. Greg always tried to remain calm, although he was not always good at it. He guessed that, like so many other things, it probably had something to do with his chaotic childhood. As a child he had been helpless to control his life. Even after becoming an adult Greg had quickly realized that there were still many things about life that could not be controlled: an asshole boss would always be an asshole boss; a paycheck would only ever be just enough to get you to come back and put up with the asshole boss for another week; stupid people were often put in positions of power and often abused those positions; most people were mostly good, but most people were also a little bad.

Regardless of all the things that Greg could not control, he had learned at an early age that one thing he *could* control was himself. Even now, thinking about his outburst after Katelin had locked him up here made Greg a bit embarrassed. There was no question Katelin deserved the verbal abuse and a whole lot more. But, regardless, it was unlike Greg to lose control of his emotions like that.

Another thing that bothered Greg was how easily his aunt had pegged him as "an angry young man." Greg was indeed often an angry young man, but he had always thought he hid it—*controlled* it—well. Was it really that obvious that he spent a good portion of his life haunted by the past? Resentful of a childhood he felt denied him by a paranoid mother? Did other people see through him as easily as Katelin had? Did people at work talk about him when he was not around to overhear them?

Thinking about work felt strange. It was like his past life in Florida was not real. It felt like *now* had always been his life, and his life in Florida was nothing but a kind of daydream. Greg found it odd how some things in the past remained in the past and quickly faded, while other experiences refused to ever be forgotten, or even fade like an old memory should, steadfastly insisting on remaining vivid, sharp, painfully real, painfully *new*.

Greg opened his eyes and looked out the window into the backyard. It looked so normal, so ordinary. Looking at the autumn leaves, the grass swaying in the breeze like a green-colored sea, Greg could half convince himself that everything was normal—he did not come from a long line of insane family members, the woods were not filled with nightmarish things, and he was not locked in this half-finished third floor until he would somehow learn how to summon the very creatures he wanted to stay as far away from as possible.

A large black bird landed on top of the backyard shed. It looked like a crow, or raven; Greg was not sure which or if there was even a difference. The bird was the deep, somehow commanding color of ink, so utterly black against the autumn colors that it looked almost unreal, like someone had drawn it into the backyard. At first, Greg assumed that it held some hapless rodent in its taloned grip, but when the bird lowered its head and stabbed at the thing it held, Greg realized that it was a flower. The crow/raven raised its head, the vibrant white of the rose petal in its beak all the more blinding due to the contrast of the bird's inky features. The bird released the rose petal. It spun away on the wind like a white teardrop. A moment later, the bird took flight. It flew upward in a circle, turned, and dived straight toward Greg.

Greg took an instinctive step back even though there was no possibility of the fragile bird penetrating the glass that was "stronger than a bullet." At the last moment, the bird shot upward like a jet fighter pilot practicing a high-speed evasive maneuver. As Greg stepped forward to the window, the rose that the bird had been carrying fell from above and landed on the windowsill outside.

Goose bumps rose over the flesh of Greg's arms. He felt a moment of profound disbelief, like when as a child you discover that Santa Claus does not actually exist and instead it is your parents who have been leaving you presents under the tree.

Although a bit tattered, there was no mistaking the large white rose with its delicate purple pink edges. It was a Moonstone rose, his mother's favorite flower.

CHAPTER TWENTY-NINE

Crying, his palms bleeding like some nine-year-old messiah, Greg runs through the park to his mother, who rises from the park bench at the sound of his voice. Greg is not badly hurt, although his hands do burn and tingle. The sight of his blood oozing from the puncture wounds on his palms is what brings the tears. They are more tears of fright than tears of pain.

His mother has dropped down to one knee in anticipation of Greg's full-steam-ahead charge toward her. Greg hurdles himself into her open arms. Her hair always smells so good. A moment later, Greg steps back and raises his palms out in front of him toward his mother.

Just the look of concern that creases his mother's smooth skin is enough to make some of Greg's fear disappear. He is with his mother now. She will help. She has Mom power, and she will make everything better.

Taking both his hands in hers, she studies Greg's bleeding palms closely for a moment before looking back up at Greg's tear-stained face. "Sweetie, what'd you do?"

Greg, huffing and hitching like an old-fashioned steam locomotive, manages to stammer, "I ... po ... poked myself ... on ... on the ... fl ... fl ... flowers!"

His mother nods and leads him over to the park bench. "Sit down, little man, we'll fix you."

Greg has been through fixing before, and although he is getting old enough to have his doubts about whether or not his mother's fixing is real, he dutifully and gratefully holds out his palms toward her.

His mother reaches into her front jeans pocket and pulls out the Invisible Little Boy Repair Kit. Opening the lid that only she can see, she takes out the special repair tools and begins to fix Greg's palms by first wiping the blood away, then tapping the wounds back together with the Repair Hammer. Next, she rummages through the repair kit until she finds some Make It Better Bolts, which she twists in the air above each of Greg's puncture wounds. Finally, she brings out the All Better Ruler and makes sure everything lines up properly.

After returning everything to the kit and putting it back in her pocket, Greg's mother looks at him with her wondrous brown eyes. "All better?"

Greg thinks about it for a moment. His palms still tingle and they do still hurt a little, but only a little, and the blood, the scary red blood, is gone. He grins and nods vigorously in that little boy way that will give any adult a headache if attempted.

His mother hugs him. "Good. Now, why don't you show me where these mean flowers are?"

Standing on the grass at the edge of the park before it gives way to thick underbrush and trees, Greg points at the rosebush that hides just inside the tree line, teasing them with glimpses of white.

His mother once again kneels on one knee and looks at Greg. "Remember what I told you about going into the woods?"

Greg nods. "Don't go into the woods. Stay where you can see me."

"That's right. Where I can see you. Always where I can see you. Those are roses," his mother says, "Moonstone roses. It's strange that they're growing out in the wild like that, but they are. Roses have thorns on their stems that will poke you if you grab them. They're like people—some of them are very pretty but they can hurt you if you don't know how to handle them properly. You understand, little man?"

Greg nods, not really caring about what the flowers are called and not really understanding, but hoping that if he agrees, he will not get in trouble for disobeying his mother and going into the woods, even though it was only a little bit into the woods.

"Why were you messing with them in the first place?" his mother asks.

"I wanted to pick one and give it to you, because they're pretty, like you."

Looking at his mother's face, Greg is convinced he has said something wrong. Then her stern gaze crumbles, her eyes well up, and a tear slides down her cheek. She grabs him and hugs him tight. "From now until forever, these will be my favorite flowers. My sweet boy."

CHAPTER THIRTY

Greg had forgotten all about the day in the park and the roses. It had been just another day, in another town, somewhere new—always somewhere new. But the memory had resurfaced with startling ease and clarity. Apparently, not all of Greg's childhood memories were bad. The bad memories just seemed to be the ones he recalled most often.

Greg was surprised to find himself crying a little. He wiped his cheeks and blotted his eyes with his shirtsleeve. He sniffed, straightened from his hunched position in front of the window, and sighed. There was no Little Boy Repair Kit to help him now—his mother had possessed the only one. Besides, he was not a little boy anymore, and if Big Boy Repair Kits existed, Greg doubted that they would have the same magic as the little boy version.

Greg stared at the rose outside the window. One of the petals caught the breeze, fluttered back and forth like a butterfly wing, and broke loose, carried away on the wind. Like a prison visitor come to spend time with an inmate, Greg put his palm against the window opposite the rose.

Regret had begun to leak into Greg's heart. It was only a small trickle, but Greg feared that if unchecked, it would grow into a raging torrent. If he had known the whole story of why his mother had been the way she'd been, maybe things would have been different. Maybe he wouldn't have been so confused, so angry about constantly moving. Maybe his mother's cryptic life lessons and warning would have made some sense, been more relevant. But in reality would he have believed her had she told him the whole story? Would it have made a difference if she told him that they were running from a crazy family that chased monsters? Would he have believed her? Would it have helped if Greg had known that he was the product of rape? The simple answer was no, not really.

His mother had by no means been a saint, and had definitely been mentally unstable. But could Greg blame her? Had it *all* been her fault? Again, the simple answer was no, not really.

Like the haunting face of a ghost, Greg recalled the hurt in his mother's eyes when he had, at eighteen, finally become a legal adult and had severed ties with his mother. He remembered how devastated she had looked as he unloaded all the years of confusion and pain on her. How he had blamed her for it all before leaving her forever, making it clear in stinging words of hate that he never—NEVER!—wanted to see her face again.

The last memory he had of his mother was that look of devastating pain as she stood outside the motel room and watched him leave. She had said nothing, had not tried to stop him, had not attempted to plead with him. She simply had stood, stoic, and taken in her son with her tearful eyes for what she had to have known would be the last time. At the time, even the fact that his mother had just stood there and let him leave had made Greg angry. Now, in retrospect, Greg suspected that his mother had probably known that the day would come, had resigned herself to the fact that it would be yet another in the long line of hurts and losses that she would have to bear.

Greg had literally been all his mother had had, and he had left her utterly alone. What had she done for the last decade of her life? How had she lived? Where had she gone? The thought of his mother, alone and heartbroken, threatened to make Greg cry again, but he held the tears back. "You're a selfish shit," Greg said to himself, relying on his old ally, anger, to help him control his other emotions.

Now that the adrenaline had worn off, emotionally spent and physically drained, Greg shuffled over to the far corner of the room, away from the desk and the bookcases, and plopped down into the corner, legs bent, his knees raised to eye level. Resting his elbows on his knees, he ran his hands through his hair, tilted his head back against the wall, and stared up at the ceiling.

What was he going to do now?

CHAPTER THIRTY-ONE

The *rattle-hiss-squeak* of the dumbwaiter descending brought Greg out of his thoughts (or lack thereof) with a start. Greg did not know how long he had sat in the corner thinking about nothing, but it felt like it had been no more than half an hour. Nonetheless, it was still amazing how fast time could get away from you.

Greg rose to his feet and walked over to the dumbwaiter in time to catch a glimpse of its top as it disappeared below to parts unknown. Greg had a feeling where it had gone. After patiently waiting a few minutes, Greg was rewarded by the noise of the dumbwaiter once again, this time ascending toward him.

Inside the dumbwaiter, Greg found a piece of lined notebook paper and a ballpoint pen. He picked up the piece of paper. On the paper, written in black ink:

Honey,

It's getting towards suppertime and I'm checking to see what you'd like to eat. You can have anything you want, anything at all. Just write it down and send this note back down to me.

Just because we have to go through this bit of unpleasant business, that doesn't mean you shouldn't eat well. You need your strength for learning. You can have anything you want, anything at all.

Staring at the note that had obviously been written by his aunt, all Greg could think about was the "steak" incident that had not involved steak at all. Even now the thought of it made Greg's stomach twitch a bit in disgust. Since the incident, Greg had eaten nothing that his aunt had prepared, instead subsisting on a diet of simple foods that Greg prepared himself: burgers, hotdogs, cold sandwiches, cereal, frozen pizzas, TV dinners—the diet of bachelors (of which Greg was one) and college students (of which Greg had *been* one) everywhere.

For a moment, Greg thought about writing something on the note like *Kiss my ass! Both cheeks!* but decided that something straightforward and truthful would be more effective in getting his point across. Using the bottom of the dumbwaiter as a writing surface, Greg grabbed the pen and wrote below his aunt's note:

I refuse to eat until I am released. I am being held against my will. I can't control what you do, but I can control what I do. You should be ashamed of yourself.

Heart pounding, Greg grabbed the rope and sent the dumbwaiter below. While the thought of not having food scared him, Greg also felt a certain satisfaction at regaining a bit of control over the situation. Yes, his aunt could lock him upstairs, but she could not make him do anything, even eat.

Greg wondered how long a person could go without food. Greg seemed to remember reading somewhere that a person could go for weeks, maybe months, without food. Could a person really go a whole month without eating? Greg felt determined that if he had to, he would find out. But despite his resolve, Greg was already beginning to feel hungry. "This sucks," he mumbled, and turned away from the window.

Because his aunt wanted him to learn to control his abilities—if you wanted to call accidentally summoning creatures that scared the shit out of you an "ability"—Greg, in another simple act of defiance, ignored the books in the bookcases and the papers spread across the desk. Looking at anything that pertained to what his aunt wanted felt like giving in to her demands, and Greg was not going to do that. *Both cheeks!*

CHAPTER THIRTY-TWO

The morning of day two had consisted of another note from Katelin asking him to eat, which Greg had ignored. Now early afternoon, Greg had spent the day seated in front of the same window that he had looked out of yesterday. With his feet propped up on the windowsill, Greg could have passed for someone spending a leisurely afternoon taking in nature, maybe with a glass of iced tea or a cold bottle of beer. Only the chair Greg sat in was made of hard pine wood instead of the canvas straps and lightweight metal of a lawn chair, and Greg was not outside on a front porch waving to neighbors, but instead locked in a room. And hungry.

Greg was surprised that he had become so hungry so fast. In fact, even though only a single day had passed without it, Greg found himself thinking about food almost exclusively. He would sit in the chair, arms crossed, and stare outside into the backyard, occasionally watching a bird land on a tree and hop around, or a squirrel dart from tree branch to tree branch. And the whole time Greg would be thinking about pizza with melted cheese and greasy pepperoni, or a cheeseburger so thick that it would cramp his jaw when he tried to get his mouth around it to take that first fantastic bite. And onion rings, he needed those to go with the cheeseburger. And some apple pie. Hell, an *entire* apple pie. And if he was going to have apple pie, he would need vanilla ice cream. Did he want a cold glass of milk? Maybe a bottle of beer? Would beer go well with pie and ice cream? Maybe he should have milk and the beer, just to be safe. Greg thought he might end up driving himself crazy thinking about all the things he wished he could eat.

Greg also now realized why being imprisoned was a punishment for committing a crime. When watching prison documentaries on television, Greg always thought that prison didn't seem that bad. Granted, Greg never wanted to go to one—being surrounded by dangerous people did not seem fun. But you were provided with food—

Pie!

—and a warm place to sleep, so it could not be that bad. But Greg had come to the conclusion that it was not the other inmates that made prison so bad, but the *time* you spent in prison that really got to you. Greg guessed that prison time was similar to what he was experiencing now. It was a different kind of time, like work time (time always seemed to slow down when you were at work, while the weekend went by in a flash) but worse, more powerful, more intense. Greg thought he now understood what made prison so terrible: an hour felt like a day, a day felt like a week, a week felt like a month, and a damned month felt like a year. No wonder prisoners said they were "doing time."

To Greg, it felt like time was no longer just something that marked the point when you had to wake up in the morning, or when you could leave work, or when your favorite TV show came on. No, time now felt like a real thing—a living, breathing behemoth of a thing that wanted to crush you under its unforgiving weight.

Greg did not know how long he had sat staring out the window, lost in his thoughts before he heard the dumbwaiter ascend. He glanced over at the wall and waited. A few moments later, the dumbwaiter finished its ascent.

Greg smelled the food before he saw it. His mouth filled with a flood of saliva and his stomach cramped painfully like a cry of surprise. Then the dumbwaiter came to rest, revealing a plate of fried chicken, mashed potatoes and gravy, and corn on the cob. A glass of milk and a glass of orange juice stood behind the plate.

For a moment Greg just sat and stared in disbelief, as if the room was a desert, and the food a mirage conjured from the mind of a desperate, lost wanderer. Before he was fully aware of having done so, Greg stood in front of the plate. The lack of nourishment had made his muscles weak, and Greg's legs quivered like taut rubber bands. His jaw muscles twitched. At that moment, an army would have been hard-pressed to prevent Greg from snatching up the food and gobbling it down in giant, stomach-filling mouthfuls. Greg, however, exhibiting his practiced self-control, grabbed the rope, and sent the dumbwaiter back down, food untouched.

It was almost physically painful to watch the food disappear from sight. In fact, in a howl of protest, Greg's stomach cramped hard enough to make Greg gasp and bring both hands up to his waist. The pain, however, subsided as quickly as it had come, and Greg was left to stand and stare at an empty hole in the wall, his emotions flipping from despair, to fear, to self-pity. Eventually, Greg rolled around to anger, where he stayed.

Greg stomped out of the room and over to the area that would have been a bathroom had it been finished. He turned on the sink faucet, lowered his head to the tap, and slurped up cold water until he thought he was going to gag. When he finally lifted his head from the tap, a spike of pain from the rush of cold water nailed the center of Greg's forehead.

Greg closed his eyes and brought his right palm up to his forehead. *You stupid ass, you should have ate it.* Greg shook his head. "No, she can't win."

Feeling angry and sorry for himself, Greg shuffled over to the bed and fell into it. He threw the old, mildew-smelling blanket over his head and tried to fall asleep.

When he had been a teenager, Greg's dreams had often been filled with nameless naked women who desired nothing but sex and more sex, sometimes in positions so strange that Greg was not sure they were possible anywhere *but* in the land of dreams. In his current state of hunger, Greg would not have been surprised if he dreamed of naked women that desired nothing but to feed him cheeseburgers and pizza until he exploded. He could hope, at least.

CHAPTER THIRTY-THREE

When Greg awoke, the sun had begun to set. A dusk shadow had settled over the room like a dark blanket. There had been no dreams that he could remember, naked or otherwise.

Thankfully, Greg's stomach had subsided from a scream of outrage to only a dull ache of protest. After relieving himself of what felt like a gallon of pee, Greg made his way to his lookout post and sat down on the hard chair with a sigh. Dusk had brought a layer of low fog that clung to the backyard and wound its way through the trees like countless smoky snakes. The effect was a bit eerie, but at least it was something new to look at. How did the saying go: simple pleasures for simple minds? Greg did not know exactly, but it was something like that.

And the ache of Greg's stomach was almost gone. Greg was not sure if that was a good thing or not. The feeling of hunger had been replaced with a sensation that Greg could only describe as an emptiness that was somehow not empty. It was a strange concept, but that was what if felt like. An emptiness had filled his body with a hollow nothing that somehow still managed to take up space. Basically, Greg felt full of nothing.

Greg wondered what he looked like. There was no mirror, which may have been a good thing. His eyes felt sunken, his eyelids tired, as if they just wanted to stay closed and dream this whole torturous affair away. His hair had a mind of its own and was always a little disheveled in the best of times, ensuring that Greg suffered from a permanent bad hair day. Without a comb to tame its wildness over the past few days, Greg was sure his hair looked like a cross between Don King and Albert Einstein. When he ran his palm over his cheeks, Greg could feel the stubble of a five o'clock shadow that was steadily advancing toward five thirty.

And, to top it all off, sitting in a hard chair for hours on end had begun to make Greg's ass hurt. Of course, after a few hours, it just went numb anyway. So, no harm no foul, Greg supposed.

Greg forgot about his ass when, at the tree line to the right of the backyard shed, the fog swirled and parted, and from the woods stepped a ghostly young woman who was as pale as … well, a ghost. As before when he had encountered the half-man (literally half a man), half-bird monstrosity at his bedroom window, Greg felt a subtle shift in his perception, as if the tether that held him to reality had been pulled taut and threatened to snap. It was how he knew that he was staring at what his aunt called an "entity."

Against her chalk white skin, the darkness of her long, straight black hair was startling. It fell over the front of her shoulders and was parted by her naked breasts before ending at her stomach. From the waist down, she was concealed behind the fog that seemed to come alive in her presence and wrap around her with eager, clinging fingers. She held something in her right hand. Greg strained to make out what it was, but the combination of fog and lack of light made it impossible to make out. Her white skin was covered in random splotches of something dark, like she had been playing in mud.

Although Greg could not make out much detail about the entity, he was sure that she was looking directly at him. As if to confirm this, she held her hands up toward him, still holding whatever it was in her right hand, and spread her arms in the universal gesture of embrace.

The thought of having her (if you could truly call it a "her," regardless of what sex it appeared to be) touch him, let alone wrap her arms around him, made Greg's skin crawl. Maybe it was only his imagination, but Greg thought he could feel a pull coming from her, like a hunger, a *need* for her (it) to touch him.

Greg stood and took a step back. He shook his head. "No," he mumbled.

The thing outside seemed to hear him. More incredibly, it actually seemed to understand. It moved backwards toward the tree line from which it had come. Its movement had an unsettling quality to it, as if it was being pulled backward on a string. It did not look behind it to see where it was going, but instead kept its gaze locked on Greg. Arms still outstretched toward him, it disappeared back into the woods, the fog engulfing it.

Shaking from a combination of adrenaline and lack of food, Greg stepped forward and sat back down on the chair. Good thing he had taken an afternoon nap, because there was no way he was going to be able to sleep for the rest of the night. Looking around the room, the only meager light coming from the single bulb of the desk lamp, Greg did not like the shadows that clung to everything. When he looked back out into the night, his imagination immediately conjured an image of the deathly pale woman standing behind him in the room, silently floating toward him behind his back, hands outstretched, now only inches from the back of his head.

Greg jumped up from the chair and whirled around. A dangerous black pulse filled his vision, threatening to bring with it unconsciousness. Greg staggered. He reached out and grabbed the top of the chair for support. He took a deep breath. The blackness receded to the edges of his vision and then disappeared entirely. Greg reminded himself that he needed to take it easy. Without food for two days, he was running on empty and his body would not tolerate too much excitement before he would be *forced* to take it easy.

On the plus side, nothing stood behind Greg ready to grab him. Just in case, Greg dragged the chair over to the far side of the room and put its back against the wall. With everything in the room in view and most of the backyard visible when he glanced sideways, satisfied, Greg sat back down, the wall protecting his back. Suddenly, Greg had an unpleasant thought: *What if that one can walk through walls?*

Greg shook his head. *No, that's not funny.*

The thing was, no one was laughing.

CHAPTER THIRTY-FOUR

The sound of the dumbwaiter woke Greg. Apparently, despite his previous firm assertion that he would not be able to sleep, sometime during the night he had proven himself wrong and fallen asleep sitting in the chair. He had slept at a bad angle, though—what could you expect from sleeping on a wooden chair—causing his neck to creak in protest when he attempted to turn his head to the left. Greg grimaced, muscles that he had formerly been unaware existed making their presence known all the way down the left side of Greg's neck, shoulder, and back.

Once again, sitting in the chair had caused Greg's ass to go numb; only this time, both his legs had gone along for the ride. When Greg tried to stand up, he almost fell flat on his face. His legs had fallen asleep to such an extent that they felt like dead slabs of meat attached to his lower body. He vigorously attempted to rub life back into his thighs. After kneading his thigh muscles like dough for about half a minute, Greg felt a cold wave wash over his legs as blood once again began to circulate freely. After a more familiar bout of invisible pins and needles poked and prodded his skin, his legs returned to normal. By this time, the dumb-waiter had ascended and come to a stop, and Greg hobbled over to it on newly awakened legs connected to a still half-numb backside. It was an odd feeling.

Greg expected to find another plate of maddeningly tempting food waiting in the dumbwaiter. The thought alone made his stomach spasm painfully. Instead of a meal, Greg found a dark blue two-way radio about the size of the average cell phone. Frowning, he picked it up. The green LCD display on the face of the radio proclaimed that it was turned to channel 2. Greg turned the small dial a notch on the top of the radio next to the stubby black antenna. The radio responded with a brief hiss of static, the LCD display changing to 3. Greg turned the dial back to channel 2.

Greg slowly turned the radio in his hands. Since food itself had not worked—Greg felt a glimmer of pride in winning that not-so-small battle—was his aunt resorting to direct lectures about his responsibilities to the family? If Greg had to hear his aunt remind him one more time in her snooty little way that he was a Dameron, that he was special, Greg thought he might start screaming and never be able to stop. Well, Greg was not going to give Katelin the satisfaction.

Greg brought the radio up toward his mouth and used his index finger to push the black button that ran up the side of the radio. "I don't have anything to say to you. You can go to hell," Greg said into the front of the two-way radio. He took his finger off the talk button and began to lower the radio before reconsidering and bringing it back up toward his mouth. "You can go to hell and you can take your fried chicken and mashed potatoes with you. And shove your corncob up your ass while you're at it."

The corncob ass-shoving remark made Greg blush in embarrassment as he lowered the radio to his side. At the same time, he giggled a little like a young child who has just learned a bad word and repeated it for the first time, feeling naughty, but also strangely empowered.

Greg jumped and almost dropped the radio when it barked a short burst of static followed by Ron's voice. "I'm not sure the old hemorrhoids would take too kindly to the corncob ass-pokin'. When I was a kid, like a lotta Iowa kids, I detassled corn during the summer. My dad said it would keep me outta trouble and teach me the value of a dollar, but all it ever did was make every muscle in my body ache and slice my hands all to shit with a thousand tiny cuts from corn-stalk leaves. But you couldn't argue with my dad. He was kind of a hard-ass that way. Anyway, ever since then I'm not too fond of corn on the cob. I *for sure* don't have strong enough romantic feelings to let it butt-plug me." A few moments of silence followed. Then, from the radio: "Bud, you there?"

"Yeah," Greg said before realizing that the radio was still at his side. He brought it up to his mouth and pushed the talk button. "Yeah," he repeated, "I'm here."

"Good. For a second there I thought I was sharin' my most intimate corn secrets with no one."

Greg walked back over to his sentry chair by the window and sat. "So ... what's going on?" he said, marveling at how conversational and laid-back he managed to sound while being locked in a room and slowly starving.

"She locked me in the basement," Ron said sardonically.

Greg stood back up. "What?"

"She says she's not gonna give me anything to eat 'til you start eatin'."

Greg fell back into the chair. "Fuck," he mumbled.

"I can probably go for a few days without food, but uh …"

Greg waited for Ron to continue. After a few moments, he said into the radio, "But what?"

His uncle sighed. "Shit, bud, I'm a drunk. We both know it. I can probably go for a few days without food. Hell, I've done it before. But I can't remember when's the last time I went without a beer for even one damn day. I'm already gettin' the shakes 'n shit."

CHAPTER THIRTY-FIVE

With his head down and eyes closed, Greg used his left hand to hold his forehead. In his right hand he held the two-way radio. Katelin was like some kind of Betty Crocker cancer, a cake mix for disaster: just when you thought you had figured out how to beat the nastiness hidden inside the pretty, innocent exterior, she added some new ingredient to the mix and knocked you back down a peg. Greg sighed and brought the radio up to his mouth. "How long you been down there?"

"Since yesterday afternoon, so not too long. But long enough," Ron said.

Greg knew what his uncle meant. Greg had only spent ... was it two days? Three days? A week? Greg did not take it as a good sign that time had become pliant, sliding through his fingers and slipping away from him. But regardless of how long it had been in reality, Greg felt like he had been locked away for months.

"Do you have anything down there at all?" Greg asked. "Anything? Water?"

"Yeah, there's a washer and dryer down here and one of those big-ass plastic laundry sinks, so I got water. Hell, damned sink's big enough I could probably climb in and take a bath if I got the notion to."

Greg leaned his head back. A headache had begun to drill a dull, aching pain into his forehead. He rubbed his temples, leaned his head forward, and reluctantly opened his eyes.

"You know ... oh fuck it, never mind," Ron said.

Greg sat up straighter in the chair. "No. What were you going to say?"

"It's just that. Well, I just never thought she'd do somethin' like this. I never thought she'd take it this far."

Even through the tiny radio speaker, the hurt in Ron's voice was unmistakable. Greg opened his mouth to try to come up with some kind of comforting remark, but decided that in this instance maybe he should just remain silent and listen. Let Ron get it all out. Greg's assumption was rewarded a moment later when Ron began to speak again.

"I mean, shit, I *know* she ain't normal. I know that. And maybe I even always knew that she was a little dangerous if pushed into a corner, but I never thought she'd go and do shit like this. I mean, so we don't love each other, I know that."

Greg winced.

"But still, there's common decency. I wouldn't lock a *dog* in a basement, not a goddamned dog."

"How'd she get you down there?" Greg asked.

Ron laughed humorlessly. "Well, when I didn't see you around for a few days, I started gettin' a bad feelin' and asked her what was goin' on. She didn't even try to deny it. She told me what she did. Well, goes without sayin' I wasn't havin' any of that crazy shit. I went upstairs to let you out. I figured she'd follow me, try to stop me, but she didn't. When I got most of the way up there, I realized I didn't have the key to open the damned door. When I marched back downstairs, Katelin came out of the kitchen with …"

"What?" Greg asked.

Ron sighed. "Man, bud, I feel like an ass. She came out of the kitchen with a can of beer. Hell, she's handed me so many brewskies over the years that even with the crazy shit that was goin' down I didn't think anything of it. I took it from her and told her I wanted the key, now. She nodded her head in that little kid way that she does and said she'd go get it for me. Said she was sorry and told me she'd made a mistake. Told me to drink my beer and she'd be right back. She played my ass.

"Well, most times no one has to tell me *once* to drink a beer, and no one ever has to tell me twice. So I stood there in the kitchen feelin' all proud and manly and drank my damned beer, that she had put somethin' in. Didn't take but a minute before I started feelin' light-headed, like I was gettin' ready to pass out, which I'm pretty familiar with. Last thing I remember is the floor jumpin' up at my face and wonderin' if the tile was gonna hurt when I hit my head on it. Then I woke up down here."

Greg remained silent, head throbbing. He rubbed his forehead absently.

"Shit, I'm sorry, bud," Ron said after a moment.

Greg shook his head. "It's not your fault."

"Well, thanks for sayin' so. But I still feel like an ass. Got any ideas what we do now?"

"Not really," Greg admitted. "I guess we just wait and see."

CHAPTER THIRTY-SIX

Greg did not have to wait long. Within the hour, the dumbwaiter again came to life, rumbling first down and then back up. This time it did not hold just a plate of food, but a virtual buffet of dishes stacked on a blue plastic serving tray that anyone who ever ate at an elementary school cafeteria is familiar with.

Each plate held a heaping portion of food. There was a bowl of salad almost as big as Greg's head. A mound of shredded cheddar cheese covered the lettuce, cherry tomatoes, and sliced green peppers. On the side were three little bowls filled with dressings: one ranch, one Italian, and another Greg could not identify offhand. Another bowl consisted of a salad of bright, freshly chopped fruit. A plate had been filled with garlic mashed potatoes, two ears of sweet corn, and some barbecue baked beans. On another plate were four dinner rolls, next to it a tub of butter. Next to that were slices of apple and blueberry pie, complete with a glass of milk. And on the final plate was the mother lode that made Greg's stomach do a lurching dance of delight: the large serving plate held a slab of barbecue ribs, a cheeseburger with everything, and a miniature mountain of chicken wings. The promised spicy-hot goodness of the chicken wings transformed the inside of Greg's mouth into a pond of saliva. He did not know how Katelin had found out that probably his favorite meal on the planet was a pile of hot chicken wings and a cold bottle of Corona. And behold, not one but two bottles of Corona, each with a green lime slice sticking out the top. It was enough to make Greg want to join his stomach in a herky-jerky victory dance.

Greg was so hungry that his instincts almost took over and made him dive into the food with his bare hands, ripping off chunks and gobbling them down like a starving animal. Greg had a flashing mental image of himself, face and shirt covered in grease and barbecue sauce, screaming in victory, both hands held high, filled with chicken wings and ribs.

Greg resisted the urge to go primal on the food, though, and instead hurried over to the desk, ripped out a piece of paper from one of the empty notebooks strewn around, grabbed a pen, and hurriedly scribbled a note:

I won't eat until Ron does.

He picked up the piece of paper, reconsidered, and added:

This is NOT NEGOTIABLE!!!

Greg walked back over to the dumbwaiter, put the note on top of the barbecue ribs, and sent the whole thing back down to Katelin. He wanted to cry as he watched the food disappear. Despite his note, if his aunt sent the food back up and refused to give in to his demands to feed Ron, Greg was not sure he would be able to resist and send the food away a second time.

Greg was so hungry he thought he was going half-mad, which would be fine around here—he would fit right in. Greg felt like one of those old cartoon characters that gets stranded with a friend on a desert island or in a boat out to sea with no food. After a while, the friend's leg starts to look like a hotdog, or his head like a cheeseburger. Pretty soon the two friends are chasing each other around the island with forks and dinner knives in their hands (never mind where the utensils came from—it is a cartoon, after all), bibs tucked under their chins.

A harsh bark of static from the two-way radio made Greg jump. He spun around toward the desk. At some point he had apparently added the radio to the jumbled collection on the desktop. "Smokey, come in Smokey. This is the Bandit. Come in, over," Ron said from the radio.

Greg smirked and picked up the radio. "I'm here."

"You're supposed to say something like 'ten-four, good buddy, I'm readin' you loud and clear, over.'"

"Why do you get to be the Bandit?" Greg asked. "You don't even have a mustache."

"Well, you don't either," Ron said.

"Good point," Greg conceded. "And wasn't Smokey the cop? Why would you be talking to the cop?"

"Hell, I don't know. I think so."

Greg heard the dumbwaiter squeak back to life behind him. He glanced over his shoulder and watched the homemade feast return. "Did she give you anything to eat?" Greg asked, walking over to the dumbwaiter. He was practically willing Ron to say yes.

"Oh, yeah, she brought me more food than I eat in a week. And a six-pack. So, hell, life is good. If I had my computer, I could stay down here forever. I …"

Greg lost track of what Ron was saying. He had something akin to tunnel vision, and all he could see was the food. He absently sat the radio on the floor, pulled his sentry chair over, and sat down in front of the dumbwaiter. Greg's hands were actually shaking as he reached out for the plate of chicken wings with one, a bottle of Corona with the other.

Every piece of candy combined that Greg had eaten as a child; every cold, rich milkshake; every bar of chocolate; all of them put together times a hundred, a *thousand*, was not one-tenth as satisfying as that first chicken wing.

CHAPTER THIRTY-SEVEN

Greg could not recall ever being this full. It felt like he had a brick sitting in his stomach. He had eaten in a couple of hours more food than he would normally have eaten over the course of a couple of *days*. More than once during his feast, he had been certain he was going to be sick, once even getting up and walking half-way to the bathroom before reconsidering and returning to shovel more food into his eager mouth. It was like an addiction: He told himself he was full, he had eaten enough, but his body was having none of it. If food was there, he had to eat it, had to have it. Maybe some ancient survival instinct had reawakened and kicked in, revving up due to Greg's starvation over the last week. It seemed his body was ensuring Greg put a little energy in the food bank in case he encountered another lean week and had to make a few withdrawals.

Greg's stomach made a noise that sounded like a gurgling sigh of content-ment. Greg put his right hand on his distended belly and sighed in response. Too full to lean forward far enough to grasp the dumbwaiter rope, Greg stood, grabbed the rope, and sent the empty husk of his meal downward. He sat back down.

"Hey, bud, you there? Or did you choke yourself to death? You gotta remem-ber to chew."

Greg smirked. The two Coronas had given him a mild, pleasant buzz. He leaned over and retrieved the two-way radio from the floor. "This is Smokey. Reading you loud and clear, good buddy. Over."

"That's the spirit," Ron said approvingly. Greg thought Ron sounded a little drunk, but it was hard to judge from only a voice coming through a little speaker. So what if he was, Greg reasoned. Greg could understand why Ron drank so much: being in this hellhole would drive anyone to drink. As if reading his mind, Ron said, "The well has run dry. I repeat, the well has run dry. We have an emergency situation. Call in the Navy, the Marines, the Air Force, and the Army!" Ron giggled. Yes, he was a little drunk.

Maybe it was the alcohol, maybe it was the food, maybe it was just having someone to talk to after days without human interaction, or maybe it was a combination of them all. But whatever the reason, Greg actually felt a small measure of contentment. Yes, he was still locked in a room, but if he did not dwell on the fact, it was easy to push it to the back of his mind and ignore it. And Ron had given him an idea about a helpful way to assist in the ignoring process.

Greg brought the radio up to his mouth. "You want to get shitfaced?"

There was a short silence, followed by a bark of laughter from the radio. "That's not even a question."

"I'll take that as a yes."

"You think she'll let us?" Ron asked. He sounded as hopeful as a little boy asking his parents if they can all go to Disney World.

Greg shrugged. "I don't see why not. As long as she thinks I'm working on learning to be all that I can be and all that bullshit, I bet she'll pretty much give me whatever I want."

"Well, hell, bud, sounds like we got ourselves a party."

With some effort, Greg stood up from the chair, walked over to the desk, and wrote another short note:

> I've decided you've been correct: I should study. Before I "hit the books" I'd like a little something to celebrate my newfound studies. In college, I always seemed to study better if I had a few cold beers. Would you please get me some more Corona? Also, since Ron is forced to be locked in the basement, please let him have whatever he wants while he's down there. From now on I'll be working hard, so I don't think I'll be up here much longer, but I'd like to make mine and Ron's remaining time as pleasant as possible.

Of course, it was all bullshit. Greg had never been much of a drinker, or a studier for that matter. Sure, like most college students, he had had his share of late-night parties and early-morning hangovers, but no more than most. Gifted with an above-average level of intelligence, and a mother who, despite her profound strangeness, had provided him with a very good homeschooled education, Greg had rarely needed to study, instead coasting through with a B average on a full-ride scholarship to Florida State University thanks to his high SAT score. He most likely could have graduated with honors, but Greg had decided early on that having a gold cord draped over his graduation gown and an asterisk next to his name in the graduation handout was not worth the hassle. In fact, Greg's entire college graduation ceremony had not been worth the hassle, so he had not gone. Besides, he had already had a job lined up before graduation, and after scraping by as a poor college student for four years, eating cafeteria food and living in a dorm, Greg had been eager to start making some real money so he could afford to live in a place where he did not have to share a bathroom and shower with a couple hundred other guys and eat barely-warm macaroni and cheese that tasted like cheese-covered cardboard on a good day, and cheese-covered ass on a bad one.

Compared to his current situation, though, Greg would have gladly moved back into a dorm in a heartbeat, ass-flavored food and all. Greg had not studied much during college, and he definitely had no intention of studying anything related to the things that roamed around outside in the woods. So, it looked like he was not moving anytime soon. But those were thoughts for another time. Right now, Greg was just going to sit here, stare out the window, and see if Katelin believed his bullshit.

As it turned out, she did indeed believe it.

CHAPTER THIRTY-EIGHT

Somewhere between Corona eight and twelve, Greg came to the conclusion that he was drunk. Greg had reached his destination of shitfaced, parked, and got out and walked around, stretching his wobbly legs a bit. Also somewhere in the magical beer range of eight to twelve, Greg had lost contact with Ron. But Ron, ever the old pro at drinking, had been kind enough to inform Greg that he was going to pass out soon, now that he had finished all his beers.

Left with no one to talk to, Greg quickly grew bored with staring out the window. He stood and wandered over to the bookcases that lined the far wall. All of the volumes—some expensive-looking leather-bound editions, others spine-creased, tattered paperbacks—were on the subject of magic in one form or another. At a glance, Greg saw volumes about witchcraft, voodoo, demonology, and a myriad of other more obscure subject matters. Even drunk and bored, Greg had no interest in reading any of the material. Greg feared it would be like opening Pandora's box.

Greg walked back to his chair, dragged it over to the desk, and sat down. On the desktop, under the layer of dust that Greg had disturbed when he had picked up the notebook he used to write to Katelin, Greg noticed a black leather-covered book about as thick as the other notebooks. Greg brushed off the dust from some of the other notebooks and moved them over, revealing more of the black books. Greg chose one of the books at random and picked it up.

It turned out to be a kind of journal, handwritten in heavy black ink. Obviously old, the thick, unlined pages had yellowed over the years. The pages made a whispery, dry crackling sound as Greg flipped through them. In some places, the pages had become stuck together. Greg chose one such place and carefully peeled the paper apart. Greg caught a glimpse of a sentence:

... some instances. Control of the entities has proven difficult in many ...

Greg closed the journal. Did he really want to read this stuff? Although the journal did not appear to be dated or signed, it had to be written by his great grandfather, Doctor Crazy Fuck himself. In a way, the journal was far worse than the books that filled the bookcases. The books contained neat, typed pages—formal, orderly. The journal, however, was personal, more obscene, covered in his great grandfather's looping handwriting. The journal suddenly felt greasy, slimy in Greg's hands.

While discretion may be the better part of valor, inebriation is often the catalyst that kicks discretion to the curb. As a result, Greg flipped open the journal to a random page and began to read.

The entities are difficult to study to any degree, as they seem to appear, vanish, and reappear at will. In some instances they will not be seen for weeks or months. Then suddenly they will become prevalent multiple times in the same day.

Classification had proven to be another obstacle to scientific understanding. Categories cannot be based on appearance, as in many cases the most benign appearance masks the most malevolent of natures. It is these more violent, malignant entities that seem to harbor the greatest power and are most promising to discovery. I am most drawn to such entities, and in turn, they seem to be drawn to me as well. Further study is needed to confirm the validity of this statement, however.

Greg flipped forward to another page.

Bait has not proven to increase the likelihood of a sighting. On multiple occasions, various mammals, both live and dead, ranging from rats to live-

stock in the form of swine and bovine, left in areas of high entity concentration have yielded inconclusive findings. In some instances, the live animals are taken; in others they are mutilated, sometimes found alive but missing various appendages.

It is worth noting that in all instances, the animals that were presented already dead remained untouched. The entities appear to have no interest in the dead, but a keen fascination with the living. Perhaps this can be tested further by carrying the experiment to its logical conclusion.

Greg again flipped forward a few pages.

The same results have been found with human test subjects as with previous animal test subjects.

Greg stopped and reread the sentence, a sense of foreboding creeping into his body.

The same results have been found with human test subjects as with previous animal test subjects. When presented with four separate cadavers over the course of days at varying times and in various locations, the entities ignored the cadavers without fail. Live test subjects will be more difficult to obtain.

Hands shaking, Greg flipped forward through the pages, scanning each briefly. It did not take long to find the entry that continued this insane experiment.

I believe I've had a breakthrough. The four live human test subjects have yielded superb results. Not only did the entities react, but in all cases, upon investigation, the entities were actually found still inhabiting the areas where the live human test subjects had been placed. The live test subjects were no longer present, but this fact is of little consequence in the present study. A separate study will be conducted regarding this matter. What is important is that data indicates that the entities can be controlled to a certain degree by the presence of live human bodies.

What is most compelling about the results is that the entities seemed to react to my presence. They seemed to know and understand that I was the one who brought them the test subjects. The entities are intelligent and aware of their environment!

Greg turned the page to the next entry.

I HAVE SUCCEEDED!

In my excitement I must not fail to record the events that led to my success. While recording results from four new live human test subjects, the fourth was found in a direct interaction with an entity! The entity in question is one that has become prevalent in my studies, and is always present during experimentation. The entity appears as a half-man, in the literal sense of the word. The entity consists of a muscular male human torso, darkly colored, with no lower body. The head of the entity is insectlike in appearance, but with a long, thin beak that is avian in nature.

"Oh, fuck," Greg said, rubbing his hand over his forehead and down the side of his face. The thought of the thing that had tapped on the window outside his bedroom actually touching a human being made Greg's skin crawl. Regardless of how horrible the outcome, Greg had to know what happened.

It is that very beaked appendage that was inserted deeply into the back of the female test subject's skull, at a downward angle into the spine. The entity had clamped its arms around the test subject, preventing escape. I can only assume that the entity was somehow feeding off of the test subject.

Although close to death, the test subject did not appear to be in pain, and in fact, appeared peaceful and lethargic. I would have liked to have seen and recorded the initial penetration.

The entity, which has previously shown extreme violent tendencies, allowed me to approach during the feeding, if only for a short while before dragging the test subject deeper into the woods and disappearing from sight.

While this is of course an amazing development, it pales in comparison to the true breakthrough that later occurred. Even as I write this, my hand shakes with excitement.

Later in the evening, while recording my findings, I heard a tap on the window outside my bedroom. Thinking nothing of it, I ignored the sound, only to have it return with a newfound persistence. Thinking it a bird, I angrily went to the window to scare it away. And upon pulling back the curtains, discovered THE ENTITY outside my bedroom window, bidding entry.

As I write this, the entity is present in the room, in the corner, watching me intently. I have succeeded! Despite its propensity toward violence, I am confident that I can control the entity and will come to no harm, for I have become the entity's provider, its caregiver, feeder of its appetite.

This is, of course, only the beginning. But I ask myself, what must God have felt like when he used Jesus as a tool of his will?

Greg threw the journal across the room in disgust. It bounced off the far wall and fell to the floor in a flutter of pages, landing open to no doubt some description of sadistic insanity poorly disguised as scientific research.

Greg's great grandfather had obviously been a sociopath, lacking any measure of compassion or conscience. How did someone like that manage to go through life undetected and become, of all things, a doctor?

Greg's pleasant bout of blissful drunken indifference had come to a complete and sudden halt. He stood and began pacing. When he encountered the thrown journal, he kicked it out of his way hard enough to send it sailing into the air, where it once again bounced off the wall and fell to the floor, this time, thankfully, closed.

This was the legacy of his family? *This* is what he had been "chosen" to continue? Well, that was not happening. There was no way in hell that was happening.

CHAPTER THIRTY-NINE

Apparently, the alcohol had affected Greg more than he had been aware of, because although he did not remember falling asleep, he obviously had, as he was currently being dragged up from that deep sleep. Greg resisted the intrusion, fighting to drag himself back down into comforting nothingness. Something, however, was having no part of it. Greg was once again nudged in the back between his shoulder blades, pulling him further up from the depths of sleep.

Greg swatted at the thing behind him, but made contact with nothing. It nudged him again, this time hard enough to rock him back and forth, causing the box springs of the bed to squeak in protest. Now for the most part awake, Greg realized that something *was* nudging him, which meant something was in the room with him. The last foggy grasp of sleep lost its grip on Greg as he sprang up from bed, vaulting around to face whatever had managed to creep up behind him as he slept. He landed upright, sitting with his back against the wall, legs out in front of him. Instinctually, Greg pulled his legs back to prevent something from grabbing them and pulling him off the bed.

For a moment, Greg did not fully register what he saw. Then Spooky, sitting on his haunches at the side of the bed, thumped his tail against the wooden floor in greeting. The familiar sound broke Greg's trance. He pushed himself off the bed, stood beside Spooky, and looked down at the giant dog that looked back up at him. Greg reached down (although he did not have to reach far) and scratched Spooky behind his brown ears. Spooky again thumped the floor with his tail in approval.

"How the hell did you get in here?" Greg asked. Greg walked into the hallway and toward the door that led downstairs. Spooky followed close behind. Greg felt a surge of excitement as he put his hand on the doorknob. The excitement quickly faded, however, when the doorknob did not turn, reaffirming that Greg was still locked in. Only now, he was locked in with a dog that had somehow managed to … what, walk through the wall? It was one thing for Spooky to be able to open doors. Strange, yes, but Greg could accept that. But Spooky could not walk through walls, could he?

Greg turned around toward the dog. Spooky had something in his mouth not much bigger than your average playing card. Greg did not remember Spooky having anything in his mouth while in the bedroom a few moments ago. Spooky dropped whatever he was holding on the top of Greg's shoes, took a step back, sat back, and looked up at Greg expectantly, turning his head to one side as if to say, *Go on, pick it up.*

Even as Greg reached to retrieve it from the top of his shoes, he realized that it was a photo, the square kind taken with an instant camera that rattles and hums and spits out a picture a few moments later that you then stare at, mesmerized, as the surface slowly transforms from a black nothing into an image. This particular photo, however, had developed long ago and was in fact faded and a little rough around the edges. The photo was, nonetheless, perfectly recognizable.

Greg held it up in front of his face, his hand shaking a little. The photo was of a young, beautiful woman standing in a field of tall grass, the warm afternoon sun shining behind her, making her look like a glowing brown-haired angel. In her arms was a young baby, little more than a newborn. And at her side, was Spooky.

Greg recognized the image of his mother. She was smiling, radiant, young, and fresh. Greg had never seen her look so happy. Obviously, he was the baby she held in her arms. And despite the photo having to be over thirty years old, there, impossibly, sat Spooky beside her, staring intently with his knowing eyes into the camera. Greg was not sure how he knew, but he knew nonetheless. As if to confirm his own thought, Greg read the short note that had been written in his mother's small, neat handwriting across the inch-wide white strip at the bottom of the photo: *You can trust the dog. Spooky is there to help you.*

A month ago, hell, maybe even a week ago, Greg would have asked, *Why? How?* He would have fought to make some logical sense of it all. But Greg was not the same person he had been a week ago. How could he be?

Greg lowered the photo a bit and looked over the top of it at Spooky, who looked back up at him. "So, I guess you knew my mother. And you and I are old friends," Greg said.

Spooky thumped his tail against the floor. It was all the answer Greg needed.

Greg put the photo in his back jeans pocket and looked at Spooky. "Okay, so now what?"

CHAPTER FORTY

Greg stood beside the desk in what he had come to call his "sentry room" and watched Spooky nose around the corner of the bookcase closest to the window. The rising sun revealed that Greg had indeed fallen asleep and slept through most of the night. The *whoof-whoof-whoof* of Spooky's substantial nose doing its work sounded like the spinning blades of a helicopter. Each time Spooky exhaled, a buff of dust from the dirty floor exploded around his face. Greg was surprised that Spooky did not sneeze.

Apparently, Spooky found what he was looking for. Tail wagging, he began to paw at the corner of the bookcase, as if he had found a bone hidden in the wood and was determined to dig it out with one giant paw. A moment later, Greg heard a loud *click* and the entire bookcase spun sideways on some kind of central axis, revealing a dark passageway, the side of the bookcase separating the two halves down the middle.

Amazed, Greg walked to the newly revealed passage and peered inside. Although filled with shadows, dust, and spiderwebs, Greg could make out the narrow hallway made up of bone white plaster and lathe that went off into parts unknown. It was an actual secret passageway.

Greg looked down at Spooky. "You've got to be shitting me."

Spooky's ears perked up and he turned his head sideways as if to say, *Who, me?* Then he headed into the passageway, went about ten feet, stopping at the corner where the passage turned right, and looked back at Greg. He wagged his tail beseechingly, striking each side of the wall like a rhythmic clock pendulum, his bulk barely clearing the narrow confines.

"Okay, I'm coming," Greg said, and stepped into the passageway. He followed Spooky around the corner and down a narrow flight of stairs. "Just for the record, I think it was Colonel Mustard, in the Library, with the Lead Pipe."

Spooky, apparently unimpressed with Greg's attempt at humor, ignored him and continued on his way.

They soon came to an area that could not really be called a room, but was bigger than the hallway. Once again, Spooky began nosing around the floor. Greg was not quite as surprised this time when he heard another *click* and light flooded the little closetlike area as another bookcase turned sideways. He followed Spooky into what was obviously the only room in the house he had not previously visited: the den.

The den was nice, in a manly kind of way. The walls were made of floor-to-ceiling walnut bookcases, almost all of them completely filled with books. It was quite a collection. Greg guessed there had to be thousands of volumes. The thickly carpeted floor was a deep purple-red, like the color of a ripe plum. Two black leather sofas sat on either side of a large walnut coffee table that was flanked on both ends by black leather recliners. The room was brightly lit by an iron chandelier that hung from the ceiling above the coffee table. The room smelled like lemon-scented furniture polish mixed with the mysterious, spicy aroma of ink and paper. Greg liked the room. It felt safe, secure somehow, like a stoic bank vault.

Greg watched Spooky begin to push the sideways bookcase back around into place with his head. Greg lent a hand. Despite its obvious weight, the bookcase slid back around with surprising ease, turning into place with a *click*.

It took a moment for Greg to realize that, yes, he had indeed been sprung from his prison. When realization hit, he bent forward toward Spooky, pointed his index fingers toward the dog, and said, "You rock." He rubbed the top of Spooky's head. "Okay, buddy, now we need to get Ron the hell out of the basement."

Spooky did not need any further encouragement, and was out of the den and into the kitchen before Greg could think about being sneaky. Luckily, Katelin was not in either the formal living room or the kitchen, and they made it to the basement door unchallenged. The door, however, presented its own challenge: it was locked.

Greg looked around the kitchen but did not see anything obvious. It seemed that Spooky was ahead of him. He stood up on his hind legs, put his front paws on the counter by the sink and opened a slim drawer with his teeth. Greg watched this for a moment before walking over to join the dog formerly known as Dogzilla, and now known as Superdog, although Spooky was apparently too modest to wear tights and a cape.

Spooky lowered himself back to the floor and allowed Greg room to rummage through the drawer. Like junk drawers everywhere, it was filled with a chaotic mix of stuff. Underneath an old phone book, its cover the victim of countless ink-drawn doodles, Greg found some loose change, a few paperclips and push-pins, some recipes scribbled on yellow Post-it notes, a single glass marble, and an authentic black Wham-O SuperBall just like the ones Greg loved to play with as a kid. You could bounce those things a mile high, which inevitably led to you eventually losing the ball in the grass, or the trees, forcing you to go buy another one. Greg thought that was a pretty good marketing strategy.

Greg, however, did not have time to dwell on the youthful days of SuperBall adventures; Ron was still locked in the basement. Following the discovery of an old pair of blue plastic-handled scissors and another marble, Greg found the large, old-fashioned brass key that had to unlock the basement door.

Sure enough, when Greg put the key in the keyhole and turned it, it slid all the way around without protest. Greg pulled the key out, put it in his front jeans pocket, and tried the doorknob. It turned easily, and Greg shoved the door open a little too hard, wincing when it bounced off the right stairwell wall with a vibrating *thud*.

Steep wooden stairs descended to the left along a rough stone foundation wall. The stones of the wall were immense and made the wall look like a massive rock puzzle pieced together by giant children.

Greg did not need to find a light switch; there was enough light from the early morning sun to illuminate the stairs most of the way down. A light source shining up from down below finished what the morning sun started, revealing the remaining stairs and the dirt floor below.

Greg hesitated to step into the basement. Regardless of whether or not Ron was down there, Greg had had enough of dark corners and shadowy places behind lockable doors. Dark places were, after all, where monsters liked to hide—just ask any eight-year-old. Hell, just ask Greg *himself*; he had recently seen his fair share of monsters. Beside him, Spooky whined softly. "I know," Greg whispered, glancing at Spooky.

Greg sighed. Well, he could stand here all day thinking about what to do, but that would not actually get anything done. "Ron, you down there?" Greg asked in a half whisper, half strangled yell. He listened, but heard nothing. "Ron?" he said louder.

As Greg began to resign himself to the fact that he would have to go down into the basement and look for Ron, a long shadow appeared on the wall at the bottom of the stairs and grew smaller until Ron came into view. He stood there, squinting up at Greg and Spooky, the side of his hand on his forehead, shielding his eyes like the brim of a baseball cap. The *actual* red brim of his NASCAR cap sat sideways on his head, comically making him look like the worlds' oldest wannabe hip-hop music star. He must have fallen asleep with it on. Despite the situation, the sight of Ron made Greg smile. A moment later he suppressed a laugh and asked, "What are you doing down there?"

Ron smirked, shook his head, and began walking up the stairs. "Yeah, you keep laughin' there, funny boy. But you should take a look in the mirror. You look about as pretty as a hat full of assholes," he said, and started laughing as well.

The laughter was cut short, however, when Greg heard from behind him, "Jesus, Mary, and Joseph, what have you done? Just what have you done?"

Well, Katelin was awake.

CHAPTER FORTY-ONE

All three conspirators turned to look at Katelin, who stood in a plush purple bathrobe, her arms crossed over her chest, her mouth set in a grim line. "What do you think you're doing? And how did you get out?" she demanded.

For a moment, Greg was apprehensive. Despite the fact that he had done nothing wrong, had in fact been the victim in this scenario, he nonetheless felt a momentary twinge of guilt, as if he were once again a child and had been caught doing something he had been specifically told not to do. Katelin had a strange ability to exude authority and privilege, even in situations like the present, where she should have neither.

Katelin's demanding question snapped Greg out of his apprehension. *And how did you get out?* As if he were some kind of farm animal that had escaped the barn. Greg scowled at his aunt. "It's none of your business how I got out," Greg retorted.

Katelin continued to stare at Greg in an apparent attempt to stare him down. When he refused to look away, she glanced first to Ron on his right, then to Spooky on his left, before bringing her attention back to Greg. "Why do you have to talk to me like that?"

His aunt never ceased to amaze him with her level of self-absorbed arrogance. "You locked me in the attic! And you locked your own husband in the basement! Why do I have to talk to you this way? This isn't about *you*! Everything in the world does not revolve around *you*! Jesus, what the hell is wrong with you? What—"

Before Greg was fully aware it had happened, his aunt had crossed the short distance between them and slapped Greg across the face hard enough to whip his head to one side. He brought his hand up to cover the left side of his face, which alternated between sensations of cold tingles and hot waves of pain. Involuntary tears blurred Greg's vision. He moved his hand away from his cheek and used it to wipe the tears from his eyes.

Spooky took a step toward Katelin and growled menacingly. "No," Greg said, and reached down. It took but a touch to halt the dog, but Greg could feel the powerful muscles of Spooky's back, as taut as the braided steel wire used to support a suspension bridge.

Katelin looked down at Spooky, her arms once again crossed over her chest. "Traitor."

"What you did ain't right. That's all there is to it," Ron said calmly.

Katelin rolled her eyes. "Shut up. You're not good for nothing except eating, drinking, pissing, and shitting. You couldn't even get me pregnant. Hell, you probably can't even get it up anymore. Do you even jerk off? Or is it like trying to get a wet noodle to cum?"

Greg was surprised at how calm Ron remained.

Ron shrugged and adjusted his NASCAR cap so that it sat properly on his head. "I've never been much of a religious man, but I think God knows better than to allow *you* to bring children into this world."

Couples who have been married a long time learn to navigate the turning roads of each others' hearts until they become so familiar with one another that they no longer need a map to find their way around. This is a precious and dangerous gift. One word can bring tears of joy, or of sorrow. And even if a marriage turns from a warm summer day into a bitter winter blizzard, two hearts who once shared love never forget how to find one another; never forget how to talk to one another, whether for good or for bad.

"I can't believe you said that," Katelin said. "You're a terrible man. Just terrible!"

"Maybe I am," Ron agreed. "But you went too far this time, Katelin. You went way too far."

It seemed that Greg had been forgotten. He remained silent, his gaze alternating between Katelin and Ron, like a child listening to arguing parents.

"I'm doing what's best for *him*!" Katelin yelled, jabbing a finger in Greg's direction.

So much for being forgotten, Greg thought.

"I'm doing what's best for this family! I've *always* done what's best for this family! And you never appreciated it! You never appreciated *me*, you son of a bitch!"

"It's hard to appreciate a woman who fucks half the town in the same bed she used to share with her husband," Ron said sardonically.

"It's for the family!" Katelin screamed. *"My sacrifices are for this family!"*

Ron nodded. "Whatever you gotta tell yourself to make it easier for you to sleep at night."

"You're a bastard," Katelin said through clenched teeth. "A worthless drunken bastard." Katelin stormed out of the kitchen.

Greg felt like he had just witnessed a tornado touch down, devastate everything in its path for sixty seconds, and then vanish to leave him standing in the aftermath, looking around at the devastation and wondering exactly how he had managed to survive.

Ron went to the refrigerator. "I need a beer."

PART THREE

TWILIGHT HALLWAYS

CHAPTER FORTY-TWO

When Spooky had insisted that Greg follow him outside by nudging Greg's thigh with his basketball-sized head, Greg had not put up much in the way of resistance. After the morning scene of insanity in the kitchen, Greg had been eager to have an excuse to get out of the house.

Now Greg followed Spooky deeper into the woods, more or less along the winding path that remained as free of debris as a well-tended cemetery lawn. Greg felt nervous about going into the woods, for obvious reasons, and a bit concerned about where Spooky was leading him. But the morning daylight scared away the shadows, and Greg trusted Spooky. It was not just the picture and message from his mother, but also something that Greg felt, a kind of instinct. It was like when you met a person for the first time. You usually had one of three reactions. Indifference was the most common—a feeling of, well, *no* feeling at all. The second was a negative vibe and, more often than not, you could never quite put your finger on exactly why you felt that way—you just did, because for some reason or another, the person rubbed you the wrong way. And lastly, and most rare, was a feeling of immediate connection; sometimes you just liked someone, plain and simple. And although it had not been immediate, Greg liked Spooky. Besides, if Greg could not trust a two-hundred-plus pound dog that liked to watch children's TV shows, whom could he trust?

As they made their way past the family cemetery, Greg glanced over in the general direction of his mother's grave. The surrounding iron cemetery fence obscured much of the area within, and the forest trees and plants further hid his mother's gravestone from Greg's view. He was not sure if he caught a glimpse of it or not, but regardless, Greg felt a twinge of emotion grip his heart. Was it regret? Remorse? Sadness? Perhaps it was a mixture of all three.

Despite the fact that it hurt, Greg decided that it was good to feel something other than a dull, hollow ache of confused anger when he thought about his mother. Not for the first time Greg wondered about how things might have turned out differently had he known about the clusterfuck of a family he and his mother had spent Greg's childhood running from.

Spooky seemed to sense Greg's thoughts, because he stopped and looked back at Greg. He wagged his tail once in a quick back-and-forth swish. Greg could almost hear Spooky in his head saying, *You can take a few minutes if you want.*

Greg waved Spooky on. "I'm right behind you."

It did not take long for Greg to realize where Spooky was leading him. His thoughts were confirmed when they came out of the tree line. In the middle of about an acre clearing stood the stone foundation of the Cooper farmhouse and the skeletal remains of the barn. This was the place Ron had warned him about, the place Ron had told him *not* to visit.

Where Greg and Spooky now stood at the outer edge of the clearing, the ground was covered with wild grass and weeds. But the closer you got to the barn, the less foliage there was, until it stopped altogether in a twenty-foot radius around the barn to reveal nothing but bare earth as perfectly flat and black as a schoolroom slate chalkboard.

Anyone with half a brain could tell that there was something inherently wrong with this place. It was as silent as death—nothing moved, nothing made a sound. A smell like burnt-out electrical wire and melted plastic permeated the area in a thick acrid stench. If hell had air fresheners you could plug into the wall, Greg guessed this place was what they smelled like. The very air seemed filled with hostility. Even at this distance, Greg could feel it pulsing out from the barn like a disease-filled heartbeat. The barn itself felt too real: too sharp, too vivid, too *there*, as if demanding that it be seen. Numerous wooden slats were missing from the barn walls, giving it the look of a giant rib cage. Although Greg was about a hundred feet away, he could easily make out the multiple layers of paint that covered the remaining riblike wooden slats. Currently, the barn was painted light blue or gray, the faded paint making it hard to tell which. The worn and chipped surface revealed that the barn had once been green, and before that, red. The twin barn doors hung open on loose hinges, revealing an entrance like a gaping, hungry maw, the inside of the barn beyond filled with an inky darkness that belied the incomplete walls and bright afternoon sunshine. No light penetrated the blackness within, as if even sunlight shunned the place. The roof sagged like a tired, broken backbone. The whole image reminded Greg of some ancient prehistoric beast that had lumbered into the field to die—an ancient prehistoric beast with sharp teeth and a hunger for flesh and blood.

Greg glanced over to his left at Spooky. "I'm not going in there."

Spooky did not take his liquid amber gaze from the barn, but growled deep in his throat by way of agreement. A short time later, Spooky began to circle to his left along the outside perimeter of the area. Greg followed, keeping as much distance between them and the barn as possible.

Soon they had circled halfway around the clearing to end up at the foundation of what had once been the Cooper farmhouse. The foundation was made up of solid rectangular blocks of what looked like sandstone to Greg. They stood half buried in the dark earth. When Greg reached down and touched one, a thin layer of the outer surface crumbled away, revealing solid stone beneath. A few hardy weeds dared to spring up around some of the stones, which made Greg feel a little better knowing that they were far enough away from the barn for something to grow.

Spooky seemed interested in one stone in particular, sniffing around its base. He pawed at it, leaving four distinct rake marks down its side from his thick nails. When he seemed convinced he had the right stone, he put his massive head against its side and began to push it up and over like a fur-covered bulldozer. Greg hurried to help, and they soon turned the heavy stone onto its side to reveal bare earth beneath in a six-inch deep crevice in the rectangular shape of the stone that had rested in it. Since there was no stone underneath the one they had moved, Greg guessed that they were standing on what must have been the foundation for some kind of porch. If it had been the foundation for the house Greg was fairly sure the stones would have continued downward below the frost line to ensure that the foundation did not heave up during cold Iowa winters.

Spooky wasted no time and set to work digging into the revealed earth, his front paws and legs working like explosive pistons, flinging dark earth behind him in large clumps.

Greg, acknowledging the superior digging capabilities of the canine species, took a step back and watched, letting Spooky have at it. Greg did not have to watch for long. Within half a minute, Spooky stopped digging, stuck his nose down into the foot-deep hole he had created, sniffed around, and wagged his tail. Greg took that as a good sign. A moment later, Spooky brought his head out of the hole. In his mouth was some kind of cylinder, which he dropped at Greg's feet. He sat back on his haunches and thumped his tail against the ground in satisfaction.

Greg bent down on one knee as if proposing to the cylinder and picked it up, brushing off bits of clinging earth. It was the size and shape of a cardboard center of an empty paper towel roll, made of hard black plastic, like PVC pipe, and capped at each end with some kind of twist-on knob. Greg tried to turn both knobs, clenching his jaw in effort, but neither end would budge. It was like trying to open the world's most stubborn jar of pickles. Greg held the cylinder up to his ear and shook it like a child trying to guess the contents of a wrapped present on Christmas morning. He was rewarded with an ambiguous soft rustling sound that could have been almost anything.

Spooky's booming, cannonlike bark was so unexpected in the dead silence that Greg let out an involuntary yelp of surprise and almost dropped the cylinder. With his heart somewhere in his throat, beating hard and fast enough to choke him, Greg scowled at Spooky for a moment. His scowl vanished when he saw that Spooky was no longer sitting happily on the ground, but was instead standing, his entire body quivering with tense muscles, his gaze locked on something behind Greg.

Greg realized with a sick kind of certainty that if the past was any indication, Spooky only barked for one reason: entity.

CHAPTER FORTY-THREE

Three things happened in quick succession: Spooky burst forward as if shot from a cannon, Greg began to twist around to face the barn and follow Spooky's path, and something hit Greg from behind between his shoulder blades with the force of a sledgehammer. The impact literally knocked Greg off his feet and sent him flying forward to land sprawling face-first into the ground.

Greg rolled over and staggered to his knees. Gagging, he spit a mouthful of dirt onto the ground. He wiped more dirt away from his eyes and around his mouth. His fingers came away from the bottom of his nose smeared with warm blood. *I wonder how you tell if it's broke,* Greg thought blearily, his ears ringing like a tuning fork.

Greg forgot all about his bleeding nose and ringing ears when he came face-to-face with the horror that had knocked him to the ground. The thing less than ten feet away from Greg was like a nightmare made real. Its entire body was the color of an oil slick: deceptively black, but shimmering with color when sunlight struck it at certain angles. Its body swam with pools of dark green, blood red, and metallic blue that bloomed into deep violet. Its body was thin but seemed immensely strong, insectlike, with overly long arms that ended in wickedly pointed fingers on foot-long hands. The thing's head, though, was its true claim to monstrosity. It looked like a cross between an oversized human skull and a giant Halloween jack-o'-lantern. The head was perfectly round, with the sunken eye cavities and nasal passage of a human. But like the rest of its body, its face was the same inky black oil color and seemed to lack eyes, instead possessing only empty sockets filled with blackness. Its mouth was stretched into an obscene grin that was easily a foot wide. The inside of that mouth was filled with thousands of black, needlelike teeth that traveled back into its throat in rows, like the mouth of a shark. Greg knew without a doubt that the thing's mouth could easily swallow his head whole and with one quick clamp, slice his head off at the neck.

Greg guessed the thing had to be at least eight feet tall—it was hard to tell, however, because at the moment, Spooky had its right arm clamped in his jaws and was fiercely yanking on it. While the entity had stubbornly planted its feet, refusing to be moved, Spooky's powerful body had forced the creature to bend forward. Each time the entity attempted to right itself, Spooky would squat lower to the ground and jerk backward, yanking the creature forward. It seemed that they were at a stalemate; neither would be moved.

Although the entity appeared to lack eyes, it also appeared able to see in some sense of the word. It stared down at Spooky and hissed in what seemed more like hatred than pain. If Greg lived to be a hundred, he would never forget that hiss; it was the most alien sound he had ever heard. It made his bowels instantly turn to water. It resembled nothing on earth so much as a chorus of snakes mixed with a choir of cicadas recorded with enough reverb to make it echo into eternity. That single hiss seemed to go on for minutes.

Apparently realizing that it would not break free from Spooky with sheer strength, the entity raised its free long left arm and brought its hand down toward Spooky with terrifying quickness. Spooky narrowly missed being sliced in half by the entity's sharp fingers, each as long as a butcher knife. When the entity raised its arm to take another swing, Spooky jerked back and, growling fiercely, shook his head from side to side. The entity hissed again in frustration and, pulled off balance, stumbled forward, forced to plant its free left hand on the ground to keep from falling. Whatever kind of intelligence it possessed, it seemed to understand that if Spooky managed to pull it completely off its feet, the stalemate would be over and Spooky would gain the advantage.

A moment later, the entity shot up its left hand from the ground, clamped it onto its right hand as if it were praying to some long-lost evil god, planted its feet, and pulled backward like a bodybuilder doing rows. What the entity had not been able to accomplish with one arm, it managed to accomplish with two.

Greg watched in horror as the entity yanked backward and brought its arms up over its head, Spooky still attached to the right one, and fell onto its back, at the same time using its arms to slam Spooky into the ground behind its head.

Greg had only been in one automobile accident in his life. And that had been in college. He had not been paying attention and had pulled out in front of a very nice Lexus in his beat-up old Toyota that, regardless of its old age, ran like a champ. In fact, Greg believed that if the world came to an end from nuclear annihilation, and if the only things that survived were indeed the cockroaches, they would not have to walk, because Toyotas would still be stubbornly running. The Lexus had not been going very fast while driving in town, not much over thirty miles an hour, but when it had made contact with the front corner panel of Greg's Toyota, it had produced a sound like an explosion that did not seem possible for two cars to make.

The sound that Spooky made when he impacted the ground was similar to Greg's one and only automobile accident. Greg was sure he heard the sharp crack of snapping bones. Spooky let out a howl of pain, releasing the entity's arm, and lay motionless on the ground. "No!" Greg yelled, and before he fully realized he intended to do so, he threw the only thing he had, the hard plastic cylinder, at the entity, which had risen to its feet with its back to Greg, still preoccupied with its canine adversary.

The cylinder spun end over end through the air and struck the entity in the back of the head, comically bouncing off with a hollow *pongggg!* The entity actually appeared to jump in surprise. Then it crunched up its substantial shoulders as if it were taking a deep breath and turned to face Greg. It bent forward, like a sprinter at a starting line, or a predator getting ready to pounce on its prey. Greg thought the second simile more apt and knew with a calm certainty that he was going to die.

Spooky, however, seemed to have other ideas. Although only moments earlier Greg had been certain Spooky was dead, he rolled over and stood, seemingly no worse for wear by being crushed into the ground. Spooky charged forward and rammed into the entity from behind like a linebacker. This time it was the entity's turn to go sprawling face-first into the ground. Greg would have cheered had the entity not landed right beside him. Although only one of its pointed fingers barely brushed the bottom of his jeans, it sliced through the material like a razor, blessedly missing Greg's flesh beneath, to leave a neat six-inch line that folded open to reveal Greg's left shin. Greg rolled to his right, scrambled to his feet, and took a few steps back, putting some distance between himself and the entity.

Spooky did not give the entity time to react. By the time Greg had managed to stand, Spooky was beside the entity's left shoulder, his jaws clamped down on the back of its neck, forcing its face full of teeth to remain planted into the ground. The entity put both of its palms against the ground and tried to push itself up, dog and all, like a soldier doing push-ups in basic training. Spooky, however, proved to be too strong and weigh too much for the entity to force itself upright from its compromised position.

Unable to right itself, the entity grabbed hold of Spooky in both hands and tried to pull him off. Greg was sure that the contact of the entity's daggerlike claws would slice viciously into Spooky, but it appeared not to be the case—Spooky seemed no worse for wear by being grabbed by the entity. Although unable to force Spooky to let go, the entity managed to twist itself sideways. Still grasping Spooky behind its back, the entity squirmed to its feet. It seemed that Spooky had taken most of the fight out of the creature, for it weaved and wobbled its way back toward the barn like a drunk walking home after a long night at the bar.

Greg assumed that Spooky was going to let go of the thing's neck, but, no pun intended, Spooky doggedly held on, even when the entity released its grip to leave Spooky hanging from the back of its neck like a side of beef.

"Let go!" Greg called out. But Spooky had decided that he was not letting go. Greg watched with a sinking feeling as the entity continued to stumble closer to the barn. "Come on, buddy, let go," Greg mumbled. "Don't go in there." But a few seconds later, Spooky did go in there. Still attached to the entity, the two disappeared into the barn.

Greg lowered his head and grabbed his hair with both hands, as if he were going to make himself go bald with one great yank. He stomped his foot. "Shit! Shit! Shit!" He began to pace until he came across the plastic cylinder, bent down, and picked it up. Greg looked at the barn. He wanted to go in there about as much as he wanted to get hit by a bus. Greg's brain told him to turn around and leave, tried to rationalize that Spooky could take care of himself and would be okay. His heart, however, remained unconvinced. He could not leave Spooky in there, alone. Could he?

Greg turned away from the barn, took a step, stopped, and sighed. "Ah, fuck me," he said, turned back around, and ran toward the barn.

CHAPTER FORTY-FOUR

Greg knew something was wrong with the barn entrance a split second before he ran through it—or, more accurately, *into* it. And then Greg was plunging into something as black as coal with the consistency of ice-cold Jell-O.

Greg involuntarily opened his mouth to gasp from the cold, and all the air in his lungs was sucked out, leaving him instantly suffocating. Worse yet, the stuff that encased him seemed alive and vile. It squirmed over his body like a million tiny worms trying to burrow underneath his skin. It was the most horrible, violating thing Greg had ever felt. Unable to see, Greg stumbled blindly forward with his arms out like a mummy, his lungs screaming for air, his skin literally crawling.

Had he somehow turned himself around? Was he wandering in circles, slowly dying from lack of oxygen? *I don't want to die in here,* Greg thought miserably. How deep could the entrance of a barn be? But Greg knew that it was not really a barn he had entered. The barn just happened to be on the same spot, but the normal laws of physics did not apply to what his uncle had called an interstate crossroads truck stop for monsters.

When Greg had convinced himself that he was hopelessly lost and was going to die, the tips of his fingers broke free into air. Greg plunged forward, falling out of the gelatinous goo onto his knees, gagging. When Greg had finished gasping for breath and dry heaving, he looked at the palms of his hands, ran them over his face. None of the goo seemed to have clung to him; it had all remained behind. Greg looked behind him, and sure enough, there was the wall, its surface pristine, as if he had not so rudely just finished ripping through it.

With his mind no longer preoccupied with thoughts of death by suffocation, Greg realized that he was *on the other side.* Greg did not know why he labeled it that, but it felt right. Greg knew he was not in heaven or hell, or anything even close, but he knew he was somewhere *else*, somewhere *between* the reality he called home and some other place. Greg did not need to know the details of that other place to know that whatever else it may be, it was not a good place.

Greg stood and looked around. The ground was covered in a fine gray powder, like ash. All around and above, the place was a featureless gray nothing that eventually blended into blackness far off in the distance. It was like being inside a giant gray box. The only feature that Greg could see was a light haze that rose from the ground like morning mist on the surface of a lake. While the mist did not completely obscure Greg's vision, it was thick enough to make it difficult to see if there really was anything out there. Although there did not appear to be any light source, a perpetual gloom illuminated Greg's surroundings, giving it the feel of that fragile twilight moment between the time that the day ends and the night begins. As Greg's eyes became more accustomed to the gloom, he began to make out vague shapes in the distance, some stationary, others appearing to move in and out of the mist. Having seen at least one thing up close and personal that existed in here, Greg hoped that whatever those shapes out at the edge of his vision were, they were not alive—and if they were alive, he hoped they did not want to make him *no longer* alive.

Greg suddenly realized he no longer had his cylinder. Although he still had no idea what it contained, Greg was learning to trust his instincts, and something told him that that cylinder was important. His heartbeat racing, Greg looked around. What if he had lost it? What if it was somewhere back there in the worm-filled black gelatin?

Greg found the cylinder casually laying on the ground next to his right foot. He must have let go of it when he had come through the wall and dropped to his knees. Greg bent down and picked it up, instantly feeling better when it was back in his hand. It might just be a few pieces of plastic, but it was something from where he came from, something made by *people*, not some oil-covered monstrosity or half a man with an insect head and a beaked face.

Greg sighed and told himself he was going to have to learn to calm down. He could not freak out every time something weird happened. A moment later, Greg almost laughed. He thought about all the shit he had been through, looked around at this twilight place that was probably going to get him killed, and smirked. Under the circumstances, Greg thought he was doing a pretty good job of not freaking out.

Resigned to his fate, and not knowing what else to do, Greg began to walk.

CHAPTER FORTY-FIVE

Walking always calmed Greg. The simple act of putting one foot in front of the other cleared out the clutter in his head. And even though he currently walked through dangerously unknown territory, Greg nonetheless felt his frantic thoughts calm, his focus sharpen, his concentration increase. He programmed computers for a living, although that seemed like such a long time ago—it felt to Greg like another life. But regardless, programming was logic: yes or no, true or false, on or off. Reduce the problem down to its simplest form, like binary machine code, all zeros and ones. When Greg thought of the problem as a computer program, it was simple. The central process, or module, was to find Spooky—that was the main program. Now, how did he make that happen? Break it down further: what subprograms did he need to create and call in his main processing? Break it down even further: what module did he need to create *first?*

Greg's thoughts were interrupted by the sound of a woman's musical laughter up ahead and off to his right. Although the laughter sounded sweet, almost angelic, Greg knew better than to trust the assumption that anything in here could be judged so simply. The wise adage of not judging a book by its cover worked as well for monsters as it did for people, and books for that matter.

Greg stopped walking and stared in the general direction from which the sound had come. As if watching a television screen slowly homing in on a weak station signal, a scene wavered into view about twenty feet ahead and off to the right of where Greg stood.

At first Greg was not sure what he was seeing, but then it became clearer. It was like watching a car wreck: Greg did not want to stare, but some morbid fascination made it impossible for him to look away. A naked blonde-haired woman was bent over on all fours. She would have been beautiful save for the fact that she was covered in shimmering silver scales like a fish and that her eyes were not eyes, but pools of blood that continually filled her eye sockets and ran down her face like tears.

Something that looked like a giant centipede was wrapped around her body. The thing had to be at least ten feet long. Its wide, flat head rested on her left shoulder; its wicked-looking mandibles opened and closed, slicing through the air. From the lower part of the centipede thing, a foot-long bony obtrusion as thick as a beer bottle stuck out of its exoskeleton. It was using this to sodomize the woman. It would pull out completely, then violently thrust forward, its whole body quivering each time it buried itself into her. And each time it did this, a gush of blood would spurt out of the woman's mouth, she would gag, and then she would laugh in her musical sing-song voice.

What he was watching was bad enough, but Greg thought he was going to be physically sick when he saw a half dozen two-inch-long centipede creatures squirm out of the pool of blood that had been created in front of the woman by the continuing spurts from her mouth. They wriggled free like maggots, glistening with blood, and scurried off in all directions to disappear into the surrounding gloom.

Although Greg stared at the creatures, they did not seem to notice him. Or if they did, they did not acknowledge his presence. Greg took that as a sign to leave while he still could. There was no way he was going to continue forward and pass within a few feet of the creatures. Greg changed his course and headed right, keeping a weary eye on the entities until they were out of sight. The image of those small maggotlike things wriggling free and scurrying off into the darkness made Greg study the ground around him. Greg thought he might freak out for good if one of those things managed to get under the cuff of his pants and crawl up his leg. The thought alone was enough to make Greg stop for a moment, lift each leg one at a time, and shake it vigorously. Afterwards he patted down his jeans to make sure nothing was hiding anywhere. Even with that done, Greg could not shake his bad case of the heebie-jeebies.

After Greg walked in a more or less straight line for about half an hour, it became apparent that while this place may fit inside a barn in his world, here it was much bigger, and for the most part, empty. The woman/centipede creature was the only thing Greg had seen, and he hoped he did not see another one of those, or them, depending on how you wanted to look at it. But not knowing how big this place actually was, Greg had no way to judge how full or empty it happened to be. Besides, if it was—and Greg thought his uncle had been correct—some kind of waypoint, it could fill up and empty again in intervals. Greg hoped not. He did not want to be here when this place flooded with creatures similar to what he had already encountered. Rush hour traffic was a bitch. Rush hour traffic *here* was probably deadly.

Greg had given up on attempting to compare his current situation to a computer program. While it had seemed like a good idea at the time, and had helped calm his mind, it was obvious that this place could not be logically compared to anything that Greg knew. And while he was reluctant to admit it, Greg had no way of finding Spooky. Without landmarks or a sense of familiarity, Greg had no way of finding *anything*. Greg was not even confident in his ability to find his way back out of here. The thought of being permanently trapped in here to wander around until he died of hunger, or worse yet, until something used him to relieve *its* hunger, made Greg's heart pound harder. He felt a little better when he noticed that he left tracks in the dust-covered ground. If nothing else, he could follow his own tracks back to where he had entered, hopefully.

The sight of his tracks caused Greg to consider a new possibility. In the short time he had known Spooky, the dog had repeatedly demonstrated an uncanny ability to find Greg. Greg had woken to find him in the same bed, and Spooky had followed him when Greg had decided to take a walk along the gravel road in front of the house. In fact, Spooky seemed to appear whenever Greg really needed him. It was apparent to Greg that he had been looking at this the wrong way: he was not going to find Spooky, because if anything, Spooky was going to find *him*.

Greg was considering whether or not he should stop or continue to trudge on when he came upon what looked like a plum tree. It was about twenty feet tall, filled with green leaves, ripe plums hanging from its branches. As Greg cautiously approached the tree, more came into view behind it, until by the time Greg stood in front of the first tree he had seen, a small forest was visible beyond.

Greg stood there, face-to-face with one of the lower hanging plums, tapping his entity-smiting cylinder against his right thigh. Could it really be just a plum tree? Could it really be that simple? Greg soon had his answer when the plum he was staring at opened up to reveal an eye filled with glistening black liquid. The eye blinked wetly and then seemed to study Greg intently.

Greg tensed in preparation for some kind of attack, but none came. More eyes opened, and Greg now had a small audience of about a hundred pieces of fruit staring at him.

After Greg stood there for another five minutes, staring at the tree while the tree stared at him, Greg gave up. He sighed, took a few hesitant steps forward, and sat down cross-legged under the tree, his back to the trunk. *If I'm going to get eaten by a tree, well then, fuck it, go for it, tree.*

The tree, however, seemed content to only watch him, and after a few minutes, Greg began to relax enough to once again become curious about what was in the black plastic cylinder.

Greg again tried to twist off one end, then the other, but only succeeded in making the palm of his hand hurt. When the throbbing in his palm subsided, he wrapped the bottom of his T-shirt around one of the knobs and tried again. Just as he thought he was going to burst a blood vessel, Greg felt the knob turn a tiny bit. Greg took a deep breath and redoubled his efforts. He was rewarded when, slowly but surely, the knob began to turn. Although it was like trying to twist something encased in almost set concrete, Greg eventually managed to open the container. His heartbeat quickened with excitement as he upended the open cylinder into his lap. Out fell a large rolled up plastic zip-top freezer bag. Inside the bag were several pieces of paper, all rolled up together like miniature posters.

Greg opened the top of the freezer bag and took out the rolled up pieces of paper. He used his thigh to help unroll the pages. The pages were normal, blue-lined, college-ruled, white notebook paper, three holes punched down the left side of each. Although they had begun to yellow with age and stubbornly insisted on rolling back up if Greg let them, the pieces of paper were in good shape. And it was obvious when he glanced at the first page that the words written on it were in his mother's handwriting.

CHAPTER FORTY-SIX

My sweet boy,

Greg's hands trembled a bit. He could hear his mother's voice in his head as he read her words. He took a deep breath and began again.

My sweet boy,

It's so strange writing this, because I hope you never read it. If you are reading this, my worse fear has come true and you're with the family and I'm not able to protect you. There's only one reason on this whole earth that I wouldn't be there for you.

Where to begin? There's so much to tell you, so much you need to know. But I don't have all the answers. I don't even have most of the answers. As I'm writing this, you're off at college. Please understand that I'm not spying on you, and I've respected your wishes to be left alone. That said, I have to make sure you're okay. I'm doing so from afar. I hope and pray that someday soon we can talk face-to-face; that you'll forgive me for everything I've put you through.

"It's not your fault," Greg mumbled. "I thought it was, but now I know it was never your fault."

After I finish writing this, I'll go back to Iowa and give Spooky what I've written to hide someplace the family would never find it. It's the one and only time I'll ever go back to Lost Haven. No one but Spooky will know about it, and I'll leave quickly after I give him what you're reading. I think Spooky is as good a place as any to start. As I'm sure you've come to know, Spooky isn't a normal dog. He is a dog, but he's also more than a dog. I'm not sure where Spooky came from, but from what I've been able to gather, he seems to have shown up around the time my grandfather, your great grandfather, began his "experiments." He's been around for as long as I can remember; he never gets old. Many Native American belief systems talk about spirit guides, or totem animals. These totem animals are there to protect and teach us about ourselves and the world around us. It's believed that a person doesn't choose his or her totem animal, the animal chooses the person. I don't think this is exactly what Spooky is, but it's close. Whatever he is, Spooky is on your side.

I'm afraid Spooky is about the only good thing that has to do with the family. God, I'm so afraid to tell you all this, but I know I have to. You need to know what you're up against.

Bill Jenkins is your father.

Greg closed his eyes and rubbed his throbbing temples with his fingers. Even though he had known it was true, some small part of him had held out and hoped that is was not. After a few moments, Greg continued to read where he had left off.

Before I go any further, know that I have never, not for one second of one day, ever regretted having you. My sweet boy, you are the one pure thing in my life. You are my life. You are everything to me.

There's no nice way of saying it: Bill Jenkins raped me and my sister when we were sixteen. He was a deputy sheriff then. I'm sure by now he's sheriff—that's how things work in Lost Haven. I won't go into any detail, but Spooky tried to protect me, and ripped apart Bill's thigh so badly it almost killed him. I'm convinced Spooky was looking to finish what he'd started, but Bill managed to get away. The Dameron and Jenkins families are intertwined in this sick game. The Jenkins role in all of it is one of protectors for the family, both physically and financially. At the time I'm writing this, there are two Jenkins brothers. Bill is the physical bully for the family, and to put it bluntly, is a murderer without a single ounce of feeling in his entire body. Bill's brother, Jerald, is the financial bully, president of Jenkins Bank & Trust. He's not a murderer like Bill, but he's as sharp as a tack, and in his own way, dangerous. Son, I want you to know that you are not your father. You are everything he could never be: kind, compassionate, loving. We don't get to pick our parents, but we can't let them define us. You are your own man. Don't ever forget that, son.

Something else you should know about the family finances that you probably don't know. I doubt that anyone would want you to know. When your great grandfather Cyril became aware of your potential, he changed his will to have the estate, in its entirety, pass to you in the event of his death. Son, you own everything. It's all yours: the house, the land, all the family bank accounts. You are worth close to twelve million dollars. You own a good portion of the land that Lost Haven sits on.

As for my own parents, your grandparents, I have no memory of them. Your great grandfather said they died in a car accident, but deep down I've always known he was lying. I think he killed them. I don't know how, and I don't know why, and trying to logically explain insanity will force you to follow it down its dangerous path. If you follow that path too far, you can get lost and not know how to find your way back. If you have not already looked at them, Cyril Dameron's research journals are upstairs on the third floor. They're filled with his sick insanity, but it may be good for you to have a basic understanding of what started this nightmare. In the end, Cyril was killed by the very forces he thought he could control. The things, the entities, he thought he was in control of were just using him. The entities cannot be controlled by anyone. They're like hungry predators: they will let you get close to them if you have something to offer, but when you run out of food, or if the mood just strikes them, they'll turn on you. But by helping to feed their desires, Cyril brought himself and this family to their attention, permanently.

Not all of the entities are evil or dangerous. Cyril, being psychotic, was only interested in the evil ones, but there are others. The entities seem to fall into three categories:

The worst ones, the ones Cyril tried to control, are what I call "lurkers." They're not from this world. They seem to drift in and out of our reality. The really dangerous ones can do so at will; others seem to do it by accident. In most cases, unless you're a Dameron, the lurkers ignore people. Again, unless you're a Dameron, most people can't even see them. The lurkers just seem to wander around as if in some kind of dream. But the really bad ones, the ones that can move between our world and their own at will, they can see people clearly, and they hate us. Luckily for most peo-

ple, they can't hurt you. Unless you can see them. Seeing a lurker seems to give it some kind of power to cause physical harm. It's like by acknowledging the lurker's presence, a person completely opens the door and lets it into our world. This forms some kind of link between the person who saw it and the lurker. Most people who see a lurker are only going to see it once, because once they see it, it will kill them. And having severed its link into our world, it can no longer hurt anyone, until it finds another person who can see it. These lurkers seem to live, if you can call it that, for the sole purpose of killing people who can see them.

Greg thought about the thing that had attacked him outside the barn, the thing that had caused him to be here now. If there ever was a lurker, that thing was it.

Not only could your great grandfather see lurkers, but he also seemed to be able to share his sight with others. He used his ability like a weapon. If someone angered him, he projected his ability onto his victim, and suddenly the poor individual could see lurkers just as easily as Cyril did. I can only imagine how horrified his victims must have been to one second be living an ordinary life, and in the next second have their whole notion of reality shattered, to see monsters everywhere. What a horrible way to die.

I think the second group of entities are some kind of poltergeists. They're lost souls. They've spent such a long time remaining on earth when they should have moved on that they've developed a weak link of their own to objects around them. They can't hurt you themselves, but they have the ability to briefly manipulate physical objects, which makes them very dangerous. A knife thrown at you from a poltergeist is just as dangerous as one thrown from a person. A knife is a knife. From my experience, most poltergeists are violent and hostile. They were bad people in life, and because of it, are afraid to move on to what comes next, afraid they will somehow be punished. As a result, they stay here and fester like infected wounds, growing angrier and more violent. Sometimes they look human, and other times their inner ugliness seeps out and they become on the outside what they are on the inside.

The third group of entities is not dangerous. They are spirits, ghosts, souls. Unlike poltergeists, these spirits are not mean or hurtful by nature, but for whatever reason, they have not yet moved on and continue to inhabit our world. Sometimes, if these spirits stay chained to our world long enough, they too develop the ability to manipulate objects like poltergeists. The only reason I would not classify them as poltergeists is because they don't manipulate objects out of harm or malice. They're more likely to steal small trinkets than slam doors, pound on walls, and throw objects around a room.

Now for what ties all the entities together. While most lurkers can't see, and don't seem to care about people, they seem to be able to see spirits or ghosts very well, and they're attracted to them.

There are paths that crisscross the earth, some visible, others not. Entities travel these paths like roads, going to who knows where. Where these paths crisscross, hubs are formed. These places are gathering points of power. Some of these gathering points are good and some are bad, just like the paths that crisscross them. Throughout history, great temples and monuments have been built on these sites when people found them. I'm sure a few of the people were able to see things like we can. But even without the ability to see and interact with entities and spirits, all people on some level have an instinct about life and death. Most people know a place is special. They may not know why, but they feel it just the same. Some of these monuments still exist, such as the Sphinx and Stonehenge. Others have been forgotten. The Cooper barn is one of these places: it's long been forgotten, if it was ever discovered in the first place.

The good gathering points help souls move on and are filled with beneficial entities. They remind me of what some religions call angels. I'm not sure if they actually are angels, but if not, they're something like them. I wish I had more concrete answers, but what we're dealing with is so far beyond our understanding that I think we can only grasp little bits and pieces, tiny truths. In a way it makes sense that we can't truly know what comes after death until we experience death itself.

Unfortunately, our part in all this has to do with an evil gathering point: the Cooper barn. Do not go there, son.

"Too late," Greg mumbled. Although, all things considered, Spooky had picked the perfect spot to hide his mother's letter. No one in Greg's family, aware of what gathered in the area, would have the courage to come out here.

Evil entities (again, you can compare them to the religious idea of demons) at places like the Cooper barn are there to torment and destroy. They enslave the weaker souls that travel along bad paths. Most of these souls were bad people in life, and while I don't know if they are being punished in the afterlife or believe they will be—I like to think that whatever created life is above such petty things as vengeance—these souls wander bad paths. Sometimes I think that perhaps they are punishing themselves. Perhaps they are so fearful of reprisals for their past sins that they would rather be tormented in this world than move on to the next, where they belong. In fact, it's speculation, but it may be that if a bad soul stays here long enough, it begins a transformation into first a poltergeist and then in rare cases, a full-fledged entity. While this is bad enough, what is worse is that sometimes a good soul gets lost and wanders off a good path and onto a bad one. I don't like to think about what terrors they encounter in pits like the Cooper barn.

Our family has a gift, or a curse depending on how you choose to look at it. Even in our family it's very rare, and often skips generations, but somehow, someway, it gets passed down. I guess the simplest way to think of it would be some kind of psychic ability. I don't know how it happens, or why—if our brains are wired differently, or if we just somehow figured out how to tap into something that all humans possess—but for whatever reason, some of us can see and interact with things most people can't. Your great grandfather had the ability. He dubbed it being "chosen," as if the entities had given the ability to him. I, on the other hand, think that we are born wired with it, like a light switch in our heads that remains off until something comes along and turns it on. I think the entities have the ability to turn this light switch on in people who have it. I also have the ability, and I believe my sister does to a lesser extent. You, however, son, glow with the ability. You have more potential power than all the rest of us combined. I think that maybe the ability is evolving, with each new generation becoming more powerful, more focused. I could see it when you were born. You were like a beacon of light. That's why I had to take you away from the family. I wasn't the only one who could see your potential; your great grandfather saw it, too. The family would have tried to twist you, mold you into some kind of sick copy of Cyril. And if you had refused to yield to the will of the family, they would have imprisoned you and used you like a slave.

Looking back on the whole thing, I don't know why I never told you about all of it. I think in some way, my ability has brought me so much pain that I tried to shelter you from it by denying your own special gift. I thought that if we just kept moving, no entities would be able to pin us down; none of them would be able to reach inside your head and flip your switch on. And that you could live a normal life. But I was so busy trying to keep you away from the entities and the family, so busy trying to give you a normal life, that I made your life anything but normal. I think I made the biggest mistake of my life by not acknowledging your gift. I made the *mistake of assuming that our family's ability could never be anything but a curse, that it could never do anything but bring heartache and misery. But you, my sweet boy, are filled with love. Open you heart, and let that love guide you. I don't know what your purpose is, or why you shine so brightly, but I know that if you follow your heart, you cannot go wrong.*

Please forgive me for the choices I've made. Please know that no matter how things turn out, I did what I did with the best of intentions. Just thinking about you off in college makes me so proud, and at the same time, makes me want to cry. I see you with my eyes, and you're all grown up, a young man, yet my heart will always see you as the sweet little boy who showed me what true love is and forever changed my life. A mother's heart never forgets her child, even when her child is no longer a child.

If you discover nothing else from the ability you possess, know this: We all go on. Somehow, someway, somewhere, we go on. And wherever that is, I'm waiting there for you now. Under the circumstances, I pray this letter finds you well. I hope in some small way it helps you. Remember, part of me will always be with you. If you ever get lost, or scared, just close your eyes and open your heart and I'll be there. I'll be the one holding the Moonstone rose given to me by the best thing that ever happened to me: you, son.

Loving you always and forever,

Mom

Greg did not realize he was crying until his tears began to hit the last page of his mother's letter like drops of rain. They turned the crisp blue letters into small blue ink puddles. For the first time since his mother's death, Greg felt the true crushing weight of the loss. As bad as it was, the loss would have been bearable had it not been mixed with a heartbreaking remorse over what might have been. Greg no longer blamed his mother for what had happened; he also did not blame himself. He could not even blame his aunt, not really, although it would have been easy to try. Should he blame his great grandfather? The entities? What made the whole thing so painful that Greg thought his heart might actually break—a concept he had always assumed had been made up by some slick writer for a book or movie—was that there really was not anything or anyone he could blame. And even if he could blame the pain on something, it would not bring his mother back. It would not allow him to start over, to try again. The loss was final and crushing. With death there are no do-overs.

Greg lowered his head and wept.

CHAPTER FORTY-SEVEN

Greg was not sure how long it was—time felt strange here, different somehow, slower perhaps—before the tears stopped. By the time they did, Greg's eyes were puffy and his throat throbbed, raw. Greg sniffed a few times and wiped his cheeks with the bottom front of his T-shirt. For a moment he considered wiping his nose on his shirt as well, but a memory of his mother scolding him when he had been about five for doing such a thing made him hesitate. In the past such a memory probably would have made him angry; now it made him smile a little. Greg realized that he had spent so many years being bitter that he had come to see all his memories of childhood smothered in a red haze of anger, including the good ones. It was strange what the mind chose to remember, and how it chose to remember it.

Greg's mother scolding him had been kind of funny, because right after she had told him not to wipe his nose on the front of his shirt, he had industriously wiped his nose with his hand, and then wiped his hand on the front of his shirt. A completely legal move in the mother-son game of Do What Mom Tells You. His mother had known it, too, because she had smirked, shook her head, and said, *Nice one. Now don't do that again, little man.*

Greg sighed and laughed a little at the memory. Now that the tears had stopped, Greg felt a tad better as if, like a river, the tears had carried away a little of the hurt and loss he felt inside. It had been only the tiniest bit, but it was something, it was a start.

Greg carefully arranged the pages of his mother's letter in the proper order, put the letter back in its freezer bag, and secured it inside the plastic cylinder, twisting the lid on tight. In a way, the letter was like a memory of his mother, a moment in time, ageless and magical. Greg wanted to ensure that it remained safe. He doubted that he would be throwing the black plastic cylinder at any more entities, regardless of the satisfaction he felt at smacking them in the head with something.

Thinking of entities, Greg remembered that he was still in their house, so to speak, an intruder. Greg glanced behind him, at the tree filled with ocular plums. Although it seemed harmless, and the only other entity Greg had come across had ignored him, how much longer before his luck ran out? Greg turned his head back around, gazing at his tennis shoe tracks in the powdery ground. Greg hoped nothing came shambling by those tracks and decided to follow them to see what sort of strange creature left such marks on the ground.

Greg was imagining what sort of horrid creature would follow his tracks and what he would do when he saw it, *if* he saw it, when a creature appeared. Only it was not horrid, and was not really a creature, but instead a big dog named Spooky.

Greg stood, wincing at the pins and needles that tingled in the back of his legs, and grinned. Spooky came fully into view about fifty feet ahead of him, parting the mist that hung in the air, his nose to the ground, tail wagging. He looked up a moment later, saw Greg, and charged forward.

"I missed you, buddy," Greg managed to say. Then Spooky bowled him over, and before Greg could recover enough to protest, Spooky assaulted his face with the canine equivalent of a handshake. Only the canine version was much wetter than even the sweatiest palm.

His face thoroughly coated with Spooky saliva, Greg managed to escape out from between Spooky's front paws. Greg stood and wiped his face with his forearm. "You've got to stop running into me like that. You're like a truck with fur," Greg said, and grinned again.

Spooky wagged his tail furiously, trotted past Greg, and sniffed around the base of the tree that Greg had, a few moments earlier, been leaning his back against. Apparently, the tree got the Spooky seal of approval, or at least did not get the Spooky seal of *disapproval*, because after a few deep sniffs, Spooky returned to Greg's side without so much as a backward glance at the tree. The tree, however, did glance at Spooky with its numerous black eyes. Greg grimaced. *Creepy. What the hell was I thinking leaning up against that thing?*

Greg returned his attention to more pleasant thoughts. He reached down and scratched Spooky behind the ears. "Okay, buddy, I'm assuming you took care of our bogeyman and you know the way back to get the hell out of here." Greg had often seen people talking to animals as if the animals could understand what the baby-talking people were saying. In the past, Greg had been guilty of doing it himself. But in this case, Greg knew Spooky really did understand what he said. And it probably helped that Greg did not talk to Spooky in that annoying goo-goo-gaa-gaa tone. Maybe all animals really could understand what people said, but they just chose to ignore the people who talked like babies. Greg could not blame the animals; if everyone talked to him as if he were two years old, Greg felt sure he would ignore them, too.

Greg raised his cylinder-grasping right hand and pointed it in the direction from which Spooky had come, back along the trail of Greg's tracks. "Lead on, oh fur-covered one."

A short time later, they stood facing the wall of black gelatin, its surface pristine and glistening. Greg looked down at Spooky. Spooky looked up at him. "I hate this shit," Greg said.

Spooky did not have a collar, but he did have that loose mastiff skin. Greg bent and grabbed hold of a handful at Spooky's shoulder. "That doesn't hurt, does it?" he asked. Spooky responded by slapping Greg on the leg repeatedly with his tail, *whap-whap-whap*.

Although Greg would have to walk bent forward a bit if he wanted to remain holding on to Spooky, it was a small price to pay. Greg sighed. "Okay, let's get this over with." Greg followed beside Spooky in a shambling sideways gate as they drew closer to the wall. "Did I mention I hate this shit?" he said. Then he took a deep breath, held it, and walked into the gelatin wall of worms.

CHAPTER FORTY-EIGHT

The second time through the wall had been no better than the first. Maybe a bit more bearable because Greg had known what to expect, and maybe a bit faster because Greg did not panic, but the short trek back through the wall had made Greg feel just as nasty as it had the first time.

Spooky seemed to share Greg's feelings, because as they once again stood on the lifeless black soil outside the Cooper barn, Spooky shook from side to side as if he were drying himself off, even though he was not wet. With that done, he glanced up at Greg and then began to walk out of the clearing toward the line of trees, back in the direction of the house. Greg followed and soon caught up, falling in beside Spooky.

They walked into the woods and began to follow the path back to the house. Greg's feeling that time moved slower while inside the Cooper barn proved to be correct, because it was nearly dusk as they wound their way through the woods. Greg and Spooky had begun their little adventure in the morning, and while inside the Cooper barn, the entire day had passed them by in what felt to Greg like only a couple of hours.

Fog moved in behind the dwindling light. It began to blanket the ground in a surprisingly thick, gray soup. Greg absently watched the fog part around his shins in swirling waves each time he took a step. "Thanks for giving me the note from my mother," Greg said after a few minutes of silence. He glanced at the cylinder held in his right hand. "It means a lot."

Spooky stopped on the path. He turned and looked at Greg with his intelligent amber eyes.

Greg stopped as well. It was obvious to Greg that regardless of what other talents Spooky possessed, he had an uncanny ability to judge character. When Spooky looked at you, he did not just see you from the outside; you could feel him looking into you, seeing your true self. "You knew my mother," Greg said to Spooky. "Did you … like her? Was she a good person?"

Spooky fiercely wagged his tail and gave a single muffled bark.

Greg smiled a little and nodded. "Yeah, I think so, too." Greg cleared his throat. "And thanks for saving my ass back there." Greg struggled to find the right words. Like most men, Greg had the it's-hard-for-me-to-express-my-feelings gene that seemed to be fed by testosterone. "I didn't always appreciate things you did for me. But, well … you uh … you saved my life."

Spooky walked back to Greg, bumped into him, and leaned against Greg's leg hard enough to make him take a stumbling step backwards. The meaning of the gesture was so obvious it made Greg grin: It would have been the same if Spooky had been a man, punched Greg in the arm, and said, *No problem, buddy. Don't worry about it. What are friends for?*

"Anyway, just wanted to say thanks," Greg continued. "My mother told me some interesting things, and I've got some ideas. First thing …"

The rest of Greg's thought died on his lips when the figure rose out of the fog that now covered the ground past his knees about twenty feet ahead on the path. The way the figure rose up from the fog and rigidly tilted forward reminded Greg of Dracula in one of the old black-and-white movies. Like Dracula, the figure was deathly pale, appearing even more so against the stark contrast of her long black hair. Unlike Dracula, the thing on the path was female and could not have been more than twenty, had she been alive. She was completely nude, and blood flowed from her eyes like tears, dripped from her nipples as if she were indeed a vampire and had given birth to a hungry baby bloodsucker. Blood also covered the lower part of her body, seeming to flow from between her legs in a steady stream, sliding down her inner thighs. And from between her legs, rising out of the lake of blood like a mythical sea serpent, was a glistening gray umbilical cord that swung like a jump rope and connected to the shriveled gray fetus she held in her left hand.

Greg took all this in with a calm anticipation of the eminent conflict. Adrenaline focused his mind, making it sharp and quick. Everything else fell away: there was only him, Spooky, and the entity. Greg surprised himself with his own reaction. But in a way it made sense: After being attacked at the Cooper farm by an entity that looked like it was in charge of death itself, walking through a black wall of worm-filled gelatin, only to find some kind of alternate dimension that seemed to be a factory that produced monsters, Greg had been overloaded with fear. To cope, it seemed that his mind had said *enough*, and shorted out the circuit that made Greg panic. Greg had read somewhere that one cure for people's phobia was to expose them to the phobia repeatedly, to drown them in their own fear. So, if you were afraid of snakes, you would be forced to handle them until your brain could not take it anymore and shut down your fear of snakes. Greg was still afraid of the thing in front of him, there was no doubt about that, but he was no longer *terrified*.

Greg had seen this one before. He was sure that this had been the one he had seen outside his sentry window when he had been locked upstairs. This was the one who had looked up and opened its arms to Greg, beseeching him to embrace it.

Spooky had also seen the entity and had turned to face it, studying it. What happened next had to be the last thing Greg would have imagined. In fact, it was so strange to Greg, that he would never have considered it at all. Instead of barking like a cannon and charging forward, hell-bent on evil entity destruction, Spooky casually trotted toward the entity, tail wagging.

Greg raised his hand out toward Spooky. "What are you doing? Don't do that!" But it was too late. If Spooky heard Greg, he chose to ignore him. Spooky now stood in front of the entity, his head turned sideways, looking up at it. Greg cringed as it reached down toward Spooky with one hand—the one not holding a fetus—as white and delicate as porcelain. Its hand, however, passed right through Spooky. To Greg, the entity looked like it had been trying to pet the top of Spooky's head.

Spooky turned and headed back toward Greg. The entity followed. "No, don't!" Greg yelled. Regardless of his newfound calm, Greg wanted to turn and run. But run where? His uncle had told him, and he had found out firsthand, that entities could move extremely fast. An Olympic sprinter could not even begin to outrun one.

The entity was now in front of him, Spooky between Greg and it. It was a small comfort, but it was a comfort nonetheless. Now that it was so close, the entity looked even more horrid. The blood that dripped from its body was thick and clotted, closer in color to black than red. Its white skin had a gray tinge and hung from it in loose folds, as if it were wearing a skin jumpsuit two sizes too big. A smell wafted from it like stagnant water filled with rotting bits of earth. And if all this was not bad enough, it was holding a fetus that looked to have been ripped out from between its legs, umbilical cord still attached. The fetus looked more birdlike than human.

Before Greg could stop it, the entity grabbed his hand. It felt like being touched by a cold, wet piece of half-rotted rubber. Greg shrieked like a girl at her first horror movie when the monster jumps out for the first time in all its night-marish glory. Greg would have been embarrassed under other circumstances. Then, everything changed.

Greg developed instant tunnel vision. All he could see clearly was the entity, everything else around him blurred like he was racing down the first steep hill of a giant rollercoaster. And like being on a rollercoaster, Greg's ears filled with the roar of rushing air. Then, a golden light filled Greg's vision, blinding him as if he had not only looked directly at the sun, but had traveled there and stuck his head into its fiery core. Greg's heart was beating so fast and so hard it felt like it was trying to pound its way out of his chest. Greg fought to breathe, gasping, afraid that at any moment he would suffer a heart attack. And then everything became instantly clear. The switch inside Greg had been flipped on completely.

Greg opened his eyes, his heart once again calmly beating in his chest. He still held the entity's hand, and it still looked as horrible as ever. But now it was sur-rounded in an aura like molten silver. Greg saw that his arm was covered in a similar aura, but golden. He brought his free hand up to his face and wiggled his fingers. The golden aura that outlined his hand moved and flowed with his fin-gers. Greg glanced down at Spooky. He was surrounded by his own gold aura.

Greg looked back up at the entity. He reached up with his free hand and touched the side of its face, completing the circle between them. The instant the circle was complete, Greg understood. The entity was not an entity at all. It was the spirit of Mary Riley, the young woman who had been raped and beaten nearly to death for daring to love a black man. In the same instant that the circle had been completed, Greg knew her whole life. It was not like a series of images flashed in front of him. It was far simpler, and far more profound. Greg just knew everything about her, in the same way he knew everything about himself. It was like he had lived two lives: his own and Mary's.

Mary had remained tied to the area of her death for so long after she should have moved on that she was slowly changing, becoming something between a spirit and an entity. Greg knew that if she remained long enough, she would eventually evolve into a full-blown entity, which would trap her here forever. Mary had not wanted to stay here. But the evil entities that surrounded this place had trapped her with fear and confusion. Greg now understood that the entities fed on souls like vampires, draining energy and sucking them dry until the souls themselves, like the victims of vampires, became entities, doomed to carry on the horrible soul-feeding.

Mary did not speak to Greg so much as Greg read her emotions. Now that Mary had flipped Greg's switch all the way on, everything was becoming clear to him. For some reason, Greg understood that the dead did not speak. Regardless of how talkative they may have been in life, in death they were silent. Greg, though, did not need speech to understand Mary. Her emotions spoke like words: *Please help me. I want to go home.*

And Greg realized he *could* help. In fact, he now understood that he was here to do precisely that: to help the dead move on, to help them go home. Because of the entities that trapped them here, the dead could not do it by themselves. But Greg was like a door between this world and what lay beyond. And he could open that door. He did so now, simply willing it to happen.

There was another blinding pulse of gold light. It lasted only a moment. When Greg's vision cleared, the ghastly image of Mary had been replaced with a beautiful young woman. She stood before him naked, but unashamed, still bathed in a silver aura. There was nothing sexual about her nudity, but instead, her nudity seemed to radiate something pure, like a beautiful painting or a perfect statue. She was so beautiful it took Greg's breath away. And cradled in her arms was a newborn baby, its hair as black as its mother's, its skin the rich color of cream-filled coffee, its big round eyes a piercing blue.

Go home. Greg did not know exactly how he made Mary understand what he had thought, but Greg nonetheless knew she understood. She looked up from her baby and smiled at Greg. Greg smiled back. As Greg watched, the aura that surrounded Mary and her baby changed from silver to gold. Mary looked into Greg's eyes. He felt her say, *Thank you. Bless you.* She waved at Spooky like an old friend. Then she began to move on.

There was not an actual door through which Mary left. There was nothing as dramatic as a white light shot down from the sky. No angelic beings appeared to carry Mary away. Instead, the gold aura that outlined her gradually grew inward, covering her, until she looked like a gold statue. Then, the pieces slowly broke apart and blew away, like tiny, glowing golden particles of sand. Soon, Mary Riley and her baby were gone.

For the second time in so many hours, Greg found himself crying. These tears, however, were not tears of pain, but tears of joy. Greg grinned. For the first time in his life, he felt whole, complete. Greg felt right with the universe, as if he had finally found his place within the grand scheme of things. In fact, Greg was sure he had done exactly that. Some found their callings in medicine, education, parenthood. It was different for everyone. Greg had found his purpose helping lost souls move on. Greg wondered how that would look on a resume, and laughed.

He thought about that M. Night Shyamalan movie with Bruce Willis and Haley Joel Osment, *The Sixth Sense*. Greg liked that movie. Greg looked down at Spooky. "I see dead people," he said, and laughed again.

PART FOUR

EMPTY ROOMS

CHAPTER FORTY-NINE

"Where have you been? I've been worried sick!" Katelin said.

Greg watched the dim gold aura around his aunt flicker like a fluorescent light that threatened to burn out at any second. Katelin's golden aura, which Greg now understood was a sign of some sort of psychic ability, was not a fraction as intense as the one that surrounded himself, or Spooky. But it was there around Katelin nonetheless. *It's going to take a while to get used to seeing glowing people,* Greg thought. *But now I'll be able to brush my teeth in the dark and still see myself in the mirror.* Greg grinned.

"And just what is so funny?" Katelin demanded. She stood in the kitchen by the back door that Greg had used to enter the house, her hands on her hips. She pointed a finger at Greg. "Just what is so funny?"

Greg watched Katelin's face grow increasingly redder. He had really pissed her off this time. Greg didn't care. Since discovering his ability and using it to help Mary Riley escape the entities and move on, Greg had been on a kind of natural high. He felt great, and was not going to allow his aunt to ruin it.

Greg glanced down at Spooky, who sat beside him. Spooky looked up at Greg as if to say, *If you want her to know, you tell her; I'm not telling her anything.*

Greg looked back up at his aunt and shrugged. "We've been out in the woods talking to entities."

Katelin looked like she had been ready to go off on a tirade about Greg leaving all day and not telling anyone where he was going. Greg's mention of entities, though, seemed to have caused her to hesitate. She looked at Greg, glanced down at Spooky, and then looked back at Greg dubiously. She stopped pointing at him and put her hand back on her hip. She set her mouth in a firm line. "That is not something you should be joking about."

"I'm not joking," Greg said. *Just lying a little,* he thought. "We … I made contact with two entities." Greg thought it might be a good idea if he did not tell her that Spooky seemed to be able to communicate with and track entities and spirits, if she did not already know. Greg doubted that she did, which in a way was odd, but in another way made sense: Katelin was so self-absorbed that she most likely never gave Spooky more than a passing thought. To her he was probably just a big dog that had once bitten Bill Jenkins, but not much else. Did she even realize that Spooky had to be at least as old as Greg, an impossible age for *any* dog? Greg guessed that most likely Katelin simply did not care.

Greg studied Katelin's face. She did not seem convinced. Then it dawned on Greg: feed her ego. Because regardless of how much Katelin professed to do for the greater good of the family, how much she claimed to sacrifice, Greg understood that it wasn't about the family, it was about her: *her* sacrifices, *her* recognition, *her* contributions. Greg cleared his throat. "Yes, your idea of forcing me to study upstairs worked. I learned a lot while I was up there. You really helped me, and uh … the family. You did a good job for the family. Thank you."

Katelin's face softened. A moment later she hugged Greg tightly and kissed him on the cheek. Greg endured it. Then she stepped back and smiled. "Oh, sweetheart, you really did contact an entity, didn't you."

Greg held up the index and middle fingers of his right hand in a V, which could represent peace. In this case it represented the number two.

"Oh, of course," Katelin cooed. "*Two* entities! Of course you would summon *two* entities on your first try. Of course *you* would. You're so special!"

"Thanks to your training and patience with me," Greg said.

Katelin beamed with obvious pride. "Oh, sweetheart, this is going to be so great! The things you and I will do together. The things we'll see! We'll get back the respect we deserve in this town. Before we're done, we'll own everything. Every single thing!"

Katelin's level of excitement seemed almost manic to Greg. She seemed barely able to control herself. It was like she was a five-year-old who had been let loose in the world's biggest candy store and told that she could have as much as she wanted of whatever she wanted for the rest of her life. Greg watched his aunt wring her hands together and practically jump up and down. "Do it again! Do it now! Can you do it now? Can you summon one now?"

Greg knew he could not summon anything. That wasn't the way it worked. That was not the way it had ever worked, regardless of what his great grandfather had thought. While Greg doubted that Cyril Dameron had possessed the ability to help spirits, he had nonetheless failed to understand what power he *did* possess. It seemed Katelin had followed in her grandfather's footsteps, and failed to grasp her ability, however meager it may have been.

Greg was not in command of anything. Greg was a facilitator, and nothing more. Something, some kind of force, flowed through him, used him as a kind of vessel, to help spirits move on to whatever came after this life. In fact, despite Greg's ability to communicate with spirits and open the figurative door to the afterlife, he could not see through that door, and still had no idea what lay beyond. In all honesty, Greg had to admit that he still knew very little about what he did or how he did it, and had a feeling that that was the way it was always going to be. Greg was not a great and mighty commander of monsters; he was simply a humble servant of some greater power. And that suited Greg just fine. His aunt, on the other hand, seemed to expect something more.

Greg tried to put on his best expression of regret. He shook his head. "I'd love to summon an entity right now. Now that I've done it, I want to do it more. But it takes a lot of energy to summon one. And with me just beginning to learn what I'm doing, I used up a lot of energy already today summoning the two that I did. I need to rest, recharge my batteries."

It was obvious from Katelin's pouting expression that she was disappointed. She now looked like a five-year-old who had been let loose in the giant candy store and told she could have all the candy, the only caveat being that first she had to eat a truckload of Brussels sprouts. "But I think I'll be able to summon more in a day or two. And when I'm ready, I'll summon them with you there. We'll do it together." Greg gazed at his aunt. "I just need to rest first."

Katelin nodded. She patted Greg's arm. "Of course you do. I was being selfish."

"It's okay," Greg said.

"You get your rest. I've waited this long; I can wait a few more days. If you need anything, honey, just let me know."

Greg nodded. "Will do. Now I'm going to go rest up," Greg said—*because tomorrow is going to be a busy day*—and walked out of the kitchen and headed to the stairs in the family room, Spooky beside him. As they walked up the stairs, Greg glanced at Spooky. Greg swore Spooky was smiling. Greg smiled back. "Yeah, I know. I laid on the bullshit pretty thick. I didn't know I had it in me."

In his room, lying in bed, Greg thought, *I'm not going to be able to sleep, not after today.* It was the last conscious thought he had before he fell asleep.

CHAPTER FIFTY

Greg awoke to knocking on his bedroom door. He rolled over to face the door, one eye closed, the other squinting in the early morning sunlight that shone in through the bedroom windows. Usually the heavy velvet curtains were closed, but apparently someone had opened them sometime yesterday before Greg had entered the room and gone to sleep. Spooky lay on the other side of the bed, also awake. They looked at each other. "You know, if I ever get married, you're going to have to sleep on the floor." Spooky yawned, apparently unimpressed with Greg's threat.

"Honey, are you awake?" his aunt called from the other side of the door. "I have breakfast."

Greg stumbled out of bed and into a pair of sweatpants. He shuffled over to the door, unlocked it, opened it a few inches, and peered out at his aunt. At her feet sat a large wooden tray heaped with food. Greg's stomach reminded him that, in his excitement, he had completely forgotten to eat anything at all yesterday. He was instantly starving. "That's normal food, right?"

Katelin blushed and actually seemed a little embarrassed. "Yes, honey, it's normal food. That was a onetime incident. I can't say I liked it any more than you did, but it was for your own good. For the good of the family." Katelin smiled. "You understand."

Greg opened the door. Katelin reached down for the tray, but Greg stopped her by saying, "No, that's okay. I'll get it," reaching down to pick it up. It was surprisingly heavy.

Katelin smiled at him. "You're such a good boy. You let me know if you need anything else," she said, and headed off back downstairs.

Greg turned with the tray and closed the door with his foot. Having smelled food, Spooky was no longer lying on his side, but was up on all fours in bed. The mattress and box spring swayed a little from side to side in time with Spooky's wagging tail, while his nose sucked in the wafting aromas of scrambled eggs and bacon, waffles and maple syrup, pancakes and sausage, milk and orange juice.

Spooky practically leaped at the tray as Greg approached the bed. "Hey," Greg said, turning the tray away from the bed and Spooky's capable mouth, "we share, okay?" Spooky seemed to consider this for a moment. Then he jumped out of bed, nose still running in overdrive.

Greg sat on the edge of the bed, put the tray beside him, and began to divide the huge amount of food in half, pushing food onto a couple plates, taking some off of others. When he was finished, he sat Spooky's portion down on the floor on two plates, figuring it would be easier for him to eat on a flat surface more stable than the bed. Besides, Superdog or not, Greg had seen Spooky eat, and Greg did not want to have to change the blanket and sheet on the bed following Spooky's food-based destruction.

By the time Greg held up a glass of milk and a glass of orange juice, letting Spooky decide which he preferred—Spooky preferred orange juice—Spooky had finished one plate and was making a substantial dent in the second. By the time Greg had eaten two pieces of bacon and a forkful of scrambled eggs, Spooky had devoured everything, even managing to drink all his orange juice from the tall glass that was only a little wider than his tongue. He sat and looked at Greg intently, licking his chops clean. Greg shook his head. "Two words for you, buddy—pace yourself."

Downstairs in the kitchen, Greg leaned against the wall and flipped through the slim phone book. Spooky watched. It did not take Greg long to find what he sought. There was only one listing in Lost Haven, which made it even easier. Greg picked up the phone and punched in the number. The call was answered on the first ring.

"Hemmings Ford, Lincoln, Mercury. This is Tricia. How may I help you?"

"Hi, Tricia, I'd like to buy a car, and I'd like to do it over the phone, if possible. And can you deliver it?"

There was a pause on the other end of the line. "I think we can do that," Tricia said cheerily. "Let me put you through to Doug."

There was another short pause and a *click*. "Doug Hemmings. What can I do you for?"

"I'd like to buy a car and have it delivered."

"No problem. You stop on by and I'd be happy to help you."

"Well," Greg said, "I'd like to just do it over the phone if possible."

Greg heard Doug Hemmings laugh. "So no test drive, no haggling? You just want to buy a car and have it delivered? Mister, I wish I had more customers like you. We can definitely do that for you, no problem. What kind of car you looking for?"

"Well, actually, probably a truck. Something four-wheel drive, but nothing too big. Normal-sized."

"We have a nice selection of Ford Rangers. We got a few decked out with all the bells and whistles. The three I'm thinking about for you even have MP3 players in them. They're four-wheel drive, and I'd say they qualify as normal-sized. They're real nice trucks. We got a navy blue one, a black one, and a forest green one in stock. And if none of those suit you, we can order just about any color you want. Of course, all our new vehicles come with factory warranties. And here at Hemmings, you get free oil changes and tire rotations for life. And I'll throw in a free bed-liner, no charge."

Greg grinned. Doug Hemmings was definitely in the right business. Even over the phone, Greg could tell he was a born salesman. "Sounds good. Can you deliver one today?"

"Sure can. You just pick your color. I'll bring it out personally this morning if you live anywhere close to Lost Haven. You'll just need to sign some papers and have proof of insurance. And if you don't have insurance, my cousin's an agent; he can set you right up in a few minutes. From the sounds of it, I'm guessing you already have financing, but if you don't, we have financing options for everyone, regardless of credit history. We'll work with you to get you in the vehicle of your choice *today*."

"Actually, provided you don't mind us driving back into town to the bank after you drop off the truck, I'll be paying cash, or at least a cashier's check."

"Well, that just eliminated half our paperwork. And if you're not financing, you don't even need proof of insurance, although as I'm sure you know, driving without insurance is illegal in the state of Iowa."

"Yeah, I think I'll take you up on the insurance offer," Greg said.

"Great!" Doug Hemmings, of Hemmings Ford, Lincoln, Mercury, sounded downright delighted. "It's always a good day when I sell a nice truck to a nice customer and get a little business for my cousin to boot, and all before lunch. Just tell me what color you feel like and where to bring your new truck and we're in business."

"I'll take the green one. And could you please deliver it to the Dameron place? Do you know where that is?"

There was a pause that grew into an uncomfortable silence. "Hello? You still there?" Greg asked.

"I'm here," Doug Hemmings said. He no longer sounded like the eager salesman. His voice had gone flat. "Look, I think jokes are as funny as the next guy, but I don't take kindly to jokes like that."

Greg glanced at Spooky as if Superdog had an answer to Greg's bewilderment. "I'm not joking. My name's Greg Dameron, and I'm at the Dameron place, and I really do want to buy a truck."

"If this really is Greg Dameron," Doug Hemmings said in the same flat voice, "and I *did* hear that he was back in Lost Haven, then you'd know you could have any vehicle you want, free of charge."

Greg had flashbacks of The Bonfire Bar & Grill. In his excitement at discovering his newfound purpose, Greg had forgotten that no matter how well his intentions, he was still a Dameron, and in Lost Haven, the Dameron name was akin to an organized crime family. Greg sighed. "Listen, Doug, I understand what you must think. But my name really *is* Greg Dameron, and I don't want anything from you but a truck. And I want to pay for the truck, the same price as anyone else would. I wouldn't feel right not paying for it."

There was another long silence. "Okay, if that's what you want. I'll bring by the truck this morning, but I'm not going past the gate. I'll be there at eleven. If I don't see anyone waiting for me, I'll be leaving."

"Okay," Greg said, his mood soured. "I'll be there to meet you. And thanks for delivering the truck."

"Sure thing," Doug Hemmings said, and ended the call.

CHAPTER FIFTY-ONE

Doug Hemmings did indeed show up at eleven outside the front gate, and Greg was there to meet him, along with Spooky. He parked the new truck sideways in the beginning of the driveway, and glanced at Greg through the driver's side window. He cut the engine and got out to face Greg.

To Greg, Doug Hemmings looked like Santa Claus's younger brother. He looked to be in his mid-fifties, with a full head of brown hair that was going gray at the temples. His thick but neatly trimmed beard sported similar gray streaks. His round face was lined, giving him a kind, wise look. A substantial stomach hung over the waist of his blue jeans, threatening at any moment to burst free from the straining buttons of his brown flannel shirt.

Doug extended a meaty hand toward Greg. Greg shook it.

"So," Doug said a moment later, stepping back, "you want to drive it into town, or you want me to?" Some of the life had crept back into his voice, but Doug's uncomfortable nervousness was obvious. He looked like a man sitting in a dentist's office waiting to get a root canal, dreading what was going to happen but knowing he had no choice, just wanting to get the whole thing over with so he could go home.

"I'll go ahead and drive into town, if you don't mind," Greg said.

Doug nodded, handed Greg the keys, and headed around to the passenger's side door. "If he's going with us," Doug said, motioning toward Spooky as he hefted his substantial bulk into the passenger seat, "he's probably going to have to ride in back. I don't think all three of us'll fit in the truck."

At the mention of riding in the back of the truck, Spooky wagged his tail enthusiastically and headed toward the back of the truck. Greg lowered the tailgate and, despite his size, Spooky jumped up into the truck bed and began sniffing around.

Greg closed the tailgate, walked around, and got behind the wheel. He took a moment to breathe in the new car smell. He looked over at Doug. "There's nothing like that smell."

Doug smiled a little. Despite his discomfort, it was obvious that he loved vehicles.

They drove in silence, Doug looking straight ahead out the windshield, Greg occasionally glancing in the side mirror to look at Spooky, who was obviously delighted at going for a ride. His big head hung over the side of the truck by Greg's window, the wind blowing his eyes wide open, giving him a look of shocked surprise, like the world's first canine recipient of a botched facelift from a bad plastic surgeon.

If Greg intended to change things, he had to start somewhere, and Doug seemed like as good a place as any. "You don't like me much, do you?" Greg said.

For a moment, Greg was not sure Doug had heard him. Then, the big man took a blue handkerchief out of his right front pocket, wiped his forehead, and said, "Look, I don't want any trouble. I'm a family man. I got a wife, and two daughters and a son that I'm working hard to put through college. I pay my property fees to the Dameron family just like everyone else. I've never been late with a payment. Not once."

Greg glanced at Doug. "The Dameron family owns the land your car dealership sits on?"

Doug gave him the same look that Deb had at the bar when all this mess had begun for Greg: a mixture of disbelief and suspicion. "You own the dealership property and the property our house sits on. You own just about all the property in Lost Haven." Despite his best effort to keep his tone neutral, there was no mistaking the hint of contempt that had crept into Doug's voice.

"And how much are the … property fees?" Greg asked, making a turn and hoping his memory served him correctly about how to get into town. So far it seemed to, because Doug did not say anything about Greg driving in the wrong direction.

"Sixty percent," Doug said, and this time the contempt in his voice was unmistakable. "Sixty percent of all profits go to the Dameron family."

"Sixty percent! Jesus Christ!" Greg exclaimed. "Well, we're going to change that."

Doug glanced at him with a look of mistrust.

CHAPTER FIFTY-TWO

Jenkins Bank & Trust stood by the southeast corner of the town square, in its own plot of well-landscaped property, segregated, as if refusing to associate with its much less descript neighbors. Greg parked the truck on the curb in front of the main entrance. Even from outside it was obvious that the bank had been built with a budget that contradicted the small size of the town. It was a two-story structure made entirely of gray, black-veined marble, polished to a mirror finish. Four Corinthian columns, two on each side, rose from the base of the stairs that led to the front entrance. Above the door, carved into a slab of black marble the size of Greg's new truck, was JENKINS BANK & TRUST in bold capital letters, as if daring anyone to defy the bank's will or question its superiority. The building was jarringly out of place in its opulence.

If anything, the interior of the bank looked even more expensive than the exterior. The floor was the same highly polished gray marble of the exterior walls. Everything was covered in deep red cherry paneling with gold-leaf accents. The single customer inside the bank, an elderly woman, gave Greg a second look as he walked to the counter with Spooky and Doug, but no one questioned him.

The counter had room for four tellers. Only two were currently working. Greg approached the nearest of the two, a pretty young woman with big, doelike brown eyes that looked Greg up and down. "Hi, I'm ... do you know who I am?"

The young woman nodded.

Greg smiled. "Great. Can you tell me where I can find Jerald Jenkins?"

The young woman pointed to her left, toward a set of double cherry doors in the far corner of the bank.

"Thanks," Greg said, and headed toward the door, Spooky following. "And Doug needs a cashier's check, please. Just take it out of my account. Or just transfer the funds from my account to his. I'll be back to sign whatever needs signed in just a few minutes."

Greg did not bother knocking. He just opened one of the doors and walked in. For a moment he was startled when he saw Jerald Jenkins; then he thought, *Figures, twins.* Jerald looked exactly like his brother Bill dressed in a navy blue business suit.

Jerald was obviously surprised when he looked up from his massive oak desk, where he had been studying his computer monitor and pecking away at the keyboard. Jerald, however, recovered quickly, standing and extending his hand to Greg over the top of his desk. "Mister Dameron, good to see you. I was beginning to wonder when you were going to stop by to discuss finances." Jerald motioned to one of the two leather chairs that faced his desk. "Please, please, have a seat," he said. He glanced at Spooky. "I hope he won't be any trouble. That's a big dog," he added, and sat back down in his black leather office chair.

No shit, Captain Obvious, Greg thought as he, too, took a seat.

Jerald folded his hands on top of his desk. "So, what can I do for you today, Mister Dameron?"

Greg made a fist, brought it up to his mouth, and cleared his throat. "Well, a few things. First, I had a question about my accounts here at the bank. I'm the primary person on the accounts, correct?"

Jerald nodded. "Yes, all the accounts are accessible by the Dameron family, but you are the primary account holder on all of them. That's how Cyril wanted it."

"Good. Then I'd like to put all the accounts solely in my name. No joint accounts."

Jerald stared at Greg. Greg had not considered what he would do if Jerald did not go along with his plans and simply refused to cooperate. Although it would be against the law for Jerald not to comply, the law in Lost Haven was controlled by Jerald's brother, which meant that around here Jerald was above the law.

Greg was mentally going through strategies to make Jerald cooperate when Jerald grinned. "Reining in the family, are we? Good, I like to hear that. It reminds me of when your great grandfather was alive. Now, there was a man who didn't take any shit from anyone. Cyril was a real man, and he ran the Dameron family like a real man. There was no doubt who was in charge when Cyril was alive."

With Jerald staring at him, Greg had considered changing his strategy to the friendly approach to get what he needed from Jerald. A little of the old office small talk: how's the wife, the kids, the golf game? But it seemed Jerald did not care about the wife, the kids, or the golf game. It seemed that Jerald cared about two things: money and authority, and how one could be used to gain the other. Maybe it would be easier that way.

"That's right," Greg said. "The family has gotten soft. But that's over now. It's time for the Dameron and Jenkins families to start making some real money again and earning the respect we deserve. I'm here to make sure that happens. I keep a tight ship. And I'm starting with the finances."

"Fantastic!" Jerald said. He picked up the black handset of his phone and punched in a few numbers. He continued to study Greg, his head turned at an angle to hold the phone between his shoulder and his ear. "Lorraine, we'll be working on the Dameron accounts today, making some changes. It's top priority, so clear some time today to get it done, no exceptions. And Mister Dameron has put me in a good mood. I feel like some pussy. I think I want to bend you over and fuck you on my desk. I liked that last time." Jerald, apparently listening to something Lorraine said over the phone, nodded and said, "Uh-huh." He grinned at Greg as if to say, *See. See what I can do.*

It was just another reason for Greg to get this over as quickly as possible. When Jerald hung up the phone, Greg pushed forward. "I would also like to see all the property deeds."

Jerald leaned back in his chair, crossed his arms over his chest, and raised his eyebrows. "*All* of them?"

"Yes. You *do* have them all accounted for, don't you?"

Jerald nodded enthusiastically. "Oh, of course. Every single one of them. I only ask because there are, as I'm sure you know, quite a number of them."

"Well, I'd like them all put together. I'll be taking them home to go through them all. I want to get an idea of where we stand. Then I'll bring them back."

For the first time since Greg had met the man, Jerald frowned. "If I may be so bold, I don't think it's a good idea to take them out of the bank. They're obviously very valuable, and secure here in the bank. I don't think it's a good idea."

"Well, I don't pay you for your good ideas. I want the deeds." Greg thought he had managed the right mix of annoyance and arrogant amusement.

Jerald lowered his gaze to the top of his desk and pursed his lips as if kissing the air. Then he laughed and looked back up at Greg. "Fantastic! So much like your great grandfather. We're going to make lots of money together!" Jerald clapped his hands together. "Goddamn, you made my day! I'm so happy I might just fuck Lorraine in the ass today, too!"

CHAPTER FIFTY-THREE

Greg felt better once he was back outside, away from Jerald. The man made him feel dirty. That was the best and simplest way to describe Greg's impression of Jerald: dirty.

Spooky had once again defied gravity and managed to heft his bulk into the back of the truck. He sniffed around the large white cardboard box filled with the Dameron property deeds that sat on the opened tailgate. There were more than Greg had imagined. There had to be at least a hundred of them, all neatly folded in thirds like brochures, the last name of the original owner of each deed typed on the outside.

With Doug standing beside him, Greg began to leaf through the property deeds. Being the control freak that he obviously was, Jerald had even kept them stored alphabetically by original owner. It did not take long for Greg to find two with the name Hemmings on them. Greg took them out of the box and unfolded one. Greg, a renter, had never seen a property deed, but it was surprisingly simpler than he had imagined. Greg glanced at Doug. "Do you have a pen?"

For a moment, Doug just stared at him. Then he seemed to wake up with a start. "Yeah," he said, patting the breast pocket of his flannel shirt. He handed Greg a ballpoint pen with HEMMINGS FORD, LINCOLN, MERCURY written down the length of the round plastic body, the slogan HONEST VEHICLES AT HONEST PRICES below it.

Greg signed both deeds in the appropriate places and handed them to Doug. "There, it's all yours. I don't know much about deeds, but I'm sure you probably have to take them to the courthouse or something, maybe the county recorder, to make them official. But there you go."

Doug looked up from the deeds in his hands to Greg. "I … I don't know what to say."

Greg smiled and shrugged. "You don't have to say anything. It's rightfully your land. I'm just giving back what's yours."

As the reality of what had just happened seemed to sink in, Doug smiled back at Greg. He once again extended his meaty hand. And this time when he shook Greg's hand, Greg sensed genuine enthusiasm. Doug released Greg's hand, took the cashier's check from his pocket, ripped it up, and grinned at Greg like a little kid.

Greg laughed. "You didn't have to do that."

"Yeah, I know I didn't. But you didn't have to do *this*," Doug said, holding up the property deeds to both his business and home.

"Yeah. Yeah, I did have to do it," Greg said solemnly.

Doug seemed to understand. He took out a business card and put it in Greg's hand. "It used to be that in Lost Haven, we cared for our own. We looked after each other. I never thought I'd live to see the day, but I have a feeling things are coming back around, and for the better. You need anything, you let me know."

"Actually," Greg said, "I could use your help."

"You got it. What can I do you for?"

"Well, I can imagine what people think of me because of my last name. And I'm willing to bet everyone in town knows you, and you know everyone in town." Greg motioned to Spooky, who wagged his tail at the attention. "Spooky's a good judge of character, and I can tell he likes you. So you must be a man I can trust. An honest man. And I bet most of the town feels the same way. If I give you all these deeds, could you start going through them, figuring out which families still live here, and which have moved away? I think I could get them all back to their rightful owners a lot faster with your help."

"It would be my pleasure. In fact, it would damn near be an honor to be part of this. This is a big thing."

"Great, I appreciate it. One more thing," Greg said. He paused. "I'm not sure exactly how to put this, but could you maybe do a little PR for me? I mean, I know I'm not perfect, but I don't think I'm a complete asshole either. If I'm going to live in Lost Haven, it would be nice not to be hated, maybe be able to wave at people once in a while and actually have them wave back."

Doug laughed. "After people find out what you did today, and once you start handing out property deeds like Halloween candy, I don't think you'll have much of a problem with people waving at you. But just the same, I'll put in a good word and vouch for you."

"Great," Greg said. "Well, let's get you home so you can share the good news with the wife."

"Yeah," Doug agreed. "Betty is going to have kittens when I tell her what's going on. I feel like we won the lottery!"

CHAPTER FIFTY-FOUR

When Greg arrived home, he found the front door locked. Greg had been gone longer than anticipated, having decided to stop at the grocery store and get something to eat for lunch. Regardless of his aunt's obvious skill in the kitchen, Greg still went back and forth about eating what she prepared. Realizing he did not have a key, Greg walked around the house, hoping that the back door into the kitchen was unlocked. Luckily, it was. Greg walked through the mudroom and into the kitchen, Spooky right behind him.

By the time Greg realized that someone was rushing out of the basement doorway toward him, it was too late. Greg had time to register that Bill had a black semiautomatic pistol in his hand, most likely service issue, and that he was raising it toward Greg. Greg instinctively put his hands up in front of his face, as if he could ward off bullets. He heard Spooky growl. Then twin reports from the pistol, one right after the other, drowned out all other sounds. The sharp *whip-cracks* of the pistol sounded like an angry teacher had taken a wooden yardstick, held it like a sword, and slammed it down on a desk. Smoke filled the air, making Greg's eyes water. The smell of spent gunpowder burned Greg's sinuses.

Even through the ringing in his ears, Greg heard Spooky yelp in pain and surprise. He turned and saw Spooky propped up against the doorway that led into the kitchen. Two explosions of blood bloomed from his chest. One of the wounds had already begun gushing blood in thick torrents that bathed Spooky's chest and stained the tile floor.

Bill stepped around Greg and viciously kicked Spooky in the head, sending him tumbling back into the mudroom. Bill slammed shut the door that led into the mudroom, leaving Spooky to die. "Fucking dog!" he yelled triumphantly.

In his concern for Spooky, Greg ignored Bill, and moved toward the mudroom door.

"Nope," Bill said, and grabbed a fistful of Greg's hair. He yanked back. Greg hissed in pain and stumbled backward, off balance.

When Bill had Greg facing the doorway into the living room, Bill released his hair and shoved him forward with such force that Greg stumbled into the living room and collided with the leather arm of one of the brown recliners, bounced off, and landed on the floor. By the time he was back on his feet, Bill had entered the room.

Katelin was also in the living room, standing in front of the archway that led into the family room. She looked at Greg with contempt and shook her head.

Bill strolled farther into the room, over to the open doorway that led into the den. He leaned against the doorframe and smirked at Greg. "Just what the fuck have you been doin', boy?"

Despite being terrified, Greg could not help blurting out, "Fuck you."

Bill laughed. He raised his eyebrows and pointed the barrel of the pistol toward himself. "Fuck me? Nope, fuck *you*," he said, and pointed the pistol at Greg.

"You're a liar!" Katelin screeched, pointing an accusing finger at Greg. "You've just been using this family! You've just been using *me*!"

Bill grinned at Greg's obvious fear. "You're such a pussy. I can't believe that a son of mine would turn into *such a pussy*. What the fuck do you think you're doin' giving back land that our two families worked hard to get? Do you have any idea how much money you already cost us? In the long run, it'll probably amount to millions, you dumb fucker."

"And how could you freeze our bank accounts?" Katelin asked, her face crumpling. Her emotions swung wildly back and forth between rage and despair, like an insane clock that kept time for madness.

"Now, freezing all the bank accounts, that was kind of funny, but that don't excuse giving away our property," Bill said. He shook his head. "You just don't seem to learn. And gettin' other people to help you do your dirty work, that's even worse. I think after I get done here, I'm gonna take a trip out to the Hemmings place and kill those two worthless fuckers."

The thought of Doug dying because he cared about a town that was being slowly sucked dry of life, because he cared enough to help Greg try to set things right, sent Greg over the edge. He picked up the Tiffany lamp from the table next to the recliner and threw it at Bill. Even as he did it, Greg half expected Bill to simply step aside, avoiding the flying lamp of stained glass. Bill, however, was apparently so shocked that someone would dare to challenge him, that he remained in place, wide-eyed. The lamp struck him square in the face, exploding in a rainbow bomb of colors.

Bill howled in pain and staggered backward, his free hand going to his face. Already, Greg could see blood gushing from around the splayed fingers of Bill's left hand that he used to cover his left eye. There was another long gash that ran across Bill's right cheek that spit blood like an angry mouth.

Greg took a step toward Bill. Greg was not sure what he intended to do. But he intended to do *something*. But Bill saw him coming; he growled like an animal, stepped forward to meet Greg, and shoved the pistol into his face. This close up, the barrel looked like a black vortex into death. "You get the fuck back!" Bill growled. *"Back the fuck up!"*

Greg complied, holding up his hands, as if that would somehow help matters.

"You fucker!" Bill screamed. *"You took out my eye!"* Bill pounded his boot heel into the floor. *"You motherfucker!"*

Despite his rage and pain, Bill took a deep breath and actually grinned at Greg. "Okay, so maybe you got some balls after all. But it doesn't matter, because you're dead."

"No!" Katelin screamed, rushing between Bill and Greg. "No, Bill! You can't kill him! We need him! You're just supposed to scare him!"

Bill grinned again ghoulishly, the left side of his face now completely covered in blood. "Oh, I think he's plenty scared. Now get the fuck out of my way."

"No, Bill, you can't kill him."

Bill sighed. "Ah, fuck it," he said, and pulled the trigger.

The back of Katelin's head exploded as the bullet exited her skull. Greg turned his head away, but too late. A fine mist of blood sprayed the left side of his face. He felt dots of pain pepper his cheek and jaw like bee stings. Greg realized in a moment of sickening clarity that the bee stings were bits of Katelin's shattered skull striking the side of his face.

Bill took a moment to study Katelin's body as it lay between him and Greg. "Stupid bitch." He brought his attention back to Greg. "Now where were we?" he said. And shot Greg in the chest.

Greg looked down and saw a black hole in the right side of his T-shirt. Powder burns radiated from around the hole. Greg looked back up at Bill. *This can't really be happening. This is some kind of joke.* He tried to take a step forward, but instead, stumbled, swayed, and fell over on his side. He rolled onto his back.

Greg had always assumed that getting shot would cause excruciating pain, but to his surprise, he felt very little pain, only a little stitch in his chest, like the kind you get in your side when you run too fast for too long. What worried Greg much more than the pain was the fact that he did not seem to be able to catch his breath. There was a terrible pressure on his chest, like an elephant was standing on it. Whenever he tried to breathe, the hole in his chest made a strange gurgling hiss, like a tire having the air taken out of it. Greg did not like the sound. A single thought kept running through his mind like a mantra: *If I can just catch my breath I'll be all right. If I can just catch my breath I'll be all right. If I can just catch my breath …*

At the sound of Bill's approaching boot heels tapping against the hardwood floor, Greg turned his head in their direction, and grinned at what he saw.

Bill must have seen Greg's grin, because he stopped and looked down at him, puzzled. "What the fuck do you have to grin about?"

Through the open doorway that led into the den, Greg watched the bookcase slide the rest of the way sideways. Greg should not have been surprised that Spooky could take two shots in the chest and get back up. After all, Greg had seen him get crushed into the ground by an entity, only to shake it off a few moments later, ready for more. He had obviously been well enough to take the back stairs up to the third floor, go through the hidden hallway, and come out into the den.

And Spooky seemed perfectly fine when he burst out of the bookcase opening and charged directly at Bill.

Greg watched with satisfaction as the confused look on Bill's face melted into fear when he heard Spooky growl from behind him. Greg closed his eyes, not wanting to see what was about to happen. The screams that followed were bad enough. Blessedly, Spooky quickly finished what he had started thirty-one years ago, and Bill did not scream for long.

CHAPTER FIFTY-FIVE

"Come on, bud, wake up."

Greg's eyelids fluttered open. Ron knelt beside him. He pressed a towel against the hole in Greg's chest. To his surprise, Greg found that it actually helped him breathe a little easier, but not much.

When Ron saw that Greg's eyes were open and focused on him, he sobbed. "Oh Jesus Christ, bud, I'm sorry. The gunshots woke me up, but not fast enough. I was too damned drunk. I saw the end of it on the cameras. I called 911. Ambulance is on its way. I wanted to come down here, I swear I did, but I was too goddamned afraid, I couldn't move. I'm so sorry, bud, I'm just a worthless, drunk coward."

Greg wanted to tell Ron that it was okay, that he had done the right thing by staying upstairs—that if he had come downstairs, Bill would have shot him without a second thought. Greg wanted to tell Ron this, but he could not talk, because he could not draw in enough breath. God, he was so tired. He just wanted to go to sleep. But when he began to close his eyes, Ron screamed at him, *"No you don't! You stay awake!"*

When Greg opened his eyes again, Spooky stood beside Ron, his giant head peering into Greg's face. Greg gazed back into his amber eyes. Those strange eyes filled with an intelligence far beyond that of a dog. Those eyes began to glow with an inner golden light, as if someone had turned on a brilliantly bright flashlight inside Spooky's head. The light began to grow brighter, and soon became so intense that Greg was forced to close his eyes.

"No, don't you go to sleep!" he heard Ron yell, but his voice sounded distant and strange, as if he were yelling at Greg from under water. "What the hell?" Greg heard Ron say a moment later.

The wound in Greg's chest suddenly began to itch. Greg opened his eyes. The golden light that had been behind Spooky's eyes had become something more than light. It spilled out of Spooky like gold molten lava, flowing down onto Greg's chest, where it filled the wound.

The itching became so intense Greg had to grit his teeth. It felt like something that was inside of him, like his very bones had been coated with poison ivy. When he thought he could take no more, it began to fade, gradually lessening until it disappeared.

Greg took a deep lungful of sweet, sweet air, and let it out. He looked down at his chest. It was once again whole. Nice, normal skin peeked out at him from the black hole in his T-shirt. Another mystery solved: Spooky was the one who had healed his black eye and his wounded leg after Bill had shot him with a nail gun.

Greg sat up on his elbows. He looked at Spooky, who sat on his right side, and grinned. Spooky thumped the floor with his tail. Greg looked to his left, where Ron knelt beside him, his blue NASCAR cap practically wrung to thread in his hands.

Ron glanced at Spooky, then back to Greg. "I'll be damned," he finally said.

CHAPTER FIFTY-SIX

The three sat on the two love seats in the family room. Greg and Ron shared one. Spooky, sprawled out and currently snoring softly, took up the other.

It was evening. The police investigators had come and gone, making it clear that they might drop by if they had any further questions or needed any clarification. It had not been difficult to make up a story about what had happened. After all, they really had only needed to leave out the stranger aspects of the truth. In the end they simply said that Bill had gone crazy and went on a rampage. Both Greg and Ron knew that it would not take much for the investigators to believe their story when they corroborated Bill's character, or lack thereof, by asking around town how people felt about Bill.

Bill's brother Jerald would have to be carefully watched. But Greg did not think Jerald was as dangerous as his brother had been. Dirty? Yes. Greedy? Most definitely. But crazy? Greg did not think so. And Ron seemed to share the same opinion. Besides, it was an issue for another day.

Lost Haven would need a new sheriff. Hopefully, there were some honest deputies that, now free from Bill's tyranny, could show the people that most cops were decent, hard-working men and women who bravely went to work everyday knowing that they could die while making the streets safe for those they swore to protect and serve.

"Bud?" Ron said.

Greg glanced at his uncle. He was once again wringing his NASCAR hat in his hands. "What's up?"

"If you want me to leave, I'll understand."

Greg shook his head immediately. "No, I don't want you to leave. I can use your help."

"What's an old drunk like me going to help you do? Which, by the way, I think I'm done drinking." Ron smiled sadly. "I lost my wife today. I know we didn't have anything close to what you'd call love there at the end. But in the beginning, we had some good years, some good memories. My wife dead, you almost dead, and me upstairs, passed out." Ron looked at Greg. "I just can't do it anymore."

Greg nodded. "I'll throw out all the beer for you."

"Well, you could keep a few around. Just to make me feel better. I won't drink 'em. It'll just help ease my mind knowin' they're in the house."

"I don't think it works that way," Greg said.

"Yeah, you're probably right. Maybe I'll start going to those meeting things. Couldn't hurt, right?"

Greg shook his head. "Nope. Couldn't hurt."

"So, what is it you want me to help you do? I'm not even sure yet what the hell even happened here today."

"Well, I've decided I'm going to stay in Lost Haven, and I could use your help keeping track of things with your cameras. I could use your help watching out for things." Greg stretched out his legs, got comfortable, and proceeded to tell Ron the whole story.

CHAPTER FIFTY-SEVEN

Katelin was buried next to her sister. Despite all the things she had done, Greg could not find it in his heart to hate her. Greg was done with hate. He hoped that in death, Katelin had finally found the peace she had not been able to find in life.

CHAPTER FIFTY-EIGHT

Over the next week, with the help of Ron and Spooky, Greg rescued two more lost souls from the entities and helped them move on.

And with the help of Doug Hemmings—of Hemmings Ford, Lincoln, Mercury, where we'll work with you to get you in the vehicle of your choice *today*—Greg managed to return most of the property his family had stolen. Doug assured him that he would track down the recipients to what remained to be returned; it would just take some time.

The next phase of the operation would involve giving back the money his family had taken. After crunching the numbers, Greg figured that if he gave back all the cash, he would still have a little over two million dollars. From what he could tell so far, the two million was actual family money, not stolen from other people. In addition, the family owned a substantial amount of land that was, likewise, actually their land. That would be more than enough for one very large dog, one recovering alcoholic, and one not-so-angry-anymore man to live on comfortably.

And so, life was not so bad. It was far from perfect, but really, is anything ever perfect?

CHAPTER FIFTY-NINE

Greg stood in front of his mother's headstone, marveling at what he saw. On each side stood a lush Moonstone rosebush, covered in fully bloomed, purple-pink-tipped white roses.

Katelin had been buried less than two weeks ago, and the rosebushes had not been there when she had been laid to rest. And if someone—although Greg had no idea who would do such a thing—had snuck in and planted the rosebushes, the stealthy planter had managed to do so without disturbing the surrounding soil by so much as a single blade of grass.

Had his mother somehow managed to reach out from beyond? Were the rosebushes a sign?

Greg realized it did not matter where the roses had come from. They were there, and that was enough. Some things were meant to be mysterious. Some questions were meant to remain unanswered. Life is not about knowing everything, or even most things. Life is not about having all the answers. Life is about the journey of living, and finding what answers one may along the path.

Greg looked at the rosebushes and smiled. "I miss you, Mom."

ABOUT THE AUTHOR

Justin was born in Iowa, where he currently resides, although he has also lived in California, Nebraska, Ohio, Oklahoma, and Pennsylvania. He has worked as a janitor, ranch hand, property manager, stained-glass window restorer, computer programmer, contracting account manager, and direct marketing account manager, among others. Correspondences to the author may be emailed to: writerjb@hotmail.com.

1519096